Island Justice

Dear Tammie and JR

Thank you for your hospitality and you kindness.

Enjoy the adventure.

JBoaden

JOHN BOADEN

PAGE PUBLISHING, INC.
Conneaut Lake, PA

First originally published by Page Publishing 2020

Cover Photograph of Rum Point in Grand Cayman,
capturing a sunset by Frank Slack, March 2007

ISBN 978-1-6624-2176-1 (pbk)
ISBN 978-1-6624-2177-8 (digital)

Printed in the United States of America

I am honored to dedicate this book to my beautiful wife, who is both a strong woman and certainly not afraid to share her opinions and speak her truth. She will listen intently but never allows another's words to bring her down. She is filled with compassion, generosity and a richness of integrity. She has a capability to be vulnerable yet shows kindness and authenticity whenever needed. No matter what the circumstances may be, she will always display that she is true to herself. Without her ~~orders~~ encouragement, this book would not have been written.

CONTENTS

CHAPTER 1

Christopher Watson—City of Bilberry Police Department

Christopher Watson was a detective chief inspector in the City of Bilberry Police Department in the United Kingdom—a medium-sized country town in the naturally beautiful northeastern corner of England—having served faithfully and dutifully for the past twenty-four years.

You'd find the English country towns tucked away in all manner of places throughout England—on rugged cliffs, in rolling green hills, near forests, on moorland, with beaches, by rivers. And despite the English weather, which was reputed to be usually wet, you'd find warmth. Even if there was no one around, there was something about English country towns that was friendly and homely. Seeing a picturesque scene of the countryside and also all manner of country towns was like getting a cozy hug from the countryside. Steeped in history, sometimes very ancient history, and packed often with old pubs and manor houses, there was a sense of security in such places. Strolling around the streets of Bilberry and falling in love with the place was the main pastime. It was also a center for long countryside walks and the mandatory tearooms for relaxation from the strenuous walks or just gossiping with both neighbors and strangers. That was the essence of Bilberry and some of its environs. In this same area and as a testament to past times in Bilberry, big stone castles were found in many areas and a lingering reminder that battles and sieges were once a part of life in this region for hundreds of years. Watson was inclined to the view that it would not get any better or more charming than this quiet slice of pastoral England. Of course, from a professional point of view, Watson enjoyed the area as it was much easier to garner and maintain relationships with the public, through both personal and professional interactions, than it was in the large sprawling and ever-developing metroplexes.

Watson was forty-two years of age, six feet two in height, and weighed about two hundred pounds. He had always been deeply, passionately, and actively involved in many sports but primarily rugby, cricket, soccer, and athletics; so joining the police force allowed him to continue those activities in organized sports after he graduated from the local grammar school with his University of Cambridge O Levels in hand. He had previously made inquiries to join the Royal Air Force and attend the Air Force college situated at RAF Cranwell in Lincolnshire, but on the basis that he was found to be color-blind with certain colors, he was informed that a flying career was out of the question. He had been offered other alternatives in the Air Force, but he had desperately hoped to fly, so he was forced to look elsewhere. Moving on, he then considered going to Loughborough College, a renowned physical education teacher training college to obtain a degree in sports management and coordination, bearing in mind his love for sports of all types. Unfortunately, although his parents were both employed—his father being a salesman and also, together with his wife, running a little neighborhood grocery store that was common in those days, especially in the rural areas of England—they had little reserve finances to sponsor such a move. Watson, therefore, after further due consideration, eventually opted to try to join the local police force.

His parents had always professed and greatly encouraged him to get a job that offered a pension scheme for when he reached retirement age. At eighteen years of age, retirement after a further thirty years of service seemed way too far-off to be of any immediate concern to Watson, but the opportunity to continue his involvement in the varied sports was a great attraction for him. The police teams were well-represented in all the sports leagues that abounded in and around Bilberry. Also, as a police officer, he would not be stuck behind a desk eight hours a day, and to Watson, that was a most worthy, if not perhaps the most important, consideration. After going through the onerous and time-consuming completion of numerous forms for the position (which covered health and safety to potentially contracting dysentery or herpes) and attending various tests, including physical and oral interviews, Watson duly received an offer from the City of Bilberry Police Department to become a probationary constable in the force and all that that entailed at the time.

Watson never forgot his final interview with the chief constable who, it seemed very quickly, formally offered him an appointment as a police constable in the Bilberry Force. The chief was an avid lover of all sports, as he recognized that involvement in the majority of sports taught an individual both the need for teamwork and also individual performance. The chief believed that through various competitions and leagues in the area, the police teams played numerous games against teams drawn primarily from the public arena that would engender further good relationships. This bred both good and lasting contacts in some areas between the police and the public, a relationship that'd be so necessary in the execution of effective day-to-day police work. The chief introduced himself to Watson and noted that during his school years, Watson had represented the county at rugby, cricket, and athletics in various age groups. Watson had spent considerable time preparing for the interview, which normally took about thirty minutes, reviewing all news reports regarding both local, national, and international happenings to be prepared to answer any and all questions the chief might pose or direct to him. Watson was ready for anything! No such questions were asked, to Watson's disbelief and some disappointment. The chief remarked about Watson's involvement across the board in the sports field and stood up to shake Watson's hand, saying that he hoped he would be extremely happy in the job! Watson was dismissed after about five to six minutes, and he even felt somewhat aggrieved that the chief had not delved further into all the various areas of concern that Watson had spent some hours reviewing.

Watson then had to spend time at the force quartermaster stores and get measured for his uniform—including winter and summer clothing, daytime and nighttime uniforms, plus helmet, overcoats, etc. to survive both the winter and summer seasons and all the accoutrements he'd have to carry (e.g., handcuffs, truncheon, pocketbook, traffic control clothing, etc.). He needed two suitcases to bring all the uniform items he was issued with home but had to make do with some large plastic bags provided by the staff. The force quartermaster was a man named Sergeant Duffin who counted each piece of equipment issued as though it was his own, and Watson was threatened with potential death should he lose any equipment or, heaven forbid, get it severely damaged. In the years that followed, Watson—for a wide variety of differing reasons, some printable and some not—had to replace certain items of equipment; and on each occasion, Sergeant Duffin asked him very direct questions as an established member of the Spanish Inquisition probably would have! Duffin was not prone to giving anything away lightly or without full and extremely convincing explanation.

Consequently, upon joining the police in earnest, Watson—along with two or three other recruits from Bilberry—attended the initial sixteen weeks of basic police training at nearby Pannal Ash Police Training Center, which was just outside the town of Harrogate in Yorkshire. This involved class work, practical training and instruction, physical training and defensive training, plus other mundane things that would become a part of his daily life. It was worthy of note that during his first two years as a police officer, which was effectively a training period, he could be fired for any reason if, in the terms of his employment and his senior officers, he was unlikely to become a useful and productive officer. Accordingly, for the first two years, all he did and said was closely monitored by his seniors and contemporaries; therefore, Watson took all efforts not to offend anyone and to do his job firmly, impartially, and fairly, according to the book.

When Watson returned to the force from training school after graduation, he was then sworn in as a police officer, along with another ten or so local recruits, before the magistrate in the local magistrate court at the Bilberry guildhall. He was then assigned to the Central Division area, which, as its name suggested, was right in the town center of Bilberry. For three years plus after graduation, he served as a bobby on the beat in the center of Bilberry; and during this time, he put into practice all that he had learned at Pannal Ash and additional knowledge he had acquired each and every day by working on the beat. His uniform sergeants were also of great assistance to Watson in showing him how the practical side of the job was done, over and above the theoretical sides that had been learned and pounded into him during his period of basic training.

The Central Division was a continually active and thriving area, with all sorts of happenings, good and bad, both day and night. Most of the entertainment spots in Bilberry were within 350 yards or so of the town center. You had to be at least six feet tall to gain entrance into the Bilberry police force in those days, and there was a total of five hundred officers. Watson on being assigned to serve in the Central Division, as opposed to the less busy and outlying Northern and Southern Divisions was six feet two, and out of the 160 officers on the division, he was the fourth smallest in height. The chief and other senior officers liked the idea of having very tall officers on the Central Division area due to the fact that during the odd scuffles on a Friday and Saturday night, the miscreants would think twice about tackling a six feet six and above officer. A large number of the 160 officers on the division were in excess of six feet six in height, and a couple were seven feet tall. On Friday and Saturday nights, about 10:30 p.m. or so, some pub fights would break out as the pubs were emptying, all for no good reason other than the fact it was a Friday or Saturday night. A Friday or Saturday night for some of the customers would have no meaning if there wasn't a fight or brawl at some time in the evening hours. There was not usually any real malice associated with the brawl! When these fights occurred, the taller officers on the division entertained themselves by sending Watson and the other smaller officers in first to quell the disarray, and then they would finally enter. Upon their imposing entrance, especially the seven feet tall officers, the place would usually go quiet, and arrests were then made. The sheer size of these officers and oftentimes the number present had a profound effect on the miscreants, who quickly lost interest in any form of rebellion. Also, when any of the miscreants decided to run away from the scene, invariably due to his athletic background, Watson was the one who was nominated to give chase! At least it saved him some hours training for his current season sport of choice on the police training ground, which was on the outskirts of Bilberry.

Subsequently following his period of three years in uniform, Watson, by way of invitation from the local detective superintendent, entered the detective branch—the Criminal Investigation Department (CID)—where, primarily his own choice, he remained for the rest of his service in Bilberry. These assignments included the general CID, the Serious Crime Squad, and the Fraud Squad. They were all frontline positions. Watson did not enjoy not being on the front line; that was what the job was all about, dealing directly with all sorts and manner of people in a multitude of circumstances and locations. He had now been assigned, on secondment, for a period of two years to the Cayman Islands—three small islands in the Caribbean and a British dependent overseas territory—to assist in helping their fraud investigation unit, locally known as the Royal Cayman Islands Police (RCIP), the Commercial Crime Branch (CCB).

Watson duly researched and determined that the Cayman Islands were in the western Caribbean Sea and were the peaks of an undersea mountain range called the Cayman Ridge (or Cayman Rise). This ridge flanked the Cayman Trough, six thousand meters (twenty thousand feet) deep, which lay 3.7 miles to the south. Grand Cayman was the largest and most populated of the three islands, followed by Cayman Brac and the smallest island, Little Cayman. All three islands were beautiful in their own way and had wonderful scenery, beautiful beaches, and azure-blue seawater with pristine white sands. They really were a small piece of heaven and paradise in the world, let alone the Caribbean. The nearest other independent island was Jamaica, which was situated some 272 miles to the southeast of Grand Cayman. The Cayman Islands were generally low-lying, though Cayman Brac had a central bluff that made up 90 percent of its landmass. The coasts were ironshore (limestone fringes with numerous marine fossils) interspersed with sandy beaches and enclosed by coral reefs. Grand Cayman was the largest and most populous island, about twenty-two miles long and eight miles across at its widest, with a total area of seventy-six square miles. It had a thirty-six-square-mile sound that was a breeding ground for much marine life. Cayman Brac, about eighty-nine miles northeast of Grand Cayman, was the next largest island; it was about twelve miles long, averaged about one mile in width, and had the highest elevation of the group, rising to 140 feet above sea level. Its total area was fourteen square miles. The smallest of the islands, Little Cayman, lay five miles west of Cayman Brac; it was ten miles long and had a maximum width of two miles and a total area of about ten square miles.

Another fact that was of great interest to Watson was the information that in the square mile or so of George Town, the capital of the Cayman Islands situated on Grand Cayman, there were—at that time—a total of 583 duly registered and licensed banks. Watson thought perhaps most of those banks helped citizens of various countries hide their wealth—in some cases, ill-gotten wealth. Surely, he thought, the local residents could not possibly need that number of banks! Bilberry had far more inhabitants but only a meager seven banks!

Up to three months prior to this assignment, Watson had not really heard of Cayman and its history, let alone know where it was actually situated! He knew from various newspaper reports and police circulations that the islands were allegedly a tax haven for people trying to avoid burdensome taxation regulations at home, wherever that might be. They also were purported to be heavily involved in assisting in the laundering of various illicit monies and drugs. Watson did note that the islands were regarded as a superb spot to relax and regenerate, and the beaches there were regarded as pristine, and the scuba diving was superb.

Early in March 1987, there was an advertisement in the monthly police magazine in the UK, the *Police Review*, seeking qualified officers for the position in the Commercial Crime Branch of the Royal Cayman Islands Police. Watson's background in the CID, the Fraud Squad, and the Murder Incident environment stood him in good stead for such a position. It particularly attracted his attention because he was getting itchy feet after twelve months in an office type of post, teaching members of the Bilberry Force the ins and outs of HOLMES (Home Office Large Major Enquiry System), a system that was invaluable to anyone running any major inquiry but one that was as boring as hell to teach. It had been born out of the infamous Yorkshire Ripper inquiry some years previously, which involved many forces in the UK, and attempts were made to standardize the way information other material was handled so that forces could relate and merge cross-border inquiries together whenever it became necessary or desirous, as reflected in the Yorkshire Ripper inquiry.

That inquiry involved the savage murders and assaults on a number of young women in various parts of the UK committed by one individual with a similar modus operandi of killing each victim. In 1981, Peter Sutcliffe, the Yorkshire Ripper, was convicted of thirteen murders and a number of attempted murders. Unfortunately, even this was not the whole terrible truth. Later revelations and evidence revealed more detail regarding his callous killings and suggested he had claimed at least twenty-three more lives and left seven others with terrible injuries. The claims highlighted what was described as a disturbing cover-up of police incompetence in molding cross-border offenses together and that the Ripper attacked men as well as women in a total of sixteen years of horror across England—not just primarily Yorkshire and Lancashire.

Consequently, as it crossed a number of county borders in the UK, the various police forces involved had to learn how to file and store information so that, if necessary, each force would store all the information received in the same way, thereby making the interchange of information and facts much easier. Initially it was a standardized manual system, and then in the mid-1980s, with the advent of technology, it was duly computerized. Watson had to get out of the teaching role, back to an operational capacity, and this Cayman opening seemed like the ideal opportunity. He missed the odd morning raid and the attendant front-door destruction plus also occasionally rolling around on the ground trying to arrest people who sometimes, for some reason unbeknownst to him, objected strenuously to that course of action.

Consequently, Watson hurriedly obtained and got together all the information and documentation required to apply and completed the same for the Cayman Islands position, sending his application off from the Bilberry post office. That was not without drama though. Watson had to convince the rather parochial and elderly staff that the Caymans, which were unknown to them as they hardly ever traveled outside the boundaries of Bilberry, were in the British West Indies! It had taken the staff some time to determine the postage needed to send the package to the Cayman Islands, so Watson was not even 100 percent sure that it would ever reach its destination and, if it did, whether or not it would be there by the cutoff date, which was only a matter of days ahead. If nothing else, he thought and hoped he would perhaps get an interview in Cayman! Watson did so more in hope than expectation. That was probably rather stretching the position, but Watson was delighted to be quickly notified a few days later that he had been selected for an interview by the RCIP commissioner of police. The package had apparently been received in Cayman on the closing date for the position, hence the quick response to his application! The post office staff in Bilberry had not let Watson down! Watson was subsequently contacted by phone by the commissioner from the islands who confirmed to Watson that he had been selected for an interview. There had apparently been a number of applicants from throughout the UK, and the commissioner had selected six for interview. Watson immediately responded, "Interview in Cayman?" more in hope than anything other, only to be told by the commissioner that it was to be held at the Cayman Islands Government Office in Central London in the extremely near future. Following this initial contact by the commissioner, it was not without some humor. A number of Watson's friends knew he had applied for the position and exchanged lots of humor with Watson about the application, living in mud huts, no cars, no bathing facilities, etc.

Consequently a few days later, Watson was relaxing at home early one evening watching a local soccer game on the TV when his home phone rang. When he answered the same by saying "Hello," a softly spoken female voice stated that the commissioner of the Royal Cayman Islands Police was calling. Watson, who had had a somewhat egregious day at work, responded abruptly by saying, "Stop messing around," believing it to be one of his local friends, and slammed the phone down. Perish the thought, but that could have been the end of his desire to transfer to and work in the Cayman Islands. He sat reflecting somewhat on the call and his response when the phone rang again. Watson was running a number of possible culprits through his mind who might have been the prankster on this occasion. Watson duly answered it politely and noticed that there appeared to be a slight delay on the line with the conversation. *Perhaps it is from Cayman,* Watson thought. This time he was not abrupt, and the same lady explained that she had the commissioner on the line. Watson profusely apologized to her for his initial response, and having been told it was no problem, he was then connected with the commissioner. The commissioner was brief but stated that Watson had been selected to be interviewed for the post in the CCB. He then stated he would let Watson know of the date and time for the interview in due course, and he thanked Watson for applying before ceasing the conversation by saying he was very much looking forward to speaking in person with Watson.

Watson was immensely pleased with this progress and, accordingly, duly commenced some additional research on the Cayman Islands, the RCIP, and also the background of the commissioner in the UK and Seychelles Police Force prior to the Caymans so that he would be well-informed about those subjects should they arise during the forthcoming interview. During his career and experience in the detective branch, Watson had been taught and advised by former colleagues that it was always advantageous to know as much as you could about a person being interviewed before you enter the interview room. A job interview, an interview of a witness or an accused person, or a promotion board interview were no exception; and accordingly, Watson prepared in his usual manner for the interview, learning about the Cayman Islands, their people, and the past policing positions held by the commissioner of police who apparently would be his interviewer.

CHAPTER 2

Cayman Job Interview in London

Watson was subsequently notified of the date, and the day arrived in April 1987. It was a cool and brisk morning, but he was delighted to travel by British Rail on an awayday round trip fare to King's Cross mainline railway station and then by London Underground to a tube station near the Cayman Islands Government Office, just off the glamorous and prestigious Park Lane in London.

While traveling in the luxury of British Rail, Watson reflected on the many and varied courses he had attended over the years, which, in part, had prepared him for the forthcoming interview. All this was allied, of course, to the frontline experiences that he had had over the years, working numerous criminal cases of many types. He had attended the initial training course of sixteen weeks when entering the police, followed by two continuation courses of four weeks duration each during the first two years. He had attended a newly promoted sergeants' course and then later a newly promoted inspectors' course. He had attended a ten-week initial detective course, an intermediate detective course, and also a six-week advanced and pretty intensive CID course. He had also attended an initial fraud course and an in-depth financial investigation course. Most of these courses were held at various police training centers all over the UK. Also, as the laws and procedures changed over the years, he had attended a number of local courses to drive these new processes and procedures home. Not only was the knowledge learned on these courses invaluable to Watson but also he met and made many new friends from police forces all over the UK and Northern Ireland, which stood him in good stead as the areas of crime grew broader and outside county boundaries. A lot of the more senior courses involved not only book-work but also many tabletop exercises, and some involved surveilling and then arresting the alleged criminals and interviewing them. The alleged criminals were mainly older detectives from the local forces, and of course, they knew each and every way to confuse and derail the newer detectives. There were also many evenings spent as a group, visiting places in the training centers' area and generally bonding together as a group. Some were educational visits, while other visits were more social! The curriculum of some of the courses, such as the advanced CID class, included forms of designed testing by which the staff were able to ensure the individual's capability to perform as a detective to a required standard. All the courses were great fun and allowed Watson to escape for a few weeks from the normal day-to-day business of being a detective. His thoughts during the journey then transferred to the sports he had played, including rugby, foot-ball, cricket, athletics (field and track), field hockey, and swimming. Rugby had taken him to numerous places all over England and— to a lesser degree—Wales, Scotland, Ireland, and on one occasion, France. Cricket, his first love, both as a player and then as an umpire and coach, had taken him all over the UK and Ireland. As the train ride progressed, Watson reminded himself of a number of actions during these courses he had attended and also the sporting exploits he had partaken in, which he could use, if necessary, to answer some of the questions he anticipated might be asked by the commissioner during the impending interview.

Watson mused and thought that this was far better than another day teaching the computer system in an office at Bilberry police headquarters as he relaxed during the train journey. Watson had further learned that apparently there had been thirty-two candidates who applied from throughout the UK for the vacant position and the commissioner had selected and decided to formally interview just six of the applicants. Of the six, three were already retired from active policing, two could immediately retire, and Watson alone would have to go on secondment to Cayman—i.e., loan. This was because a thirty-year retirement pension was the optimum in the police service at that time. However, Watson had perceived there was a downside, and this immediately meant to him that he would be a more expensive proposition for the Cayman Islands to engage, as they would have to pay his continuing pension contributions back in the UK, whereas the other five would all just be on a straightforward two-year contract with the Cayman government. Nonetheless, he was eternally optimistic that he would be well-received; after all, he was pretty professionally qualified on a number of fronts. The jaunt involved a round trip for the day to London and what turned out to be a fifty-five-minute-plus interview with the commissioner.

The train ride was about three hours, followed by fifteen minutes on the underground tube and then a short yet brisk walk in the cooler air to the address of the Cayman Islands Government Office in the swanky Green Park and Park Lane area of London.

Upon arrival at the government offices, about fifteen minutes before the appointed time, Watson took the elevator to the appropriate floor of the building where he saw a sign indicating the UK offices of the Cayman Islands government. Following good protocol, Watson knocked firmly on the door and duly entered. It was a reception area and a desk, behind which sat a very pretty young lady, dressed impeccably and probably in her early thirties. She stood up from her desk and came to the entrance desk where Watson duly introduced himself and stated that he had an appointment scheduled with the Cayman police commissioner. She was obviously expecting Watson and asked him, in the best Queen's English, to please take a seat and said the commissioner would be with him very shortly. She asked Watson if he would like a drink of something, but Watson declined. Although he did consider a beer would be appropriate, but it was far too early in the day. The office had a large perfunctory photograph of Her Majesty the Queen in all her formal regalia and also a photograph of the current governor (the Queen's representative) of the Cayman Islands on prominent display.

Watson, true to detective form and protocol and as mentioned previously, had already researched and knew the commissioner's policing background and the fact that he had never served as a detective and his career had always involved posts in the uniform branch of the police service. The commissioner then came from an office at the rear of the building and politely introduced himself, and they shook hands. He led Watson to his office, and they duly sat around a small conference table with a window view overlooking the street a few floors below. The commissioner had six files alongside him, each in a brown manila folder. The commissioner then mentioned to Watson that he was the first of six potential officers to be interviewed that day. Watson perceived this as somewhat of a disadvantage as he would be setting the bar to be considered against the other officers, but there was nothing he could do about it at this time. The commissioner then indicated that he had joined the police service many years ago. Watson immediately responded, "1951, I think." This visibly caught the commissioner's notice and, Watson believed, subconsciously told the commissioner that this man had done some homework on him, in accordance with the old detectives' adage of knowing all you could about the individual you were sitting in front of.

After forty-five minutes or so of conversation setting out an overview of the position and what benefits Watson could bring to the position, including the management of major crimes that the commissioner was extremely interested in, together with some pleasantries between the two of them, the interview was curtailed, with the commissioner explaining that he would let Watson know the result of the interview very shortly but Watson was free to add any further thoughts or comments he wished to. Watson concluded by informing the commissioner that he would view the posting as an opportunity to help the CCB officers to learn how to simplify frauds—which can, by their very nature, be inherently complex—to enable jurors to understand the simplicity of a fraud scheme. Also, Watson mentioned the requirement for managing serious crime, such as murders or robberies, and how it was essential for it to be managed in a thorough and methodical way, recording all information received and issued to detectives, looking for any inconsistencies revealed, and oftentimes corroborating statements and the like. Watson made the point that having information was one thing, but if you wouldn't have the ability of recovering that information, say six or twelve months into an inquiry, you might as well never bother getting it. Watson's impression was that these points really seemed to resonate with the commissioner.

Watson further spoke at some length to the commissioner about the voluntary organizations and positions he held, especially in the sporting field and the possibility of continuing this volunteerism in Cayman. The commissioner seemed pretty keen on that idea; it was always good for the police to be involved in matters such as that with the public. It was only later that Watson found out there was no such major incident room system currently used in the Cayman Islands. Although it did not guarantee success in every inquiry even if used, Watson knew that it provided a more than even chance of the inquiry being solved.

Watson did ask one final question that he told the commissioner was totally unrelated to the post but would greatly add to Watson's ability to cultivate resources on the island. Watson said the question was whether or not cricket was played on the island; surely, being in the West Indies, cricket would be enjoyed there? Watson knew of the love for cricket in Jamaica and elsewhere in the Caribbean and therefore was pleased by the answer that there was a very active cricket league on the island, plus the commissioner added that there was even a rugby club, although he was not sure when or whom they played! There was just one rugby club in the Caymans! It was a source of amusement to Watson that the Cayman Rugby Club often advertised in the international publication of *Rugby World* for teams from other countries to visit Cayman and play with them! The commissioner also mentioned that in performing the duties in Cayman, oftentimes travel to other countries was necessary, and he asked if Watson would be averse to that. Watson used his police experiences to date in varying parts of Europe and Africa to illustrate to the commissioner that that would not be any sort of problem. A number of Watson's colleagues in Bilberry had often christened Watson as "Have passport, will travel!"

Following the interview and after bidding the receptionist a nice and sincere thank-you and goodbye, Watson—not one to miss an opportunity to see the bright lights of London—met up with a couple of longtime detective friends and rugby adversaries from the London Metropolitan Police and together had a few beers with a very satisfactory meal in a local hostelry before catching the last train back to Northern England from King's Cross. Upon arrival, Bilberry was noticeably quiet, which was not surprising as it was nearly midnight, and Watson was well-fed and watered. He was tired following the whole day and was greatly looking forward to his bed!

The next day dawned far too quickly, and Watson dragged himself to the office early to continue instruction with a HOLMES training course that had been ongoing for a week or so. All his contemporaries were deeply interested in how the interview had gone, quietly hoping for a place to stay when they'd visit the Cayman Islands— wherever they were! Much fun and good humor as could be expected from detectives was made of what style of mud hut would Watson be living in, were there cars on the island, was electricity available, and so on. These nonbelievers surely did not appreciate that at that time, the Cayman Islands was the third largest financial center in the world and had good communications and all that being a leading financial center entailed! Having said that, the questioners were all trying to ingratiate themselves to Watson to ensure that their request for a trip to the West Indies for a vacation would be well-received by him once in place in the islands, assuming he was selected!

Midway through the afternoon, a phone call was received in the training room, and Watson was instructed by the caller to immediately visit with the chief constable of the Bilberry force. This was very, very unusual—very unusual. Usually if an officer were in some trouble, they would normally see the Complaints Department first. Watson knew this from past experiences, so this summons directly from the chief was highly irregular. Watson's mind was racing as to what he had incorrectly done recently or whom he had upset to warrant such high-office intervention! He moved slowly but deliberately toward the chief's office on the top floor of the headquarters with some trepidation and his mind in turmoil. *What have I done now?* he thought as all manner of events went through his mind.

He went through the gatekeeper or secretary's office, with whom he was well-acquainted, and she joyfully welcomed him and just waved him on to the chief's office, like a police officer performing traffic duty, with a big smile on her face. Perhaps Watson's trepidation was somewhat misplaced?

The chief was speaking on the phone and, immediately by a hand signal, motioned Watson to sit down. After a few minutes or so, during which Watson picked up no clues as to the reason for him being called to the office, the chief handed the phone to Watson, saying, "Someone wants to speak to you." Watson took the phone and, being in front of the chief, introduced himself in the appropriate manner rather than just saying the usual perfunctory hello. The softly spoken commissioner of the Royal Cayman Islands Police Department, whom Watson had met the previous day, was on the other end of the line and introduced himself. Watson immediately thanked him for the hospitality and kindness shown the previous day and how much he had enjoyed speaking with him. Watson also noticed that the chief constable had a wry smile on his face; it was obvious he knew something Watson did not. The commissioner then said, "I am offering you the job in the Commercial Crime Branch of the RCIP for a two-year secondment. I would very much like for you to consider taking it. Do you want time to consider it?"

Watson replied without missing a beat, "Thank you, sir. I would." He then immediately continued, "I have considered it and would dearly like to take it."

The commissioner said, "Don't you want time to consider it?"

Watson replied, "No. If I had not wanted the job, I would not have applied, nor would I have wasted your time in the interview." Watson refrained from saying he wanted the hell out of the job he was currently doing in front of his chief constable! Watson then added in an abundance of caution, looking anxiously at the chief, "I am saying yes, but of course, I do not yet have my chief constable's permission."

With that, Watson handed the phone back to the chief who primarily gave his permission for the secondment but explained that he had yet to run the appointment by the local watch committee who oversaw the force's duties and responsibilities, but he did mention he saw that as a foregone conclusion in that they would probably agree. The chief shook Watson's hand and slapped him on the back, then Watson was summarily dismissed and allowed to leave the office.

As Watson walked past the chief's secretary on the way from the office, she immediately asked Watson whether or not she could visit when he got to Cayman. It was obvious to Watson that the secretary had known all along about the reason for him being called to the chief's office. Watson responded, "Of course, you especially are very welcome anytime," which seemed to cheer her up immensely, while his mind was now racing with 1,001 things to be done and settled before he left Bilberry and the UK, albeit—he thought—temporarily. Although not sure of the actual date of commencement of the secondment, everything was apparently being geared toward July 1, which was less than three months away.

On arrival back in the training room, everyone was highly delighted with Watson's forthcoming appointment and the fact that they now had a place to visit in the British West Indies during the long and dark and wet British winters, which sometimes seemed to last for months and months. Watson had no doubt he would need at least a two-bedroom hut in Cayman to cater for all the Bilberrians and other friends who were promising or threatening to visit. Some people whom Watson did not know were friends suddenly became friends! That evening was spent in a local hostelry with some close friends and sporting colleagues having a few more beers to celebrate the forthcoming appointment. Outside was a harsh wind and lashing rain. *Not exactly like April in the Caribbean,* Watson thought.

One thing that really concerned Watson and occupied his mind greatly was that by going to the Caymans, he would not be able to go to his favorite local breakfast place called the Mill Café. The people with Watson in the pub that evening kept driving this point home to Watson; they knew it was one of Watson's most favored local dineries. The Mill Café was situated not far from the main arterial road, the A1, which ran from north to south in England. The Mill was a favorite haunt of police, ambulance drivers, firemen, hospital workers, mail workers, and long-distance truck drivers—all of whom would arrive early in the morning. Watson and his detectives would usually arrive there after an early morning raid and possibly kicking in a door or so to arrest some miscreant, who would then be locked in a prison cell at the police station to think about what he had done while the detectives went for a large saus before going back to complete the interviews and processing. The food was excellent and sold at reasonable prices. The waitress and table cleaner had been there since its inception in the 1800s, or so it seemed. She collected used crockery and brought ordered food to the table, and when the table was vacated, she cleared the table, emptied the ashtrays, and then wiped everything down with the same scruffy cloth. The health and safety experts would probably have had apoplexy over the procedures adopted! The favorite sandwich served was a large saus sandwich along with a mug of really hot tea. It consisted of hot sausage meat placed between two thick pieces of bread and spread with a brick trowel! Missing the usual breakfast at the Mill did cause Watson to have a few second thoughts of concern about the steps he was taking to leave Bilberry, but the thought of even more time spent with HOLMES training was equally—if not more so—overwhelming to Watson! Consequently, the procedures for a transfer went ahead.

The next two months were a whirlwind of activity to clear up all the outstanding work and personal matters that Watson had to put into place, but as time passed, so did the list of items to be attended to diminish. The Cayman government in the UK London office was in constant contact regarding arrangements, letters of authority, and a miscellany of other items and documents that needed to be sorted out prior to the commencement date. Eventually a start date was agreed among the UK, the Bilberry Police, and the Cayman government for July 1, 1987.

Finally, a few days of annual leave from his work before flying out were taken by Watson, which included a tonsillectomy at a local hospital to ensure the repetitive sore throats that Watson had recently been plagued with would not occur in the islands and need attention by a local witch doctor—according to his colleagues! A going-away party was also held at the local cricket club with whom Watson had been involved for many years as first a player, then coach, and finally, umpire. It was well-attended by many cricketing and police friends Watson had met over all his years of involvement in the local cricketing and policing scene, and almost everyone showed enthusiastic and devout interest in a necessary—almost mandatory—visit, as some regarded it, to the Cayman Islands during Watson's tenure there.

CHAPTER 3

Travel from Bilberry to Cayman Islands

Consequently, on July 1, 1987, Watson made the long trek from Bilberry to London's Heathrow Airport and subsequently checked in at terminal 4 for a British Airways flight to Miami and then transfer on to a Cayman Airways flight destined for Grand Cayman. He checked in two medium-sized bags, which, God willing and with the assistance and cooperation of BA and Cayman Airways ground staff, he would next see on Grand Cayman island much later that same day. Watson went through security then through the duty-free area, buying sustenance for the trip and having a final full English breakfast with bacon, eggs, and all the trimmings (which was excellent—although not up to the Mill Café's highest standards) at the Irish bar in the departure lounge before subsequently boarding a British Airways Boeing 747 en route to the USA. Although he had traveled extensively, pursuing his job and some vacations in the UK and throughout Europe and North Africa, this was his first trip across the pond and certainly his first visit to any Caribbean island. He was looking forward not only to the challenge but also to the opportunity in two years' time to get back to his home force and out of the dreaded HOLMES environment and back into a fully operational one. Surely in two years' time, his bosses in Bilberry would either have changed or alternatively forgotten all about DCI Watson and the dreaded connections with HOLMES?

He boarded the aircraft and took his seat, a window seat 27A, and looked forward to the cross-Atlantic trip. He was comfortable and well-settled—good leg room in the seat, his carry-on bag stored, and the seat next to him still open, which was an added bonus! The aircraft doors had been closed, and he was waiting for the perfunctory preflight announcements when he was approached by a gentleman who was obviously with the crew—Watson's powers of observation for some twenty-four years stood him in good stead. The gentleman introduced himself as the purser on the flight and asked if Watson would come with him. Being the obedient type, Watson got up and was told by the purser to bring his carry-on bag with him. Watson took it down from the overhead, thinking he had been thrown out of better places than this in his past life, and dutifully followed the purser up the stairs of the 747 to the upper cabin and then forward toward the cockpit area. Once there, he was immediately introduced by the purser to the captain, the first officer, and the flight engineer. Usual pleasantries were exchanged, and Watson was astonished when he was kindly offered by the captain the jump seat in the cockpit for however long he wanted to stay in there—from takeoff to landing if he so wished!

A meeting some weeks previously that Watson had totally forgotten immediately came to his mind. He had been at the local British Airways office in Bilberry, and a lady friend of his worked there and helped him book the flight to Miami and the connection to Cayman. Watson had remarked to her that he would love to see the cockpit of the 747, and she said she would do what she could—although she then continued to reproach him and said she was disappointed he was leaving the UK for a couple of years. She did say that as a BA employee, she could always visit Cayman at very advantageous prices! Watson was pleased with that and secretly hoped that she would! She would certainly be welcome at the Chez Watson guesthouse! Well, did she ever make an arrangement? Watson immediately took the captain's offer and strapped himself into the cabin jump seat, directly behind the captain's seat. Looking down from this height as the aircraft was pushed back from the gate was in itself an amazing sight. He thought, *These 747s are large aircraft—the wing walkers look like miniature people!* Watson did not get the usual safety demonstration that the normal passengers had to endure. He was given instructions by the first officer about escaping through a hatch in the roof of the cabin in the event of an emergency. Watson clarified that as he was not the captain, he did not have to stay with the aircraft and, accordingly, could leave the aircraft in front of him! How one could get up to the hatch was not immediately clear, but Watson rested comfortably in the knowledge that on a number of occasions throughout his career, necessity had become the mother of invention, and he was certainly under no doubt that such would apply in an emergency on this aircraft! Watson also got some consolation and reassurance from the fact that the 747s were then one of the safest aircraft flying at that time. It was a workhorse for long-distance international flights.

The aircraft taxied for quite a while until it finally reached the end of the designated runway and waited for permission to take off. Watson, through the headsets provided to him, could hear the transmissions between air traffic control (ATC) and the aircraft, BA Speedbird flight number 292. The signal came over the intercom that BA292 was finally cleared by ground control for takeoff. And after acknowledgment, the captain pushed the throttles of the four Rolls-Royce engines forward, and they built up slowly and so very deliberately in power. The brakes were then released, and slowly the 747 lurched forward down the seemingly endless runway. At a certain speed, the word *rotate* was uttered by someone on the flight deck, and the big bird began to climb up slowly but so effortlessly into the cloudless blue sky of a July morning, heading west toward Windsor Castle on to Lands' End, Isles of Scilly, Bermuda, and finally into Miami.

Watson's adventure and his planned escape from HOLMES had started, and he loved every minute of it. Although he had many apprehensions about leaving his many friends and acquaintances in the UK and entering a totally unknown world in the Caribbean. He was convinced it would only be for the two-year attachment, and two years in the Caribbean could not be that bad, could it?

After exchanging further pleasantries with the cockpit crew about his position as a police detective and his attachment to the

Cayman Islands together with being fed copious amounts of soft drinks and the like by the friendly flight attendants, he watched Land's End and the Isles of Scilly slip by beneath the aircraft and sat back to prepare for the scheduled nine-hour flight to Miami. The only land they would now see en route to Miami would be Bermuda—cloud cover permitting. Watson soon realized that flying this large aircraft was primarily achieved by punching various coordinates into the on-flight computer and responding to the odd garbled message from ATCs along the way. Everything seemed so simple and was handled equally adeptly and professionally by the cockpit crew.

Given time yet again to reflect on his decision and the change of lifestyle, he had time to wonder what waited for him in Cayman. Did they have electricity on the island? Were there cars available? Would there be women to date? Did they have organized and a good standard of cricket—his beloved sport of interest in the UK? Was there a viable rugby club he could frequent (purely on the social side; his playing days were over some five years ago)? Strange how Watson mused all these concerns and more, but not one had anything to do with work! He knew that he could more than adequately cover the work aspect with the background and experience that he had in the UK police and based on his telephone conversations with the Cayman commissioner and the force administration chief inspector. It was the finer things in life that were of immediate and pressing concern to him.

Watson was jolted back into reality by a flashing light above the copilot's console. He noticed it immediately, but no one else on the flight deck appeared to be concerned about it until a computer-generated beep began to resound in the cabin. It was really a soft noise to begin with but escalated in decibels as it continued in an unrelenting manner. This now had Watson's full attention, and also all the three crew members were looking at the persistent but unrelenting light. The captain asked the first officer, "Peter, what's that?"

The first officer said "I don't know" and turned to the flight engineer and said, "Smithy, what's that?"

In an effort to assist them—as a UK police officer finely tuned and trained to react in any emergency—Watson hastened to tell them he had absolutely no clue what it was, which really did not seem to help them. The computer-generated warning continued, and Watson was already beginning to eye the escape hatch and trying to remember the evacuation instructions he had been given while on terra firma in Heathrow. Smithy, muttering unintelligibly to himself, looked under his console where there were three large in-flight manuals stored, each at least four inches in thickness. None of the crew looked too concerned, and Smithy continued flicking through the manuals. After what seemed like at least an hour to Watson, but was probably one or two minutes, Smithy pressed a few buttons. And thankfully the noise ceased, and the flashing light was extinguished. Watson was relieved to say the least but did not want them to think he had been *too* concerned. Apparently, it was some sort of minor malfunction, if there was such a thing when flying at forty thousand feet, with the fuel control and flow system.

Bermuda came and went, and the 747 was still flying in a beautiful clear sky over an azure-blue sea. It all looked pretty calm, although from thirty-eight to forty thousand feet, it was rather difficult to tell. Watson had once again lapsed into thinking about the Cayman Islands and what was waiting for him there when they entered the Miami airspace to prepare for the next stop in his long trip.

From the cockpit, they first spotted the Bahamian islands set in a stunning blue sea, and then appeared the long sweeping coastline of the Eastern Florida shoreline. The clouds over Miami were large cumulonimbus; it was the perfunctory July afternoon thunderstorm. And the captain then took over control of the plane from the autopilot. The headsets were alive with much chatter backward and forward between the ATC and what seemed like hundreds of aircraft. How they kept control of all those flights they were in contact with was beyond Watson. He had had enough trouble keeping fifty detectives on a major inquiry in control! It was also of concern to him that with the aircraft flying wherever they wanted, the chance of a collision was remote. Then why did the air traffic controller's force them into specific flight corridors, thereby making the chance of a collision higher?

With the typical July afternoon thunderstorm activity centered it seemed in the Miami area, the captain was now flying the giant aircraft very adeptly between the large thunderclouds. It really was quite an experience to view it from the cockpit. The first officer, copilot, and flight engineer were busy with various checklists and adjusting instruments as they approached the coastline and were gradually descending. They crossed the coastline, and Watson could see Miami and the Venetian Islands to the right of the aircraft and Southern Florida stretching down toward the Florida Keys to the left. They then viewed Miami International Airport off to the right and flew by it to gradually make a slow lumbering 180-degree turn and make the final approach to land from the west into Miami Airport.

All the time, the captain was weaving the plane like thread through a needle through the massive storm clouds. The aircraft shuddered slightly as they felt the undercarriage come down and lock in place. Warehouses and residential areas below passed by quite slowly, and Watson marveled at the fact that some eight hundred thousand pounds of airplane and passengers could fly at such a low speed. They then lined themselves up with runway 9R and gradually descended until they felt the first impact of the wheels on the tarmac. Watson had landed in Miami. He then felt the nosewheel come down, and the pilots placed the engines in reverse thrust to assist in stopping the aircraft—what a wonderful experience to be there and witness all that happened in those last few miles of flight! The Caribbean experience had got off to a wonderful start, and Watson thought if the rest of the secondment was as good as this, then he would be in for a memorable time on his two-year attachment to the Royal Cayman Islands Police in the beautiful Cayman Islands.

CHAPTER 4

Arrival in and Welcome to Miami FL

Slowly the plane taxied for a few minutes and eventually came to rest at concourse E, gate 30. Watson noted that they were seated almost higher than the terminal concourse roof! Watson duly and sincerely thanked the three persons in the cockpit for allowing him the privilege of flying with them and wished them much luck and good fortune on their return journey. He also thanked the flight attendants who had made the trip so pleasant and made a mental note to drop a line to his friend in the BA office at Bilberry and thank her most sincerely for the arrangements. Watson thought at the very least, he would owe her a nice dinner and a bottle of wine at some exclusive restaurant when he returned to the UK after his secondment or in Cayman should she decide to visit. Failure to do so would be remembered by her for all eternity!

Well, so far, so good. He did not have to worry about his checked luggage yet, as BA had booked it all the way through to Cayman, connecting with Cayman Airways. He was just transiting through Miami and consequently did not have to clear US Customs with his bags. He made his way through the US Immigration lines, which were quite extensive at that time of the day, numerous international flights from all over the world having just arrived. When he finally found himself in front of an immigration officer, he explained that he was on his way to Cayman and quickly was allowed to proceed. He followed the signs down to the Customs Hall and through there before he duly appeared outside and went immediately following the directional signs to the Cayman Airways desk on the main concourse for check-in. Here he was to experience his first dealings with the Caribbean world and the frustrations that one could sometimes meet.

Watson had a three-hour-plus layover in Miami and figured he would get checked in and then relax and try his first American beer—of which he had heard varying descriptions. Oh, how the plans of mice and men can often go awry. Watson got in line at the Cayman Airways counter and realized things did not necessarily move too quickly in the islands. After waiting quite a while, he was standing in front of a Cayman Airways customer service agent and duly produced his ticket at the counter along with his UK passport and also two bag checks from BA. The customer service representative or agent looked at it, reviewed every page of his passport and also the two BA baggage checks, and asked, "Where is your return ticket?"

Watson said, "I don't have one. The government is contracting me for two years, and consequently, I just have a one-way ticket."

"Well, that's no good. You need a return ticket!"

Again, being highly trained and ready—so Watson thought—for any emergency, he produced his letter of engagement from the Cayman government for two years and his letter from the British Foreign and Commonwealth Office together with the British Overseas Development Corporation announcing his secondment. These were duly digested by the CSA who immediately summoned assistance from a supervisor. Watson thought good progress was now being made. *I'll shortly have my boarding pass.* The supervisor listened intently to all that was being said and seemed to be taking it all in. Watson was confident until he was asked the crunch question by the supervisor: "Where is your return ticket?"

He reiterated the whole scenario to the supervisor and waited for his boarding pass to be issued.

"We can't give you a boarding pass unless you have a return ticket, sir."

Obviously, judging from her stern and officious look together with her tone of voice, Watson concluded that persuasion was out of the question. It was hard to believe he was a customer! He then suggested to her, trying to find a solution, "Listen, I know I will be met by two senior officers of the Royal Cayman Islands Police Force. Send a fax or telex to the authorities in Cayman telling them that an illegal is on board flight KX242, and they can arrest me when I arrive there, or alternatively, I promise I will give myself up to the immigration officers when I land." These suggested arrangements seemed rather draconian, but at least he knew (well, hoped) the situation would be resolved once he landed on Caymanian soil. This suggestion seemed to curry favor with the supervisor, and it was agreed Watson would return to the check-in desk in about one hour to see what they had heard—if anything!

He left and went for a beer—his first Miller Lite—and discovered some of the descriptions he had heard of American beer were well-founded, although he did find the taste quite acceptable. After slowly drinking the beer, he decided to take a walk outside the Miami terminal to while away some time. He had left England in temperatures of sixty-five degrees. In Miami, he thought he had stepped into an oven. It was ninety-five degrees and 80 percent humid—totally alien to him. He began to have second thoughts there and then, plus he determined that if he did not get on the Cayman flight that evening, the next day he would fly back to the UK. His rationale was that if the Cayman government and police department couldn't arrange for him to get on a flight to Cayman without a return ticket on a two-year secondment, their police department was probably beyond redemption and needed much more help than he could give or perhaps wished to offer.

Forty minutes or so went by, and Watson could stand it no longer outside in the humidity and decided to wend his way back toward the Cayman Airways check-in counter. On the way, he noticed out of the corner of his eye that a scuffle had developed in the main thoroughfare of the concourse near the escalator down to the baggage claim. Some unkempt, unwashed youth of about twenty years was rolling around on the ground with a lady police officer from the Miami-Dade Police Department who was trying to handcuff him. Watson decided he could and probably should assist a fellow law enforcement officer. He went toward the fracas and made his way past numerous people who were purely viewing the free spectacle without lifting a finger to help the officer! Watson used the time-honored British police technique of introducing himself to the female officer and then securing the miscreant's shoulders and head on the hard floor with his knee while pulling his arms behind his back and handcuffing him for the by-now-distraught Miami-Dade officer—with her handcuffs. Watson then helped her up and then stood him up for her and produced his British police warrant card—his UK police identification—to her. Suffice to say, she was delighted for the assistance. By this time, they were surrounded by numerous other police officers and security personnel; some of whom immediately led the miscreant away. The Miami-Dade police officers all seemed delighted with the assistance rendered to their officer.

Watson shook himself down, picked up his carry-on bag, and made his way again toward the Cayman Airways check-in counter. An old lady who had stood in the vicinity watching the evening's free entertainment remarked, "Good job, young man. It's exciting here! Does this happen every day?" And after being assured by Watson that he didn't think it was a daily occurrence, she waddled off with her walking stick in hand. Watson smiled to himself and thought life was really interesting here. Back at the Cayman Airways counter, Watson made his way slowly but surely to the head of the line and was spotted by the supervisor who immediately told him, "We sent a telex to the immigration authorities in Cayman, but as yet, we have had no response."

Watson retorted, perhaps rather abruptly, "Well, I have shown you everything I have, and if I don't get on the flight tonight, I'll just go back to the UK tomorrow. It isn't worth all this hassle."

The supervisor said, "I know. I'll give you a standby departure management ticket that will allow you to go to the designated gate and wait there."

Watson thought, *This is good. Progress is being made.* But he also understood she was probably just shifting responsibility to other

Cayman Airways staff at the gate. He said, "Okay, but it is vital I am on the flight tonight, and the police are meeting me, so I am sure they will resolve any immigration problems." At least he hoped they would!

Consequently, he made his way through the security procedures that then existed and carried on to concourse F and gate 20. It was quite a walk from the security checkpoints to the gate, but Watson was in no hurry at this stage. It was an interesting sight to him to see the people waiting at the gate for flight KX242 to Cayman. There were young couples obviously going on an idyllic honeymoon or some special occasion, families going for a family vacation of sun and sand in the azure-blue Caribbean, a number of returning residents and locals suspiciously decked out in new clothing that he was sure they would never declare to Her Majesty's Customs in Cayman, and finally there were a number of businessmen and bankers dressed in the best London Savile Row suits, wearing Rolex watches and carrying alligator-skin briefcases, either reading the latest stock prices in the *New York Times* or the *Wall Street Journal* or alternatively with their heads buried in lever arch files containing voluminous sheets of paper and spreadsheets, possibly cooking up some kind of nefarious multimillion-dollar international deal.

Just to think in the two years immediately ahead of him, some of these people might well become his clients and, as a natural progression, residents of Her Majesty the Queen at the prison in Northward, Grand Cayman, at very advantageous prices. It really was an education watching the people waiting in the gate area to board Cayman Airways flight KX242 to Grand Cayman, a Boeing 727. Little did he know at the time, although he was to discover it later, one of the people waiting to board the aircraft was Jim Noone who was the deputy chief immigration officer in Cayman, and he could have been the panacea for all the problems Watson was encountering regarding having no return ticket. Obviously, the Cayman Airways staff did not know this either—shame on them! Another who might have been able to help was the wife of the uniform superintendent of police in Cayman who coincidentally knew from her husband that Watson was scheduled to be on the flight but could not recognize him! Watson had many laughs with her later in his sojourn in Cayman regarding that—there were not many six feet two, two hundred pounds individuals with short well-cut hair on the flight!

The gate agents duly started boarding the flight, and the name Watson was not called by the agents. He was becoming more and more resigned to an overnight stay in Miami and possibly returning to Heathrow the next afternoon when the gate agent paged his name. He approached the counter in trepidation of what he was to hear next. "Well, sir, we still haven't got the okay to board you, but because of the documentation you have provided, we are going to board you and notify the immigration in Cayman that you are on board without a return ticket."

"Eureka," he said, but this was lost on the gate agent. She duly handed him a boarding pass, and he immediately made his way down the Jetway to the aircraft before they could change their minds. The aircraft was about half-full, and he had a window seat, 17A. Luckily, again, he had the whole row of three seats to himself. He placed his carry-on in the overhead bin and took his seat and buckled up. He had finally made it on the last leg of the trip and flight to Cayman, although Watson did not really relax until they closed the boarding door and the aircraft commenced pushback.

The 727 was pushed back from the gate then taxied out, and after a wait of a few minutes on the runway, the three Pratt & Whitney jet engines roared into life and hurtled the plane down the runway, easterly toward the city of Miami. After takeoff and flying over Downtown Miami, rapidly gaining both speed and altitude, the plane changed course toward the South, the Florida Keys, Cuba, and on into Grand Cayman. It was a short flight, about fifty minutes, but nonetheless interesting as when the plane flew over Cuba, the passengers were severely warned against taking any photographs (from thirty thousand feet plus and at night, what photos could they get?) as they traversed the island because apparently, Fidel Castro would not allow it. On the odd occasion, just to exert his authority, Castro would apparently close the airspace and force aircraft to divert around the western end of Cuba, adding some forty minutes or so to the flight time to Cayman.

Not far into the flight, Watson noticed some liquid dripping from the vicinity of the overhead bin near him. Quick analysis by Watson using the senses of taste and smell confirmed it was a genuinely nice smooth Scotch. Watson quickly notified the lovely Cayman Airways flight attendants and asked for a glass to collect the spilling Scotch. However, unfortunately, the flight attendant was far more proactive and retrieved the bottle that was leaking and wrapped it in a bag and stood it in the galley to prevent further loss! Watson later learned that the bottle belonged to the superintendent's wife and that he was therefore drinking the senior officer's Scotch before he even met him.

The plane began its descent into Grand Cayman, and Watson could see off to the left of the aircraft the prime tourist area of Grand Cayman, Seven Mile Beach, with its hotels and condominiums and other buildings of note. The plane banked sharply to the left and then lined up for landing at the Owen Roberts Airport. As they flew in over the Walkers Road area and South Sound, Watson saw downtown George Town off to the left and a number of oceanside bars—of which he made a mental note. About 9:00 p.m., they landed in Cayman, and the plane braked heavily, together with applying the reverse thrust of the engines. Watson understood why when they turned around to travel back up the same runway and he glimpsed the North Sound clear waters under the wing of the aircraft—he guessed it could be pretty hairy in a tropical rainstorm!

This thought came back to Watson during his later tenure in Cayman when he and a colleague arrived back in Cayman from some inquiries abroad during a tropical rainstorm and the Cayman Airways flight braked heavily upon landing before turning and going back to the terminal. A few hours later that same evening, another Cayman Airways flight landed and, due to the prevailing conditions that had not eased, aquaplaned and skidded off the end of the runway and into the North Sound where the plane came to rest. The passengers, all of whom were uninjured, were subsequently ferried off the plane and taken to the terminals. Apparently, one young American visitor on the flight who probably had too much to drink was most excited by this and thought that this was how they always landed in Cayman!

For some time after the accident, it was quite unnerving to be at the airport and see a Boeing jet aircraft sitting in the North Sound just beyond the end of the runway. It was eventually lifted from the water and moved away!

CHAPTER 5

Arrival in Grand Cayman

Upon landing, the aircraft turned off the main runway onto a side taxiway and then finally drew to a halt in front of the terminal. The captain turned off the engines and, after a few minutes' delay, also turned off the seatbelt sign. The cabin entry door was opened, and there in place was a set of mobile stairs for the passengers to disembark down. Jetways were not the means of disembarking from the aircraft in Cayman. Watson awaited his opportunity and made his way to the door of the aircraft and out into Caribbean air for the first time. It was 9:20 p.m. at night, and the temperature was still about eighty degrees and humid! Watson began wondering how good the air-conditioning was on the island, a luxury he had never experienced in the UK.

At the foot of the steps from the aircraft, Watson was instantly recognized by two persons—one was Chief Inspector Alan Courtney, the administration chief inspector in the RCIP, and the other was Detective Inspector Barry Martin, Watson's predecessor in the post who was leaving after two-year attachment to return to the police force in the UK. Their powers of observation were obviously better than the superintendent's wife! After the usual introductions, they led Watson quite succinctly through the immigration lines notwithstanding that he didn't have a return ticket and on into the baggage hall where they awaited his luggage with some trepidation. Miraculously (according to Martin), both bags arrived on the only conveyor belt in the building, and Watson was ushered through the HM Customs line without any problem and out to the car park where they had a vehicle waiting to transport him to his hotel, which was to be his home for the first week or so in Cayman.

Inspector Martin said in the time-honored tradition of British detectives meeting up for the first time, "You've had a long day." It was now 3:40 a.m. UK time—a six-hour time difference. "Do you want a drink?" he asked.

Not wishing to be inhospitable, Watson responded, "Yes, that would be great."

"We'll go and check you in at the Royal Palms Hotel on West Bay Road, adjacent to Seven Mile Beach, where a reservation has been made for you, and then we'll have a drink at their beach bar."

"Sounds good to me," Watson retorted, secretly hoping it wouldn't be too late a session. He was fading quickly!

They drove from the airport, passed Fosters Food Fair, then turned down Shedden Road and on into George Town. To say it was somewhat of a culture shock would be an understatement—they saw goats and cows wandering about on the streets, numerous chickens meandering in all sorts of directions and pecking away aimlessly, and near Funky Tangs, there was loud reggae music that was obviously the precursor to or part of a party being held. Although Watson was really beginning to wonder what he had let himself in for, that changed as they reached the business area in downtown George Town—the city of five hundred banks plus and fifty thousand corporations plus, most of which no one had any idea who the beneficial owners were! The buildings all looked relatively modern and, in the fading light, appeared well-kept and maintained.

They continued to speak idly regarding Watson's trip and his position back home, and they answered his many questions regarding electricity and the like—the points that he regarded as specifically important to him and his well-being in the weeks and months ahead.

They then drove onto the West Bay Road—where Seven Mile Beach was situated—and after a couple of miles or so, they turned into the car park at the Royal Palms Hotel. It was an older building, but it looked well-cared for and exceptionally clean. Watson unloaded the two suitcases, and assisted by Courtney and Martin, they all strolled confidently into the reception area of Royal Palms. Here Watson was to see his second concern regarding the RCIP organization within a few hours. Chief Inspector Courtney proudly announced, "We have made a reservation for Mr. Watson for about ten to fourteen nights."

"Certainly, sir. One moment, please," retorted the receptionist, a young girl in her midtwenties who had beautiful bronzed skin, was impeccably dressed and very demure, and had long dark hair. She looked an absolute picture and was apparently eager to serve the guests. Watson briefly considered asking her out for a drink after she finished work but decided against it on the basis that it might offend his two new colleagues in that he would rather be with her than them! Watson took comfort in the fact that he believed she would still be there in the days and weeks ahead.

Check-in cards were flipped backward and forward in a box on the reception desk and then backward again before she said, "How do you spell the last name, sir?"

Courtney, who by now from his body language was appearing to Watson to be slightly concerned and somewhat agitated, responded, "Watson. W-A-T-S-O-N—Christopher." Martin also was looking slightly concerned, albeit somewhat amused, as though to say, "Typical administration cock-up!" Watson, as a longtime detective, understood that on many occasions, admin officers did have an innate capability to mess even the simplest arrangements up! It must be something that was bred into them during the admin officers training sessions they attended.

The young receptionist said, "I am very sorry, but we don't appear to have a reservation in that name."

"Well," Courtney said, "I made one and have a confirmation fax at police headquarters, but it's not with me." The evening was now beginning to degenerate rapidly again. *Typical admin cock-up*, thought Watson. *Why would he not bring the fax with him?* Trying to rescue the situation as Watson and Martin looked on with some bewilderment and a little hilarity, Courtney said, "Do you have a room available?"

"Yes, but only one directly on the beach, and those are not normally rented out to government."

"I'll take it," Watson interjected, only trying to quickly spare Chief Inspector Courtney any further embarrassment and, to a lesser degree, considering the opportunity to have a beachside hotel room! *This is an added bonus,* he thought.

"Can you give me a credit card, sir?" asked the receptionist. Watson looked directly at Courtney who immediately pulled out some credit card from his pockets—Watson didn't know if it was a personal one or a government-issued card—and offered it to the receptionist. Another couple of minutes or so and Watson was handed the keys to a suite from which he could walk out of the entry door to the suite and step directly onto Seven Mile Beach. What a beautiful beach and view that was in the rapidly fading light, and it was complemented by the sea gently lapping on the shore in an almost hypnotic rhythm. It sure beat Ingoldmells beach in Lincolnshire—a popular boyhood vacation retreat of Watson and his parents and sister! The whole vista of Seven Mile Beach was spectacular, and the thought of spending time here was becoming more and more interesting and alluring to Watson. All along Seven Mile Beach, there were lights twinkling in the cool breeze and reflecting off the beautiful blue water.

Courtney and Martin helped Watson with his luggage, which they basically threw into the room, checked that the air-conditioning was on and fully functional (Watson relied on their experience in this regard; there was no such apparatus in the UK), and then locked the room and made their way to the bar. Suffice to say that the evening dragged on rather longer than Watson would have wished, but at least he was getting used to drinking out of a bottle rather than the usual pint mug and also spending some brand-new US dollar bills obtained from the bank in the UK! Due to the exchange rate, Watson also discovered twenty US dollar bills equated to Cayman Island sixteen dollars and consequently was rather shocked initially to discover the dearth of change provided in CI dollars. After the goodbyes had been said for the evening, Watson made his way back to the room, which was to be his home for the next week or so. Martin arranged to collect him from the hotel next morning at about 9:00 a.m. in the reception area to allow him a little extra sleep! Fat chance of that, as Watson discovered the next morning.

On arrival back at his room after having drank a couple of nightcaps, Watson hurriedly unpacked his suitcases, determined to at least get all his clothing out from them and hang the same in the closets in the room. Watson knew that they would all need ironing, but at least he had them all hanging up. He then got ready for bed, checked the wonders of the air-conditioning unit again—setting it, as advised by Martin, at seventy-two degrees—and jumped, or perhaps *fell* is the better word, into bed. He didn't remember another thing that evening after a long and exhausting day traveling from Bilberry to Heathrow to Miami and finally to Grand Cayman plus the effect of the nightcaps consumed at the hotel bar.

CHAPTER 6

First Days at Work in the Cayman Islands

At about 4:30 a.m. (Cayman time) the next morning, he voluntarily awoke—this being the equivalent of 10:30 a.m. UK time, which his body clock was still on. He had had five hours plus of deep sleep. He tossed and turned for about thirty minutes or so and finally decided that as he couldn't get back to sleep, he'd take his first opportunity to swim in the Caribbean Sea. He put his swimming trunks on and quietly left the air-conditioned room and stepped outside in the calm night air and a temperature of about seventy-five degrees. It felt like a good English summer temperature. He made his way down the beautiful pristine white sands and placed his toes into the water that was gently lapping up on the seashore. The water was almost as hot as bathwater in the UK! Having been used to swimming in the North Sea on the Lincolnshire coast as a boy, he couldn't believe just how warm the water was at this time of the day. It could only get warmer once the sun rose. He was also amazed at just how clear it appeared, and with the moon reflecting off its steady undulations, he could both see and understand why many regarded Cayman as such a romantic place, notwithstanding its rather checkered history in the financial world. Watson left his towel, shoes, and shirt on a nearby lounger belonging to the hotel, near the high-water mark on the beach, and duly experienced the Caribbean Sea for the first time.

It really was amazing and beat the North Sea or, for that matter, any other sea or channel around the UK.

Well, Watson suffered the sea for half an hour or so, gently swimming up and down parallel to the beach and taking in the whole surreal experience. The lights of George Town were still flickering further down the beach and also reflecting off the azure-blue water. It was an idyllic scene, and there was no one else to disturb the view at this hour of the day. Watson then decided to go back inside and prepare his clothing and other items for the day. He also made a mental note to open a Cayman account in CI dollars as soon as possible to ensure that he did not get caught again on the exchange rate with US dollar and also for his salary to be deposited by the Cayman government.

Once back inside the suite, he turned on the local TV only to discover that the signal was coming in from Detroit; and consequently, he soon learned all about the Detroit sports teams, obstructions and others on highways leading into and out of Detroit, plus the Detroit weather! Watson couldn't understand why this was of any interest to him, but nonetheless, it was all a part of his Cayman learning experience and not least life's rich pageant.

Watson got out the clothing he planned to wear that day, a Thursday, and quickly pressed them and hung them up ready for the day ahead. He managed to iron quite a few pairs of trousers and also shirts, so he felt as though at least the day was starting off in a useful manner. By now it was almost 7:00 a.m., and Watson had shaved, showered, and got dressed, ready to go to the hotel dining room for breakfast.

He was greeted most affably by a big Jamaican lady who had the most beautiful smile and who readily and happily led him to a table overlooking the beachfront where he had been swimming a few hours earlier. She was really nice and welcoming to Watson, and upon learning that he had arrived in Cayman to work for the government, she treated him as a local and went out of her way to ensure he had all he needed. In the days ahead, as soon as Watson entered the dining room, she was always available to help him. Watson decided that this beat Bilberry Town Square on a damp November day! She then proceeded to hand him the menu and explain that the break-fast special that day was codfish and ackee—apparently a particularly tasteful Jamaican dish that was unknown to Watson at this time and was never known or experienced in Bilberry! It had certainly never been on the menu at the Mill Café. He decided that this was way too adventurous for him on his first day in paradise and accordingly opted for the American cooked breakfast with toast and coffee.

After a good, well-prepared, and hot meal together with unlimited coffee while taking in all his new surroundings, Watson felt ready to take on the world. After thanking the Jamaican lady, Watson returned to his hotel suite, tidied up, and then returned to the lobby about ten minutes early to await Martin, as arranged. Watson sat in the lobby watching residents at the hotel checking out or setting up tours for the day to the Cayman Turtle Centre or Stingray City. These were attractions that Watson would get well used to in the days and months ahead. Some thirty minutes after the appointed time, Martin arrived and walked in most nonchalantly—this was where Watson quickly learned another lesson for the day, the lesson of Cayman time. Cayman time, for the uninformed, ran between thirty and forty minutes after the appointed time, hence Watson's appointment with Martin for 9:00 a.m. was really set for 9:30 a.m. or thereabouts—Watson just didn't understand or comprehend that fact at the time.

After exchanging the usual pleasantries, they jumped into a Commercial Crime Branch police motor vehicle, a beat-up old Chevrolet Caprice, which could carry some seven people, but the air-conditioning had apparently ceased several years ago and didn't work. It just blew hot air into the vehicle! Consequently, they sweated their way to the Tower Building where the Commercial Crime Branch office was situated and where all the top hierarchy of the RCIP were domiciled. It felt good to enter the building; the air-conditioning was working well. At that time, no building in Cayman was allowed to be taller than five stories high, and the police offices were on the top floor of the building. HM Customs were also in the building along with the Land Registry and the Corporate Registry, both of which would be visited many times by Watson during his tenure in the islands for work-related queries. They entered the elevator, and Watson determined quite categorically that the elevators in the Tower Building were the slowest in the world; if not the slowest, they were certainly within the top three! It seemed like an eternity before they jolted to an unceremonious halt on the fifth floor, and Watson finally reached the CCB offices, more than twenty-four hours after he left Bilberry.

The offices were directly next to the Police Training Department offices where a former UK police officer, Superintendent Neville Smithley, held court in his bailiwick, and the commissioner and deputy commissioner's offices plus the headquarters administrative offices were also nearby, a few steps down the hallway. The CCB offices had a reception area, where the secretary resided and four other offices that were utilized by the CCB staff. There was also a storage room and a reasonably sized conference room that was used for all manner of purposes. They were all adorned in the usual governmental drab colors, and all held similar furniture, which Watson presumed had been purchased years earlier on a large and, perhaps more importantly, to government a cheap contract. Nonetheless, Watson had an office to himself from which he overlooked the town area, the courts building, the old library, and also the waterfront and cruise ship landing area. It certainly had Bilberry beat on a winter's day! Watson was introduced to all the current staff and the current CCB secretary, Jessie, who was an elder Canadian lady who had lived in the islands for a number of years. She was to become a special friend, and they had many laughs together as Watson became acquainted with the island and the multitude of idiosyncrasies that existed there. Her husband was a banker on the island, and consequently, Watson's path crossed frequently with both the husband and wife.

The police officers in the CCB at this time were Detective Inspector Wes Rawson, a Bajun (Barbadian) by birth and an excellent cricketer; Detective Sergeant Joey Johns, a born-and-bred Cayman Islander and excellent fisherman; Detective Sergeant Henderson Lunn, another Bajun by birth who also played cricket; and of course, Detective Superintendent Goodley, the head of CCB. Watson had no doubt that with the cricketing backgrounds of the staff, there might be some real rivalry whenever England played the West Indies, and that was certainly the case! Many a bet between them had to be settled by purchase of a beer or two. Watson was also pleased to learn that Johns was a good fisherman, and he began to dream of excellent, very fresh fish recipes he might experience in the months ahead. As time wore on over the following years and months, other new members would join the CCB as the branch and their duties and workload expanded. Each and every one of them brought unique skills and knowledge to the position as they learned the intricacies of investigating frauds and also major incidents.

Later that same day, Watson was ushered down to the commissioner's office and very warmly renewed his acquaintance with him from the interview some three months earlier that year in London. Watson was also introduced to the deputy commissioner who then administered the oath of office, swearing Watson in as a member of the RCIP and thereby bestowing upon Watson all the powers that that rank carried to perform his duties in the Cayman Islands. Then in another whirlwind of introductions, Watson was taken by the commissioner of police to the local government offices—locally known as the Glass House—where he was introduced to various members of government, including His Excellency the Governor, who was Her Majesty the Queen's representative on the island. He was a tall affable man, and judging by the strength of his handshake, Watson had no doubt he had played many a game of rugby in his earlier days, a fact that the governor acknowledged during one of his further meetings with Watson. All in all, it was a day spent being introduced to people and not remembering half the names that were introduced or passed to him! By the end of the visits, Watson had met so many people, he didn't know who was who or what they did; but he was sure that in the fullness of time, as any good policeman or detective, he would get to know those especially important to him to allow him to effectively function in the execution of his duties.

Watson then took the opportunity to visit one of the 583 banks in Cayman, a well-known and respected British-based bank named Barclays Bank PLC. He met the manager there who was an expatriate from England who had been with Barclays for many years. He was most helpful to Watson in setting up a current account that Watson could use for his salary to be paid into by government and also that Watson could use for receipt of wire transfers into the account and also for sending out monies to the UK as and when needed. He also set up a savings account that Watson funded with some traveler's checks brought from the UK, which he could then use as necessary. The whole meeting took about twenty to twenty-five minutes, and Watson was all set to not have to face the dreaded CI dollar and US dollar exchange rate problem again. Watson and the manager would meet many more times in the future over all manner of matters, both professional and also on the cricket field in Cayman or after-match activities. The manager was an enthusiastic playing member of one of the island's many cricket teams, and accordingly, Watson also spent time on the cricket field with him.

By the end of another full day, Watson was ready for a cold beer, and Martin duly suggested that they go to a bar near the Tower Building, in fact a bar just walking distance across the road from the Tower Building, where he would be introduced to even more people! The bar was on the waterfront with a covered patio and restaurant at the rear. It was locally known as CB's, in deference to the owner, Captain Bryan Banks. It was a fully functioning small bar and was by no means pretentious. There were two bar areas and then a restaurant at the back of the property. As with all good police stations in the UK that have a pub usually directly opposite or adjacent to the main entrance, it was refreshing for Watson to find a bar almost next door to the Tower Building. They arrived there about 6:00 p.m., and the bar was already pretty full with all manner of persons there—dive masters from the dive school next door, accountants, tourists (including honeymoon couples), bankers, and lawyers. Martin immediately started introducing Watson to people whom he knew and also knew would become invaluable to Watson in the fraud and money laundering investigations and other things he would become involved in. Two accountants in particular whom he met that evening became remarkably close friends of Watson and drinking buddies. The evening went by very quickly, and after a copious amount of beer and much joviality, Watson coerced one of his newfound friends to give him a ride back to the hotel farther away from town, down West Bay Road, reflecting on the fact that perhaps Cayman, for a couple years, would be quite acceptable. It would be worth mentioning that CB's would become a place often visited by Watson and colleagues during his tenure in the islands. It was frequently visited on Friday evenings for happy hour, a well-known phenomenon in Cayman that consisted of cheaper drinks and CB's also provided free snacks, which were always excellent. Many businesspeople, lawyers, accountants, police, judiciary, etc. visited on a Friday evening after a harrowing and busy workweek, and many relationships were formed during those visits.

Another oft frequented place that was visited also on Friday evenings for happy hour was the Sunset House, which had a nice patio overlooking the sea toward the west so that many a delightful sunset could be witnessed. Watson enjoyed this spot also because he was able to meet many people in the business and banking sector but mainly because of a dog that frequented the area. The dog would work his way around the area and would greet regulars like a long-lost friend. His name was Tripod, a testament to the fact that he only had three legs, having lost one of his legs when he was younger in a road traffic accident in Cayman. Tripod was not inhibited in any way by the fact that he only had three legs and could still move very swiftly when called upon to do so. Watson thought that Tripod didn't realize he was supposed to have four legs, and he and Tripod got on really well due to the fact that Watson would often share part of his meal with Tripod and also applied the necessary petting to Tripod when required, which was often.

Once Watson was back at the hotel from his relaxation at CB's and having exchanged a few pleasantries with the beautiful receptionist, who seemed really pleased to see him again, he quickly went to bed and into a deep sleep—the transatlantic flight was catching up on him!

Next day, after having a nice breakfast and being collected by Martin from the hotel upon his arrival at work, Watson again went through some of the indoctrination processes, including meeting other senior police officers who would become friends over the years.

Watson was particularly pleased to meet the head of the CID branch, Detective Chief Superintendent Lindsay Brown, and Detective Superintendent Ken Hallsworth, his deputy. Both were experienced officers in the field of criminal investigation, and during his tenure in the Cayman Islands, Watson would work directly for them during various major inquiries. Both officers thrived on the work undertaken and did their jobs with earnest hard work and devotion. Watson also appreciated that they were usually great fun to be around, and an added bonus was the fact that both loved their cricket. Watson was beginning to understand what he already knew from the UK, and that was that cricket was particularly important to the people of the West Indies. This was excellent news!

Watson spent some time with Martin catching up on investigations he was already involved in and that would, of necessity, be handed to Watson for completion. One of the jobs was an alleged on-island fraud that in the fullness of time would prove to be the disaster that Watson forecast it would be from day 1. Most of that day was spent with Martin going through the ongoing cases that he would become responsible for and learning of the outstanding matters still to be investigated. At the same time, he was also learning the caseloads of the other officers in the department. It was all pretty boring but vitally necessary to ensure a smooth transition and an understanding of the matters being handled to ensure the smooth transition. Time was also spent with the CCB senior officer Detective Superintendent David Goodley, a police officer who originated from Barbados and was now living and working in Cayman, plus Watson also met other senior officers in the detective branch. Police detectives might not always know the answers to certain problems, but over the years, they'd build up such good associations and relationships with persons of all experiences and standing that they would usually know someone who would know the answers to specific questions. Watson quickly realized that operating in an offshore financial tax haven, it was going to be imperative to engender some relationships in the business and financial sector, and that became an objective for him in many meetings that took place over the following days, weeks, and months. CB's provided a venue for a number of these associations, as on Friday evenings, all manner of people gathered at CB's for happy hour, and of course, contacts could be easily bred in such an atmosphere.

At one of the very first formal team meetings he had with the CCB officers and also whenever a new officer joined the unit, Watson took the opportunity to tell them that as a boss, if any of his officers did anything wrong or incorrect that might invite a complaint from the public or even a person being arrested or if they did anything that they thought might come back to bite them in the backside at some stage, he wanted to hear solely from the officer(s) first and learn the story as soon as possible. Watson's logic for this was that when a senior officer of higher rank would learn of any complaint or possible infraction that the officer(s) had committed, the senior officer would invariably first approach Watson and ask Watson questions, sometimes very awkward questions. Watson explained that he did not want to be in the position of not having a clue what the senior officer was speaking about. Watson wanted to be in the position of saying, "Yes, I know about that, and here is the story." Watson also told them that he would always expect the truth from them regarding whatever actions they took. He continued that as long as it was a reasonable and understandable decision and action made solely upon the facts and evidence as known to them at the time, they would always have his support whenever needed. Lastly, if they made a mistake—and everyone would at some time—he did not expect them to make the same mistake twice! Watson summed it all up by explaining that if he were approached by a senior officer and he didn't know about a potential incident, then Watson would be very unhappy; and he assured the staff that they, too, by natural progression, would also be very, very unhappy! It was a grouping of messages well-received by the detectives, and this was shown by the fact it was adopted a number of times during Watson's tenure in the Cayman Islands.

During this day, Watson also visited the force tailor who equipped him with his officer's dress uniform to attend officer's mess nights and other such ceremonial happenings. This was all rather rushed, as he learned that same day that during the evening at the Holiday Inn, an officer's mess night was scheduled in their ballroom.

The majority of the ranking officers in the RCIP attended, and it was a great opportunity to get to know each of them by face and name. The food and wine served was excellent, and newcomers were welcomed. The host was the commissioner of the RCIP. After dinner, officers told various jokes; and more importantly, drinks of port and brandy circulated the dining table afterward. And as the drinks circulated, it was inherently noticeable that the room seemed to get louder! It was a very pleasant evening and was another great opportunity for Watson to get to know his future colleagues and workmates.

The next day, Watson found it rather hard to get out of bed but nonetheless made it to work on time. Some of his colleagues were not so fortunate! It was pleasing that most of the day was spent with boring documentary matters and again researching the ongoing case matters. He also got to spend time meeting and speaking with his future colleagues in the CCB, one detective inspector and two detective sergeants. They were all very enthusiastic, and Watson seemed well-received by them. Watson's predecessor in the post, Martin, had been heavily involved in one particular case and, accordingly, had not been able to provide as much on-the-job training to these officers that perhaps they would have wished for or was the intention of the Caymanian authorities in bringing expatriate officers to the island. Watson made a mental note to ensure that that did not occur during his tenure and subsequently tried to involve his colleagues in most actions and inquiries that he undertook during his time in Cayman.

His first weekend in Cayman was spent going with some colleagues to look at various rental properties that were available on the island so that he could move out of the hotel as soon as reasonably possible. There were all sorts of properties available, but he was fortunate in that a colleague, Chief Inspector Courtney of Watson's initial reservation fame, found a ground-floor one-bedroom apartment with an additional sofa bed directly on Seven Mile Beach that was available and just what Watson wanted to call his home during his two-year secondment to the Cayman police. The complex had a mixture of holidaymakers and also some long-term tenants, and it was fortunate in that the long-term tenants all seemed to be in one area of the complex. There were two swimming pools, a tennis court, and also direct access to the beach and the Caribbean Sea. Later that following week, following negotiations with the site management team, he was able to move his belongings, which filled two suitcases into his new ground-floor apartment. It really was a nice place to spend two years and would do him fine, especially in that it had air-conditioning to be used as and when necessary. As a bonus, it was also within walking distance of the office, and also just down the road was the Ramada Hotel and the current in place, Treasure Island Night Club! A midsize grocery store and a Kentucky Fried Chicken restaurant were across the road from the complex, plus a wonderful restaurant overlooking the Caribbean Sea named the Wharf was but a short walking distance away. One fact that Watson considered, in accordance with British tradition, was that the chosen apartment lay within the maximum staggering distance (MSD) of CB's as and when necessary (i.e., as and when driving a vehicle, due to the evening's activities, was not an option to be reasonably considered).

During that same first weekend, he found his way to the local cricket ground, the Smith Road Oval, and found a couple of teams playing a Cayman league match there. Unlike pitches in the UK, Watson noticed it was not a natural grass strip that they were playing on; it was an artificial turf wicket that Watson thought made it a more difficult and lopsided game for the bowlers than for the batsman. Nonetheless, both sides were thoroughly enjoying the rivalry being played out. Cricket was his first love in the UK, and accordingly, he mentioned to some of the people at the ground his background in cricket. And although past the optimal playing age, he was currently qualified internationally as a cricket umpire with the Association of Cricket Umpires that was headquartered in London and would like to umpire some games during his tenure in Cayman, if they needed any umpires. Suffice to say that at the end of the game, Watson realized there were a substantial number of cricketers on the island who had clearly played the game at a high level both in Cayman and elsewhere, including other Caribbean islands, India, Pakistan, the UK, and Australia. This was most encouraging for him; he loved all there was about cricket and the people who played the same. Following the culmination of the game, Watson was approached by a number of the more senior players and invited to share the odd beer or two at the ground, and he did so willingly. The cold beer served from ice chests did indeed taste most acceptable and refreshing. Following on from this visit, the following week, he was besieged with phone calls in the office from various cricket officials on the island; and as a result, the very next weekend, he started umpiring games on almost a weekly basis, subject to the exigencies of police duties allowing. Apart from being an artificial pitch, the other more noticeable downside to the venue was that it was at the end of the runway at Owen Roberts Airport; and every time a passenger jet came in to land—a Boeing 727, 757, 737, an MD-80, or numerous private Gulfstream jets—the play had to be suspended momentarily while the airplane passed overhead by a hundred feet or so. The primary advantage to becoming involved in cricket was that first and foremost, Watson was involved in one of his primary loves; and second, he immediately began making new friends with numerous locals and also expatriates on the island who, in the months and years ahead, would assist him in many ways in fulfilling his duties and obligations as a Caymanian police officer. There was no better way to integrate himself with the locals and make friends from all walks of life. In fact, as time progressed, Watson was duly elected as the secretary of the Cayman Islands Cricket Association, and this thereby spread the news of his presence on the island and engendered more relationships with the teams and players in the league. Some of those friendships still subsist in the modern day for Watson.

Watson, who had been using a loaned Cayman government motor vehicle for his personal transport, met a banker during the weekend who was looking to sell his spare car, an older Toyota Corolla. It had about eighty thousand miles on the odometer. The air-conditioning didn't work too well, but the engine ran like a charm. The seller was asking US $1,500 for the car, and following a bit of negotiation, Watson bought it for $1,300 cash. Bodily it appeared surprisingly good, although there were a few rust spots on the roof, which Watson duly sealed to the best of his ability with polymer, and all appeared well. It served the purpose for Watson—to get him to and from work—and it allowed Watson to return the government vehicle to the government compound. Over the next two years plus, the Toyota ran like a well-oiled machine, and the only repair Watson had to have done was a new cylinder head gasket, which one of the local garages subsequently did for him. That effort was a story in itself, but nonetheless, Watson thought Toyotas were good even if this one did not present itself too well. Some of his colleagues laughed at his choice of motorcar, but it suited Watson perfectly for what he would need for the next two years.

Also, during this same weekend, Watson learned that there were generally no street names or house numbers in Cayman at the time. Coming from the UK, this was somewhat of a shock for him. *Everybody has a postal address, don't they?* He asked a member of his staff how to get to the banker's address to view the Toyota Corolla. The answer was to take the main road out of town to the right, go down there about one-half a mile or so to a gas station, turn right and go down there until you see three palm trees in the yard of a yellow house, turn right and go down there until you see a garbage collection bin next to a commercial building, and then turn left, and it is the salmon-colored house on the left! Watson learned the distance traveled from the Tower Building to the home was about two miles, give or take a hundred yards or so. Suffice to say, it took Watson almost seven miles before he found the property in question, and his anxiety in getting there was only exceeded by his thoughts of how he would get back now! Watson had one more such exploration adventure when he had to first visit a property in Bodden Town. Again, the simple instructions given turned into a nightmare, and he arrived forty-five minutes late for the meeting with a potential informant. Whenever Watson went out looking for people following these two adventures and the Tour de Cayman he had undertaken in both cases, he thought it wise in the future to always take a local officer with him. It greatly expedited the whole process, and oftentimes the local officers knew exactly who lived or worked where and in which properties. The time to locate people by Watson was cut exponentially and made his decision look most sensible and well-founded.

Regarding the bar near the Tower Building colloquially known as CB's, Watson recalled that there was an incredibly good outcome to one of those many visits to CB's that took place over the weeks and months ahead. Watson entered CB's after one particularly harrowing day wherein he had completed one inquiry and had been assigned two further inquiries to deal with! It was a Tuesday evening and not usually a day where drinks were taken after work. Following the harrowing day, he accordingly called a local accountant friend and expressed the dire need for a beer after work. And the accountant thought for a millisecond, and they agreed to meet at CB's for a couple of drinks. Watson wandered over to the bar about 5:15 p.m., and the regular bartender, Jasmine, a lovely Jamaican lady who seemed to spend most days working there, gave him her usual warm and friendly hello and opened a can of Miller Lite that was immediately put on the counter for Watson to savor. Jasmine was a blessing to Watson in that he would get quickly served by her when the bar was crowded. There were two American ladies sitting in the bar, one was drinking a piña colada and one a Johnnie Walker Black whiskey. Apparently, they were sisters on vacation for a few days in Cayman from their homes in the USA. One lived in Dallas, and the other in Phoenix. They had just been visiting their elderly mother who lived in Pompano Beach, Florida, and they had decided to come to the Cayman Islands for a few days of rest and relaxation and to get away from everything. How fortuitous was that decision? Neither they nor Watson had any conception of it at that specific time.

They had been out all day enjoying Cayman and had visited a place of some repute in the jurisdiction, namely Stingray City, and there they swam with the families of stingrays who frequented that area, including hand-feeding them with small pieces of squid. They had also witnessed the captain of the tour boat preparing some conch that he had just plucked from the sea for a quick lunch, although Sarah was not too taken with this as a lunch. After their daytime adventures, they had finally stumbled upon CB's having been in George Town looking for a store to buy a cheap camera. Sarah (from the Dallas suburbs) and Elizabeth (from Phoenix, who had visited Cayman once previously) were now, by chance, in CB's looking for a nice place to eat dinner. When asked by the ladies where to eat, Jasmine, the bartender, directed them immediately to Watson, explaining that he knew all the places to eat! Watson, accordingly and to assist Jasmine, got into a casual conversation with them and was going through the necessary exploratory questions to determine exactly what they wanted to eat, the budget available, and other ancillary matters (e.g., views from the restaurant). Watson found himself particularly attracted to Sarah, a slim-built, pretty, and vivacious woman originally from Chicago who now lived in the suburbs of Dallas, Texas, in a small town called Roanoke. Watson had heard lots of small talk on the island over the months he had been there about the virtues of a good Texan girl, all of them good. Sarah was extremely sweet and most interesting, allied to the fact she had many interesting airline stories. Apparently, she was a flight attendant with United Airlines, a major domestic and international airline headquartered in Chicago, Illinois, and had been for a considerable time. Sarah, although trying her best, could not fully comprehend Watson when he spoke and even tried reading his lips to see what he was saying! She did think initially, with some conviction, that Watson was originally from Australia judging by his accent. Accordingly, Watson could not help but explain that he was not; and more importantly, he had no convictions, which was probably lost on Sarah and Elizabeth at that time! Watson then had to explain the meanings behind that to both the ladies. Following up on their preliminary question to Jasmine about eating, Watson suggested that perhaps CB's and the waterside patio would be a good place to eat. He knew the food there was consistently good—both meat, fish, and chicken dishes—and the view over the Caribbean was most romantic at night, the city lights reflecting off the water and the sound of waves gently lapping the supports upon which the patio deck had been constructed. While this conversation was developing, Watson's accountancy friend arrived, as did numerous other lawyers, bankers, accountants, dive masters, and business directors well known to Watson—some for good reasons, other for not such good reasons. Watson was not quite sure what happened next or how it happened, but within a short space of time, his friends and colleagues had packed the bar and further had six or seven piña coladas lined up for Sarah and the same number of Johnny Walker whiskeys for Elizabeth. This was not, strange as it might seem, an unusual phenomenon in Cayman. The evening gradually became rather boisterous and loud, and to save the ladies from any potential embarrassment, Watson suggested that they go onto the dining patio, which was a lot quieter, and eat some dinner at CB's.

Accordingly, Watson took them to the patio and ordered some dinner along with bringing their drinks from the bar. The setting, though not pretentious, was most romantic in the night air, with the sounds of the waves and small scented candles burning on each table. The atmosphere was 180 degrees diametrically opposed to that that was inside the building. Both the ladies were pretty mellow and, after a day out and about in Cayman and North Sound in the fresh air and due to the copious amounts of drink inhaled, were both fading rapidly. Jasmine came and took the orders after everyone had reviewed the menus and then brought Watson another drink to the table, smiling broadly at Watson and telling him what good choices he had made—relating to the food, or so Watson thought. Jasmine, in her usual and efficient manner, happily served the meals, and they were enjoyed by everyone, although Watson was not sure that the ladies would remember the same the next day. A nice meal and good conversation made the evening especially pleasant, although it'd be fair to say that Watson thought that both the ladies were acting somewhat on autopilot, following the drinks consumed in the bar. After dinner, Elizabeth got a lift back to the hotel with an accountant friend of Watson, while Watson asked Sarah to go for a drink with him at the nearby Hyatt Hotel pool bar. She agreed, and they went to the Hyatt, where there were some beautiful gardens and a nice pool bar at the rear of the main building. The atmosphere was first-class and more subdued than at CB's; accordingly, Watson enjoyed a nice drink with Sarah in the beautiful surroundings. In the warm evening air, it really created an atmosphere of both contentment and enjoyment. Much was spoken about that evening, but the one thing that Watson determined was that he definitely wanted to see Sarah again. After walking her through the grounds, hand in hand, Watson took Sarah back to her hotel and agreed if they wished to meet him the following evening that he would take them both to dinner so that they would at least remember fully one dinner in the Cayman Islands. Sarah jumped on the opportunity and said she thought that Elizabeth would also. They were planning to take a trip on the Atlantis Submarines the next day and were due ashore about 6:15 p.m., so Watson arranged that he would pick them up about that time from the submarine landing dock. Sarah seemed quite excited by this and duly agreed, although in her heart, she doubted she would ever see Watson again. Watson, to the contrary, had absolutely no doubt that they would meet again.

Watson finally arrived back at his apartment after the long day and the very pleasant evening he had spent. His mind was busy thinking about Sarah; she really was a beautiful lady. As soon as his head hit the pillow that evening, he was in a deep sleep until morning light! Little did he know at the time that the chance meeting with Sarah and Elizabeth was to have a profound impact on his life in the days, months, and many years ahead.

The following evening, following another remarkably busy day, Watson left work about 5:30 p.m. and went to his car and drove to the car park directly adjacent to the Atlantis Submarines store and boarding center. He arrived there about 6:00 p.m. and spoke to some members of the staff, some of whom he had already made an acquaintance with in the past months, and he was allowed by them to go deck side to where the ferry from the submarine would bring the passengers ashore after completing their dive. He was sitting there enjoying the relaxation and the view out to sea and saw the submarine surface about two hundred feet from shore, and the ferry, which was nearby, quickly attached itself to the submarine to allow the passengers to transfer. After a few minutes, the ferry came back to shore, and the passengers—totaling about thirty people—exited and came ashore. Sure enough, Sarah and Elizabeth were among them, and Watson beamed at this fact. They both seemed pleasantly surprised to see Watson waiting on the deck for them. They did not realize what being a chief inspector in the local police could do for a person. The warrant card carried as a form of identification could open all sorts of doors, formally and informally. They exchanged a quick hug and greeting among them, and they went to Watson's car.

They drove from there to a nice restaurant in Coconut Place on the West Bay Road, not far from their hotel, where they got a table for drinks and also a meal, which Watson had experienced on a number of previous occasions, and the food was excellent. Watson ordered a steak, and both the ladies had fish. A bottle of tasteful white wine was also ordered. The food was well-prepared and served excellently, as was the drink. Conversation was easy, and all sorts of seemingly important matters were covered. Much laughter also took place that evening. Watson was really attracted to Sarah, and the feelings he had following their meeting the previous evening were being expanded on and confirmed greatly.

After the meal, he took both the ladies to the Treasure Island Night Club, where a few more drinks were taken and some time was spent on the dance floor, dancing to hits from the '60s and '70s. Both Sarah and Elizabeth were fading fast, having had another full day out in the sun and fresh air, and Elizabeth wanted to go back to their hotel. Watson accordingly drove her to the hotel, but Sarah was more than eager to spend additional time with Watson, as was Watson with her. The atmosphere between them was charged; no one had to say anything. They called at another beach bar nearby for a cocktail, and then Sarah accepted an invitation to come back to Watson's apartment for a final drink or cocktail. Once there, they quickly fell into each other's arms, and the action quickly moved from the couch in the living room into the bedroom of the apartment. Suffice to say that when Watson awoke the next morning about 6:30 a.m., Sarah was lying alongside him! She looked an absolute picture. Watson smiled, put his arm around her, and pulled her close to him. It felt so natural, and Sarah responded in such a natural way. Watson was already hoping against hope that he wouldn't do anything stupid to mess this potential relationship up. Who would have believed this, so far from his home in the UK? Sarah awoke slowly, and Watson told her he needed to be at work about 8:00 a.m. that morning to go and rattle someone's cage. Accordingly, she quickly showered, and Watson took her back to her hotel. Elizabeth and Sarah were flying out of Cayman to Miami about midday that day. Once back at their hotel, Sarah and Watson cuddled, and they parted reluctantly but swore to keep in touch with each other.

About midday that same day, during his lunch hour, Watson traveled to the Cayman airport and, once there, went through security into the departure lounge. In the lounge, which was full of departing visitors and also residents going shopping in Miami, he found Sarah and Elizabeth sitting there and chatting away. A big smile came on Sarah's face when she saw Watson, and they had about fifteen minutes to interact before she and Elizabeth were called and boarded their flight back to Miami. Sarah again expressed great interest in seeing Watson in the future if and when he visited the USA, and accordingly, they exchanged their home phone numbers. Watson thought he saw a tear in Sarah's eye before she got up to board the plane and, based on his interactions with her so far, resolved to keep in touch with her.

The phone number she provided was used by Watson the following weekend. He had to travel to Atlanta, Georgia, to complete some inquiries about one of the cases he was investigating in Cayman, and accordingly, he called Sarah and let her know that he would be there in Atlanta from Sunday through the following Thursday. Being a flight attendant, she could easily travel to Atlanta from Dallas, and she duly arrived on Wednesday and left on Thursday about the same time that Watson left to return to Cayman. That Wednesday evening, they had a nice meal at a restaurant in Downtown Atlanta, and then Watson took her to the revolving bar at the top of the Peachtree Hotel Tower, where there were fabulous views to be had of the city of Atlanta and the surrounding countryside. Sarah's drink of choice was a B-52 Bomber, which, coming from Northern England, Watson had no idea of what it was, although he did know of the airplane, a B-52 Bomber! She certainly enjoyed them. Afterward, Watson and Sarah returned to the hotel where Watson was going to reserve a room for her, but no room was ordered—it was not necessary according to Watson's thought processes. And yet again, Sarah woke the next morning in Watson's room. That morning, after a hearty breakfast, they drove to the airport. Sarah returned home to Dallas, and Watson went to Miami and on to Cayman. Watson was really feeling a lot of affection for Sarah, and going forward, they met in many places and times when Watson was conducting all manner of inquiries at various places in the USA and, a few times, in other places offshore. And as for Sarah, she visited Cayman on many occasions when she could and when her flying schedule allowed to spend time with Watson. Being a flight attendant gave her the privileges to get up and go at a moment's notice and at very advantageous prices and certainly helped fuel a quickly escalating long-distance relationship.

October had arrived in 1987, and Watson found that the islanders were extremely excited and incessantly speaking about the Week! The reason being that as part of a celebration to their heritage and the Caribbean, Pirates Week had once again arrived. Watson thought perhaps pirates from other islands invaded Cayman together with ancillary and mandatory pillaging. It was not so. The first day of Pirates Week, a group of fearsome-looking pirates and wenches, most of whom seemed to originate from Seattle for some odd reason, came ashore in small boats at Hog Sty Bay and formally seized the governor to take control of the island. The first night, a big street party was held in downtown George Town. Throughout the following week, the pirates went to different parts of the island—such as West Bay, East End, Bodden Town, and North Side—and generally just partied in each location. Avid followers of the celebrations went to each district as the pirates went around the island. Watson noticed that due to these celebrations, trying to get anything achieved in the normal course of business was exceedingly difficult. But nonetheless, it was a most enjoyable week, and much fun was associated with the celebrations. Watson dutifully, or that was how he explained it, threw himself into each and every celebration on the island that he could find! The final day of the week was spent having a big street party and fireworks in the heart of George Town, which had been closed down for that purpose. A group of people each and every year, soon after one Pirates Week was finished, started the planning for the following year. Watson, having experienced his first Pirates Week, made sure that going forward, he was always available to help the Cayman islanders and visitors from near and far to celebrate the Week; each and every year, he was there. *Perhaps Bilberry should have one of these,* he thought. *Perhaps they could call it Vikings Week instead of Pirates Week.*

CHAPTER 7

First Week—an Undercover Drug Case

Watson was an experienced all-round UK detective, and the local head of the RCIP Drug Squad was also a former UK police detective who had noticed with interest Watson's recent arrival on the island. Watson was called from a meeting to introduce him to the government's computerized management system at the government headquarters by the Drug Squad's head and was asked if he was able to assist in an undercover drug buy at a local hotel, the Cayman Islander. The Cayman Islander was a rather tired and older hotel on the West Bay Road, and for a long time, the Drug Squad had quite rightly suspected that it was used for many nefarious activities, not the least of which was small-time drug trafficking. It had all been brought to the Drug Squad's attention by a number of local informants, and having been duly researched and investigated, the Drug Squad had decided to act on it. Watson was first introduced to the informants and then subsequently carried to the Cayman Islander where he was taken to apartment 137, and left there in the company of a Jamaican lady named Pearlette.

There was another Jamaican lady present named Elizabeth who left soon after Watson arrived. Watson thought that the two women were in their late twenties or early thirties. Watson introduced himself as Chris Gill and said that he'd been brought to her because he was seeking the purchase of some cocaine. He told her he had

US $4,000 in cash available and produced the roll of banknotes for Pearlette to see. Pearlette stated she had eight ounces of cocaine available but Gill would have to buy the entire lot. Gill stated it was okay, but he just wanted the $4,000 worth to begin with. There was a back and forth between them regarding buying the whole amount, and finally Pearlette agreed Watson could buy the rest of the package later in the day. Pearlette was initially rather circumspect as to why the money was in US dollars and not Cayman Island dollars, but as a recent arrival in the islands and having last worked in the USA, Watson or Gill explained he had not yet had the opportunity to set up the Cayman Islands banking accounts that would be needed for ongoing business. As she looked at the US dollars, she was then worried that they might be counterfeited; but Gill explained that if they were, then the Bank of America in Miami would get some hassle from him when he returned next to the USA. Pearlette then said she trusted him and made an internal call on the room telephone. Shortly thereafter, Elizabeth came back into the room and spoke quietly with Pearlette. Gill saw Elizabeth hand Pearlette a package in silver paper, and Pearlette handed Elizabeth the $4,000 in cash. Elizabeth left the room, and Pearlette handed Watson the package, which contained a small plastic bag containing a substance that appeared to him to be cocaine. Watson then spoke with Pearlette about obtaining the remainder of the cocaine about 3:00 p.m. that same day when they would have it available at the hotel. Watson was, of course, aware that room 137 was under observation from outside by the Drug Squad detectives, and Superintendent Smithley and his wife were also observing the comings and goings to the room from the nearby poolside bar at the hotel. They would know which room Elizabeth had been coming from and going to.

Shortly after Elizabeth left the room, things happened pretty quickly when the Cayman Police Drug Squad forcibly entered the hotel room, and both Pearlette and Gill or Watson were arrested. Watson handed the cocaine to the Drug Squad detectives, and both were taken separately to the Drug Squad offices at the Central Police Station.

Of course, Elizabeth had also been arrested earlier as she left the apartment for the final time and was also at the Central Police Station together with the US $4,000 that had been recovered from her and also the remainder of the drugs being offered for sale. Both women were interviewed by Drug Squad officers and subsequently charged with possession of the illegal drugs with intent to supply. Ultimately, they were each sentenced to three and a half years in jail plus fined $5,000 each following guilty pleas in the Cayman Islands Summary Court. Following the operation, two things came to mind to Watson regarding the events that had occurred. The $4,000 offered for the drugs was indeed very good counterfeit dollars the police had confiscated at some point in the recent past, and also the operation took place on the very same day that, by coincidence, a photograph of Christopher Watson was on the front page of the daily *Cayman Compass* newspaper welcoming him to the Royal Cayman Islands Police Department, the CCB, together with a narrative setting out his background in the UK police service. Thank goodness, neither Pearlette nor Elizabeth read the *Cayman Compass* that day, and Watson mused that thank goodness, he was not aware of that at the time too! It might have turned his hair prematurely gray! Nonetheless, nothing ventured and nothing gained, and the Drug Squad caught two people whom they suspected had been involved in the trafficking of illegal drugs for quite some time.

Also, as one of the first undercover enforcement actions he had undertaken since arriving on the island, a valuable lesson was taught to Watson over how matters could transpire in the islands compared to the UK and the work that went on behind the scenes. The Drug Squad was delighted with the outcome and subsequently used Watson again on a number of occasions in various undercover drug operations. Certain members of the Drug Squad in the Cayman Islands were very proactive in the enforcement field, and a number had some excellent informants whom they cultivated and subsequently cooperated with in a large number of ongoing drug cases. Watson always enjoyed working with them as and when necessary. Their eagerness to take illegal drugs off the streets and also to incarcerate the bad guys was impeccable.

During this first case, the Drug Squad detectives often pulled Watson's leg about him not being able to understand their Jamaican Patois, which was initially exceedingly difficult to comprehend. However, Watson always got his own back on them by speaking in a broad Northeastern English accent, and they soon learned that they could understand even less of that! Jamaican Patois was spoken by a number of Jamaicans as a native language, and Watson had had some experience with it among the Jamaican communities in various regions of the UK, a fact that he did not tell the islanders. Patois originally developed in the seventeenth century when slaves from West and Central Africa were exposed to, learned, and nativized the vernacular and dialectal forms of English spoken by the slaveholders in days gone by. By the end of his tenure in the islands, Watson became reasonably proficient with the Jamaican Patois.

CHAPTER 8

First Formal Interview in the Cayman Islands

A few days later, Watson discovered yet another idiosyncrasy of working in the islands. At the request of the FBI in the USA and as authorized by the Cayman Islands attorney general, he had to arrange an interview with the managing director (MD) of a large multinational corporation at their Cayman offices. An appointment was made for the interview to take place at the company office, and Watson prepared a list of questions to be asked to obtain the information being sought in the matter. He also briefed Detective Sergeant Joey Johns (a born-and-bred Caymanian) to go with him and make a contemporaneous record of the answers provided by the interviewee. Joey was most enthusiastic about the task at hand and enjoyed the briefing on what would happen during the interview. It should be noted that the interviewee, although he had been in the islands for some time, originated from deepest and darkest Scotland and had still retained a broad Scottish accent, which to Watson was reasonably understood when spoken slowly but might prove more difficult to a Caymanian.

The day arrived, and Watson and Johns went to the company offices, which were situated in one of the multistory office buildings on the island. The offices occupied one floor of the building and, in stark contrast to the government offices, were well-appointed and contained very high-class furnishings. They were ushered into the managing director's office and were seated in a plush air-conditioned conference room adjacent to his office. Introductions were made, and the interview commenced with Watson asking the prepared questions and the MD answering them as best he could. Detective Sergeant Johns noted his responses as each and every question was asked and duly answered. At the end of the interview and following the production of four pieces of correspondence pertinent to the facts in hand, the MD read over and made a few corrections to the answers given, which he duly signed and subsequently agreed with. The problem lay in the fact that the questions were asked by an Englishman, answered by a Scottish person, and the answers recorded by a Caymanian. This was the subject of some amusement among the parties. As an example, a question asked about specific circumstances of the matter was answered with, "Och aye, I have no idea what occurred." It was recorded in true Caymanian fashion: "Oh, wha'appened?" Another question delving into the depth of the MD's knowledge of certain parts of the transaction was answered by saying that he had no knowledge of the same. The answer recorded was, "Me no know!" Yet again, it was an important lesson for Watson to learn that this might be a British-protected Crown Colony; but as far as language was concerned, the similarity sometimes ended there.

Another thing learned from these initial encounters was that by Watson consistently working with members of the CCB, the officers in the department were eager and willing to learn the techniques used in good fraud investigation and were always willing to try new ways of organizing, maintaining, and executing the files and other matters. It was always very gratifying to work with them and help them in demonstrating how to deal with frauds and similar matters, how to accumulate and preserve and log the evidence, and finally how to prepare the interviews and submit the files for consideration. Also, they learned how to preserve and retain evidence so that the chain of custody, which could be so important in some cases, was always being preserved and integrity maintained.

Unlike normal interrogations to determine if a person broke into a property or murdered an individual, fraud matters called for interviews, not interrogations. Generally, in fraud matters, Watson told the officers, "You are showing the suspect various documents, and often, you don't care what he or she says, as you know the next document may well prove to show that they are lying. It is a totally different technique to normal interrogations where you are actively seeking admissions of certain facts or actions." At the same time, the CCB was getting well-known in the local community as a branch of the police force that always tried to do the very best they could in the best way they could while being cognizant of the rights of the people they arrested or dealt with. The CCB tried to always make themselves available to the public, the business community, and the lawyers, be it on the prosecution side or the defense attorneys. These first two primary interactions with the Drug Squad and the CCB taught Watson a lot about the manner and effectiveness of policing in the Cayman Islands.

This was further illustrated in one particular case where a defense attorney, during a trial, made a submission to the court of a particular exhibit that needed to be submitted to a lab in the USA for forensic examination to be taken to the USA and submitted for the same and then brought back to Cayman for the trial to continue. Some disagreement ensued between the prosecution and defense over how to achieve that objective. The defense attorney, who was well-known to Watson, stated to the court that he would object to any of the officers directly involved in the case taking the exhibit for examination, and then he suggested that DCI Watson be given the task and the exhibit for completion of the same. Watson was duly called to the court and informed by the court that the defense attorney had asked if he would undertake the task and bring the exhibit and a report on the same back to the court when completed. Watson asked, "Why me? I have had nothing to do with the case." The court told him that was why and that both the prosecution and defense agreed with the request and trusted that it would be properly and expeditiously completed. Consequently, Watson made an arrangement with the laboratory in West Palm Beach to arrive there with the exhibit and submit it along with the examination request. The laboratory would expedite the examination, and then by lunchtime the day after, they would return the exhibit and a report to Watson. Watson duly arrived at the lab about lunchtime and dropped off the exhibit and the request. The following day, he explored West Palm Beach and Boca Raton and had really nice meals. Sarah flew to West Palm Beach and met Watson for a nice afternoon stroll among the rich and famous shops, and then they had a wonderful meal and dessert on Wednesday evening. On the third day, Thursday, Watson collected the exhibit and a full report on the analysis made from the laboratory before going back to Miami to fly to Cayman. The following day, by arrangement, he took the exhibit back to the judge's chambers where he presented the exhibit and report to the judge and the attorneys. All the individuals were most grateful for Watson's actions in the case, and before leaving, Watson mentioned to them, "If you need anything further like this completing in the future, please don't hesitate to ask. I would be delighted to assist." Watson noted that each of them had a wry smile on their faces as he left. *This sort of police work is great,* he thought.

It was also around this time that Watson's knowledge and understanding of the idiosyncrasies of working in a jurisdiction such as Cayman was extended by the CCB secretary, Jessie, who provided him with a paperback copy of Herman Wouk's classic novel *Don't Stop the Carnival.* Jessie told Watson that he should read it and that it would further enhance his understanding of how things happen on a Caribbean island. It most certainly made for good reading over the following weekend and enhanced Watson's breadth of knowledge and comprehension. The story basically covered the trials and efforts of two slick New York businessmen or entrepreneurs to travel to a Caribbean island and set up and renovate a failing hotel business and the many pitfalls and humorous happenings that befell them in dealing with local authorities and agencies. Jessie said that she had withheld from providing the book to Watson until he had been on the island for a few months in order, as she explained, for Watson to have had the necessary experiences in that time to fully appreciate the humor spread throughout the book. Watson thought it was a classic reflection of the things that could happen on an island, and he had already experienced quite a few.

On one occasion, Jessie asked Watson if he could give her a lift at lunchtime to the dry cleaners she used on the island to launder some of her and her husband's clothes. Watson, of course, was delighted to assist her and, about lunchtime, took Jessie to the car park, loaded her bags of clothing in the car, and set off for the laundry. Once there, Watson carried the clothing in for her, and the laundry attendant welcomed her. Jessie explained she had some laundry in need of cleaning and handed over the two bags full of clothing. The attendant counted out the clothing and types and was entering it all into a computer system at a terminal on the counter. The attendant asked Jessie her name and was provided with the name Jessie followed by her surname. The attendant asked for Jessie's middle name. Jessie responded that she did not have a middle name. The attendant asked again what was Jessie's middle name. Jessie responded without a second's hesitation, "Elizabeth." All seemed well at that stage, and Watson left the laundry with Jessie and her laundry claim slip in hand.

Watson said to Jessie with a degree of incredulity, "I didn't know your middle name is Elizabeth."

Jessie replied, "It isn't. I don't have a middle name." She then continued, "You have to understand, Chris, that sometimes when you are asked questions like that in the islands, it is far easier to answer them than to try and debate the situation and thereby get past a possible impasse." Watson thought this was classic and typified but just a part of the enjoyment of living and working in the Cayman Islands.

Sadly, shortly thereafter, Jessie had some profound family problems in Canada that had to be attended to and needed to travel to Canada in an attempt to resolve those problems. While she was there, the worry and circumstances compounded on her, and she unfortunately and suddenly passed away. Everyone in the CCB and other police departments in Cayman were devastated by the news. Efforts were made to immediately reach out to her husband and remaining family to offer them whatever help or consideration they needed during this tragic time. The CCB were represented by Superintendent Goodley at her funeral in Canada, and in due course, efforts were made to find another secretary to shepherd and control the detectives in the CCB.

An outstanding replacement was found in a lovely lady named Garnet Ebanks. Garnet was a born-and-bred Caymanian who had served as a police officer and was now handed the position of secretary and receptionist at the CCB offices. She was an absolute rock to the officers there, and more importantly, she stood no nonsense from them. She was the single mother of a young man whom she loved deeply, and she tried to do everything she could to ensure his growth and success. She was always available to help in any way possible with the work of the CCB and would work whatever hours were required as and when needed. Garnet was first-class as the secretary in the office and kept all the officers in order with good humor and persuasion. Occasionally and when necessary, she would demand immediate subservience from them and often prefaced her remarks by saying, "Now listen here…" Watson learned over time that beginning a conversation with such a phrase meant that Garnet was profoundly serious in what she was about to say. She would willingly complete all tasks given to her, and when her time was needed outside normal hours, she was always on hand to provide the same. Garnet was one of the best, most dedicated, and most likeable support staff that Watson had ever encountered in his career. Watson had a lot of fun working with Garnet, and he oftentimes brought her lunch or snacks into the office, which never went amiss in Garnet's eyes. Bringing lunch to her was only superseded in her eyes by taking her to one of the local restaurants for lunch! She was a joy to be around.

CHAPTER 9

The DA's Chief Investigator from Clovis, New Mexico, Seeks Help from Grand Cayman

Watson was trying to clear a large volume of paper from his desk and also arrange some exhibit files for an upcoming fraud case scheduled for trial. This was by no means Watson's favorite pastime, but in each and every case, it had to be done. He had had quite a good run during the day completing his objectives, but then the phone rang with its usual urgency, and Watson—after silently cursing to himself—answered it in the expected formal manner, "Detective Chief Inspector Watson, CCB. How may I help you?"

A voice responded, "Good morning, Chief. My name is Jim Reimer, and I am the chief investigator for the district attorney's office in Clovis, New Mexico. I don't know if you are the person I need to speak to, but I am looking for some assistance in a large-scale fraud we have been working on here in Clovis, and I think it touches on Cayman. I wonder if you could either kindly help me or perhaps direct me to someone who may be able to?"

Watson responded, "You are probably speaking to the right person. If you would like to give me an outline of what your problem is and what you are seeking, I will try to see if I can assist you. If not, I will ensure you speak to the right individual. By the way, where is Clovis in New Mexico?" Reimer thanked Watson and then continued to set out his story. He explained that Clovis was the county seat of Curry County, which was on the eastern border of New Mexico (the Land of Enchantment as it was commonly described), with Texas. It had a population of about thirty thousand persons, and the city of Clovis had been around for about one hundred years. The district attorney in Clovis had been alerted by a local banker that a seventy-eight-year-old widow in the town had run up an unusually high credit card balance, over $9,000, which was totally out of character for her. Reimer, acting on the information, decided he should make a few inquiries and went to see the widow and told her that if there was anything possibly wrong, he would like to help her in any way he could. She then showed him numerous items of cheap merchandise—vitamins, household items, and the like—and told Reimer she had obtained them from a company styled L&N Marketing, which apparently operated out of California. At one time, they told her to buy more items and she might win a car or TV. Reimer said to Watson that she did, but of course, she didn't win! She had also told them to stop sending her stuff, but they didn't, and items kept arriving at her home, for which she was paying extortionate amounts for basically rubbish. After hearing what the lady told him, Reimer decided—and she agreed—to hook up her phone and record the calls that she was getting on a regular basis from the firm. When Reimer subsequently listened to the tapes, he heard personnel from the company berate and threaten the poor lady in both a rude and, more egregiously, a most objectionable manner.

Reimer decided to call L&N thinking it was probably just a rogue salesperson, and he was eventually put through to a man who claimed to be a customer service manager. He told the manager that L&N shouldn't call the lady any further, and indeed, following the call, Reimer thought that it would not go any further. Unfortunately, it did, and the lady received many more calls of a threatening nature, and they even falsely claimed in the calls to her that Reimer had endorsed them and their services after their call. It was following on from these calls and a further meeting that Reimer and the DA had with a member of the firm that the DA authorized an investigation be commenced by Reimer.

L&N was the brainchild of three individuals whom Reimer discovered had operated a plethora of shady telemarketing companies for years. Consumers had complained about them in almost every state they had operated in, but they had always kept ahead of the law and paid numerous pecuniary fines that were assessed on them. The three men had become millionaires through these nefarious activities, and as a result, they owned and maintained large homes in Dana Point, California, and also in the Las Vegas area. Watson, by this time, was hooked on the story and asked Reimer to continue. He did continue, and the scope of the fraud was such that he involved a number of FBI offices in the search for more evidence and to get an idea of the totality of the enterprise.

Reimer explained that following the gathering of some evidence, they had previously arrested some of the people lower down on the totem pole at L&N and allied to the information they got from them as cooperating witnesses, in April 1992, the three primary owners of L&N were formally indicted on twenty-eight counts of fraud and also racketeering. Their lawyers arranged for their clients to duly appear in Clovis to face the charges, but on the date of the hearing, the lawyers attended the court but the offenders, the most important people in the process, all failed to show up at court and thus became fugitives. Arrest warrants were issued for them, and the FBI stepped up their search for the offenders on a nationwide basis. L&N was eventually shut down by the US federal authorities, and it was estimated at that time that they had defrauded consumers of some $58 million, making it one of the largest illegal telemarketing schemes in the nation. Reimer's sole objective at this time was to locate and arrest the three principals who were on the run and who had large amounts of money to support them in hiding and keeping a step in front of the posse searching for them. Reimer had seized a substantial number of documents and an encrypted computer and was continuing to obtain lots of information from those sources.

Watson's interest was now piqued, and he had heard enough to ask, "Why are you calling Cayman? You obviously have some information, or a cooperating person has told you of a Caymanian connection." Watson's suspicions were right on target.

Reimer explained that a relative of one of the men sought had provided the investigators with persuasive leads indicating that monies had been transferred through banks and other money movers in Las Vegas to the Cayman Islands, and research made by Reimer showed that one particular bank in Cayman had received the monies and equally then returned the money in various forms to various addresses in the USA as and when requested by the three individuals. He said if they could find what address or place the Caymanian bank was returning the money or other items to, then Reimer and the FBI might be able to arrest the fugitives or, at the very least, progress inquiries in the nationwide search for them.

Watson stated that he would see what could be done on an emergency basis to assist in locating the trio. First he checked in Cayman with the immigration authorities to see if they happened to be in the jurisdiction or had been recently, but all this turned up a negative response. There was no record of them having visited. Watson then spoke to a manager at the bank with whom he had had a number of previous working interactions to question regarding the money coming in from various sources, particularly in Las Vegas, and if so, what was happening to it from that point on. It was a day or two later that the manager confirmed the presence of an account in Cayman that money had been received in and also the fact that money and other documents requested were being sent to the USA on a fairly regular basis and oftentimes to different addresses. These actions were being taken following specific instructions they received when money was needed to be transferred. Watson asked by what form the money or requested documentation was sent, and he was informed that it went always by Federal Express. The manager asked, "When money is next requested, do you want to be told of it being sent?" Watson replied that he was not really interested but if the manager wanted the FedEx package carried to the FedEx office in George Town, he would be pleased to collect it and convey it for him and thereby save him the hassle of a journey into town. The manager said that he would be near the Tower Building in two days and Watson could walk across to the FedEx office with him and then perhaps they could have a coffee together. The manager duly arrived at the Tower Building as arranged, and Watson walked with him to the FedEx office in the downtown area near Elizabethan Square and then had a pleasant coffee and snack with the manager in a nearby snack bar.

Once back at the Tower Building about an hour later, Watson updated the commissioner on the events happening and then immediately called Reimer and passed him the pertinent details of the package and the address to which it would be delivered in about forty-eight hours' time, if there were no interruptions or delay regarding the delivery. Watson thought the tracking of FedEx packages was a wonderful thing if you were searching for fugitives. Reimer added hopefully that perhaps one or more of the three fugitives would pick it up. The day of the expected delivery in the USA, the mail drop was put under surveillance by a full surveillance team of federal and local officers regarding this package; and later that same day, two out of the three named fugitives were arrested, much to their surprise, when they unknowingly arrived to collect the same. With these two now arrested and at last charged and in custody, it was not long after when the third party surrendered himself to federal authorities with his lawyer and was duly charged. After many months of backward and forward with the case, plus some other members of the men's families being exposed to potential arrest, in August 1993, all three pleaded guilty to fraud and racketeering charges. They were sentenced to terms of imprisonment from eighteen years down to thirteen and a half years.

The DA and Reimer, plus the FBI, were delighted that the case had finally been brought to a conclusion and three people who had defrauded primarily the elderly and infirm were brought to justice. It was yet another case of law enforcement across a number of domestic and international jurisdictions working hand in hand to stop the plague of major fraud and, perhaps more importantly, for the protection of elderly citizens who'd often find themselves victims in such cases.

At one time during this matter, Watson was returning to the Tower Building after having conducted some basic inquiries with an accounting firm regarding a potential fraud committed on one of their clients. Watson had agreed to return and review what documentary evidence they had available to them, and he would then advise them on the next steps to take. Watson took the slow elevator to the fifth floor. When he alighted from the elevator, he was met by Agent Bob Puller, a supervisory special agent with US Customs Service who was well-known to Watson. They exchanged pleasantries, and then Puller said, "Chris, I would like to introduce you to Agent Dave Domenico, who is taking over for Agent Keith, who—as you know—has moved on to bigger and better things." Keith Freeman had been a stalwart of Watson over a substantial period, and following his promotion, he would be sadly missed in Cayman. Watson and Dave shook hands, and Watson warmly welcomed him to Cayman and said he looked forward to working with him in the future. Some other conversation took place, and the US Customs officers left, en route to the airport to return to Miami. Certainly, during Watson's stay in Cayman, the relationship with the US Custom's officers was first-class. They were always incredibly supportive of anything Watson and his team required from the USA, and of course, the CCB and other police departments in Cayman were very responsive to their needs and requests. It was during a few meetings later with Puller and Domenico that Watson learned that following his first meeting with Domenico at the elevator in the Tower Building, Domenico had remarked to Puller, "I don't think I can do this job, sir. I didn't understand a word that Chris Watson said to us!" Puller assured him he would, and Watson later learned that either his speech had become more Americanized or Domenico became more Anglicized in his word comprehension. Domenico and Watson formed yet another good, strong, and enduring partnership. Watson learned that working with US Customs was always a first-class experience.

CHAPTER 10

Maximum Security Breached at Northward Prison!

It was about midday on a beautiful day in May 1988 when Watson was summoned by the commissioner to immediately go to the Central Police Station and meet with Detective Superintendent Ken Hallsworth. Watson had been recruited to be Hallsworth's right-hand man to inquire into the circumstances surrounding the escape during the previous night of four prisoners, each of whom was detained in the top maximum-security wing of the prison following convictions for separate offenses of murder. They had escaped from the wing after apparently overpowering a prison guard and unlocking the individual cells in the wing. It was also found that some of the mortise locks in the wing had been stuffed almost full of paper, and this made those locks and doors not really secure, and it was reasonably easy to push the doors open. Once out of the maximum-security wing, they then made their way out of the prison grounds through the fencing at the rear of the prison. Of course, following the escape, when the escape became known to the prison staff, the police and other emergency services had been pressed into action to cover the island in an attempt to recapture the escaped prisoners as soon as possible. A control center was quickly established at the Central Police Station to field the inevitable calls that would be received from the public when the details were released to them. Using the public as the eyes and ears of the search often bore fruit in such circumstances and particularly in a community such as the Cayman Islands.

Accordingly and simultaneously, Watson and Hallsworth, together with a scenes of crime officer—Detective Sergeant Joseph—traveled to the prison, which was in the center of the island and quite a few miles east of downtown George Town. On arrival at the prison, they found that it was in total lockdown, and hordes of prison officers and staff were scurrying left, right, and center. Hallsworth and Watson met with the prison hierarchy, while Joseph began processing the crime scene, namely the maximum-security block. Outside the prison, under the guidance of the uniform senior police officers, various areas were being searched, and a team of uniform officers and voluntary special constables (unpaid volunteer police officers) was responding to supposed sighting of the escapees, whose details had been widely circulated on the island by this early stage. Each and every potential sighting made of the escapees was checked and researched and logged. Also, various roadblocks and the like were set up at points in the vicinity of the prison, and they were manned throughout the days and nights that followed.

Meanwhile, Watson, along with Hallsworth, was totally involved at the prison; but the more inquiries he made there and the more he saw of the location where the prison itself was situated, the more he realized how oppressive it must be for the escapees to survive in that environment. Plus at dusk, they were probably being eaten alive by the mosquitos that thrive in that area, particularly where there was standing water. Watson also could not understand what the escapees thought they could do in a jurisdiction like Cayman. People at the prison who were interviewed included other prisoners who were in the maximum-security area, along with the prison officer who had been working at the time of the escape. He was overpowered by the prisoners and locked in a cell. One of the prisoners in maximum security whom they interviewed had watched his cellmates escape after unlocking his cell, but he chose to sit in his cell, which was not then secure, and wait for the authorities to arrive. He was fearful of adding to his already extensive prison sentence and therefore had no wish to jeopardize his potential forthcoming date of release from the

prison. Other staff who were involved in the scheduling of the officers and the movements of prisoners, which occurred on occasions,
were all interviewed in-depth, and witness statements were taken
from each and every one of them. During some of the interviews,
Watson found that one or two of the interviewees had a capacity for
equivocation, the like of which he had not seen before. He figured
that being incarcerated gave them plenty of time to consider all sides
of each and every statement or argument, together with responses
that went on for a few minutes, but they said nothing meaningful.

Hallsworth and Watson worked twelve hours plus at the
prison each day on Thursday, Friday, and Saturday, plus the following Monday. Over twenty people were interviewed at length, and
extensive witness statements were obtained from fifteen of those
interviewed. Following the interviews and other physical inquiries,
Watson prepared a draft report and exhibits for Hallsworth, and
together they fine-tuned the report for submission to the governor
of Cayman Islands and also to the attorney general for consideration
as to any criminal actions that might have been committed, together
with suggestions as to what procedures could be made better and
enhanced to prevent such a reoccurrence in the future.

Following on from the inquiries, sometime later, one of the
prison officers who had been allegedly overpowered in the incident
was shot and killed in an incident while at his home in Cayman.
Following extensive police inquiries, his assailant was thought to be
another former prisoner who had a long record and had been in and
out of prison. Following the shooting, the former prisoner had fled
the country before he could be arrested. There was a further irony in
this case that after many years, he himself arrived back on the island
and he was shot and killed not long after he arrived back. The memories of some of the gang members that abounded at the time in some
of the Caribbean islands were obviously exceptionally long.

The report that Watson and Hallsworth had prepared and the
exhibits attached to it following their interviews and inquiries at the
prison formed the core of a report that, in due course, would be the
basis of an inquiry and subsequent report that Her Majesty's inspector of prisons from the UK, Judge Stephen Tumim, held and subse-

quently reported on. The judge's inquiry took place over a number of days in Cayman, and a number of witnesses were called to the same. At the conclusion of the inquiry hearings, Judge Tumim compiled a comprehensive report, and copies of the report were supplied to the governor of Cayman Islands and the director of prisons, and various copies were also supplied to various authorities in the United Kingdom. Changes in the prison system and also regarding staffing and the welfare of prisoners were duly implemented, as recommended, in Cayman. This wasn't the first prison escape that had happened there, nor would it be—as time showed—the last.

On the exterior of the prison, the uniform police presence and their activities had been quite successful. Two of the escapees had been separately sighted and, acting on reliable information the police received, had been quickly apprehended at separate locations without any undue incident occurring. They would now be slated to be charged with escaping from legal custody, but of course, already facing life imprisonment, this was perhaps a waste of time and money for the Cayman Islands. Due to the fact that it had taken a while for these two to be recaptured, the police commissioner—working with the uniform and detective branch senior officers—through the governor, had made a request to the Miami-Dade Police Department to allow some of their dog handlers and the dogs to come to Cayman to assist in investigating sightings of the escapees, all of whom, because of their previous offenses committed, were regarded as dangerous. Accordingly, the Miami-Dade Police Department sent four officers and their four dogs to Cayman on board a Cayman Airways flight. If you boarded that flight, Watson learned that in the first-class cabin that had eight seats, you would have seen four handlers and four dogs, large German shepherds, sitting proudly and comfortably in first class. The handlers wanted the dogs to be with them in the main cabin so that—if needed—the moment they landed in Cayman, following the hour-long flight from Miami, they could be off the plane and be working. If they were transported in the hold below the aircraft, that could not have happened. Watson smiled a few times to himself wondering what the hell passengers thought on seeing this scene in first class as they boarded the plane!

After the first two escapees had been recaptured, all efforts were poured into locating the remaining two escapees. Regular visits were made by the search parties to the prisoners' former haunts and hideouts in Cayman, and additional inquiries were made in Jamaica in the event that they might have been able to flee Cayman via a canoe or other means. Nothing bore fruit until one day there was a reported sighting of two men described as similar to the two remaining escapees being seen on the ironshore near the site of Pedro St. James Castle, which had originally been built on Grand Cayman about two hundred years previously. Immediately, two of the dogs and their handlers were taken to the vicinity. Visually there was nothing readily apparent, but in the ironshore that was mainly the terrain of that area, there were lots of little fissures and crannies where a man could hide. The two dog handlers led the way, walking into the breeze. One of the handlers saw his dog react and immediately told everyone to stand still. It was readily apparent that the dog had scented something. The handler called for the person to come out or he would let the dog go. There was no response, so he called again, but there was still no response. Accordingly, he unleashed his dog, and it took off toward a cluster of brush that grew in that terrain. As the dog got near the brush, a hand appeared from out of the brush. It turned out it was one of the prisoners who foolishly set out to run and outpace the dog! However, as trained, the dog secured the prisoner by his arm before he had taken a second step and refused to let go. His handler was making his way toward the dog when the other prisoner emerged from some brush a few yards away and decided to try to outrun the dog, which he thought was now preoccupied! That was also a bad mistake. He did not see the second dog that was unleashed by his handler and rapidly closed the gap on the escaping prisoner, bringing him down on contact and holding him on the ground until his handler arrived. Both men had been quickly recaptured without incident to any of the good guys thanks to these wonderful animals. Watson thought to himself that throughout his career, he had never seen such two dumb decisions as these escapees had just made. They had just both made first place in the dumb sweepstakes!

Both the prisoners suffered bite marks that needed a substantial number of stitches, and they also had extensive small cuts caused by their falling on the ironshore, which also needed deep cleaning and stitching. When Watson saw the prisoners at a later stage back at the Central Police Station, he was of the opinion that if the prisoners needed to be interviewed, to get the truth out of them, you could have brought in a miniature dachshund to the interview room and the prisoners would have confessed to anything, including the Kennedy killing. They were certainly *afraid* of dogs, and Watson was sure they would never want to mess with dogs again!

The two dogs involved in the capture were also treated by a vet on the island for some small lacerations on their pads, but both were fine. When Watson was near them, they really were beautiful animals, but he noticed that they seemed far bigger than the normal German shepherd. They were immensely powerful and so acutely aware of their surroundings while always looking toward their handlers. Watson was subsequently informed that a local butcher and store owner had brought some prime steaks for the dogs to Central Police Station as a sign of thanks from the community. However, the handlers refused to let the dogs eat the steaks, as they were used to and always had their normal dry food supplies. Watson additionally found out that although the dogs missed out on the prime steaks, the handlers didn't! They enjoyed good company, some food, and drinks in the nearby police club before returning to Miami, courtesy of Cayman Airways, after a more than successful conclusion to their mission. The Caymanian public really loved the dogs and were relieved that all four escapees were now back in prison.

CHAPTER 11

Hurricane Gilbert Visits Cayman Islands

Watson was totally ignorant of the coming threat; sometimes ignorance is bliss! He had taken a couple days off work on the eighth and ninth of September to host Sarah who had a few days off work also and flew to Cayman to spend a long weekend with Watson—to enjoy the sea, sun, and sand and whatever else the weekend would throw at her. She had flown in on the eighth, and Watson had met her at the airport, and they had gone back to his condo on Seven Mile Beach. They were thoroughly enjoying each other's company and, accordingly, did not spend any time watching TV and the ongoing reports of the impending storm. After spending three whole days in each other's company with good food, access to the sea and the beach—together with two swimming pools—and touring the island on a rented 125cc motorbike, it truly was an idyllic time for each of them, and their relationship was becoming a really serious one. One interesting place Watson took Sarah to during the weekend was to Hell, a small township on the west end of the island. The rock formations there of ironshore, jagged and dangerous, reputed to give any visitor a view of the conditions that could reasonably be expected in hell! Also, what visitor to the island, including Sarah, could resist the opportunity to visit the post office in Hell and mail cards and letters to friends and relatives all over the world that were postmarked from Hell! Watson thought quite a few of his close friends in the UK would not be at all surprised to receive a card from Watson posted in Hell.

Regarding Watson's relationship with Sarah, Watson knew that the more time the two of them were spending together, the more he wanted them to be together. *What could be wrong with the world?* he thought. He found out the next day!

After the enjoyable and interesting weekend was over, on Monday morning, Sarah packed, dressed, and was ready to go to the airport to ride with one of the airlines on a space-available basis back to Dallas through Miami. Watson drove her and her baggage to the airport and was incredibly surprised at the large number of people milling about in and around the airport terminal. Consequently, he parked the car in the staff car park and went into the terminal where he met Allan, who was a longtime reservation and counter agent with Cayman Airways. Allan was his usual bundle of energy trying to herd people into the right lines and appropriate areas to be checked in for one of Cayman Airways's departing flights. Watson cordially greeted Allan and asked what was going on with all the crowds in the terminal. Allan looked aghast and said to Watson, "Chris, where have you been all weekend? Haven't you heard the news?"

Watson knew immediately he had missed something! He asked, tongue in cheek, "I've been remarkably busy. No, I haven't heard the news."

Allan responded, "Chris, man, there is a big hurricane coming, and we are getting all visitors off the island as part of our preparations for the same."

Watson retorted, "Oh, well, I've not heard that!" He was embarrassed to say the least. Nonetheless, after laughing greatly and deeply at Watson due to his failure to have even the slightest hint that a hurricane was coming, Allan worked his usual magic; and although he could not get Sarah a seat on the aircraft, using her privileges as a flight attendant, he was able to secure her a spare jump seat in the cockpit—thanks to the kind authorization from the pilot of the next Cayman Airways flight to Miami. Obviously, following this news, Watson knew he had to get to the office as soon as possible, and Sarah had to go through security and get into the departure lounge to get on the flight. Watson found out that the airlines that day were basically flying round trip after round trip to Miami, evacuating any and all visitors to the island to ensure their safety in the event of potential catastrophic damage. It was both a sad and sudden parting, but nonetheless, Watson and Sarah made arrangements as soon as possible after the event to keep in touch and meet again.

The tropical storm had strengthened over the weekend, and it became Hurricane Gilbert late on September 10 and further strengthened to category 3 on Sunday. Shortly thereafter, Gilbert was classified as a major hurricane with sustained winds of 125 mph.

On September 12, Gilbert made landfall on the eastern coast of Jamaica, and its fifteen-mile-wide eye moved from east to west along the entire length of Jamaica. Gilbert strengthened dramatically after emerging from the west coast of Jamaica, and as it continued in a westerly movement, it passed about twenty to thirty miles away from the south coast of the Grand Cayman island. On September 13, one of the reporting stations on Grand Cayman recorded a wind gust of 156 mph. The front right quadrant, according to what the locals told Watson, was the most dangerous aspect of an approaching storm, and the East End area of Cayman would be caught fair and square in this quadrant.

As the storm left the Cayman area, explosive intensification continued until Gilbert reached maximum sustained flight-level winds of 185 mph. The pressure reached was the lowest ever observed in the Western Hemisphere, and it made Gilbert the most intense Atlantic hurricane on record until Hurricane Wilma in 2005. Gilbert made landfall on the island of Cozumel and then later on the Yucatán Peninsula as a category 5 hurricane. Hurricane Gilbert eventually spawned twenty-nine tornadoes in Texas on September 18.

After arriving at work on Monday, Watson and his staff were busy for eighteen hours plus ensuring that the Tower Building was as secure as it could be and then visiting with people in certain districts to ensure that they were preparing appropriately for the oncoming storm. Watson learned a lot in a noticeably short space of time about hurricanes and preparations. He mused a few times that this was far more then he had ever wished to know! He was extremely impressed with how the locals and the government were working together to safeguard government buildings and private residences, plus trimming some trees that could be of particular risk during a storm. Also, some evacuation centers were now fully stocked and ready to receive residents from some of the more vulnerable areas on the island. One of the last things the government did was to take down the huge satellite dishes to protect them during the storm. These satellite dishes were used to provide communications with the rest of the world, as at that time, Cayman was a leading world financial center, and worldwide communication was essential.

During the day, DS Johns asked Watson where he would be staying during the emergency. Watson responded by saying he would shelter at his condo on Seven Mile Beach. Johns looked at him in horror and said, "You can't stay there. There is a hurricane coming, and Seven Mile Beach could vanish!"

Watson said, "Oh! Okay. Well, we don't have hurricanes in England, you know!"

Johns responded by taking the lead over Watson's welfare, "After we finish work this evening, we will collect a few things from your condo, and you can stay with me and my family at our home in Bodden Town. It is a very safe area there. You can have my children's room."

Watson was moved by this and, really unaware of what to expect during a hurricane, readily thanked Johns for his kind hospitality. Watson had no real concept of the benefits or otherwise of being in Bodden Town, but he was sure that the locals knew far better how to prepare for such an event rather than a native from the North of England.

One of the last jobs Watson did during that day involved an elderly lady who lived in an old single-story stereotypical Caymanian home situated right on the beach at East End. Watson and Johns found her sitting in a rear room at the house looking at the waves that were gently lapping on the shore. Watson had been informed this area would be landfall for the dangerous quadrant of Gilbert and, in the direct line, could suffer catastrophic damage. Most of the nearby residents had already left the area and secured their houses as best they could. Johns tried to persuade the lady to pack a few things and said she would then be driven to a nearby shelter, a church building on an elevated lookout point that was nearby and had been constructed to hurricane standards. Protesting loudly, she objected to the move, stating she had lived through other hurricanes, but she was eventually persuaded it would be the right thing to do because of the ever-strengthening power of Gilbert. She was taken to the shelter, much against her better judgment, where she continued her protestations and demanded that the instant the storm had passed, Watson and Johns return and collect her to take her home!

Later in the evening, Watson finally drove his car to Johns's home in Bodden Town where he was warmly welcomed by Mrs. Johns and also the two young children in the family. All police and emergency vehicles at this time had now been ordered to stay off the roads due to the escalating storm. The children had given up their bedroom to allow for Watson to stay for the next couple nights or whatever was necessary. Watson was so grateful for this selfless act, but by now, he was appreciating that it was very typical of the kindness and generosity shown by the Caymanian people. Sheila Johns had cooked an excellent meal, and Watson enjoyed the friendship shown to him during the meal. It really was heartwarming to a stranger. After dinner and helping Johns further prepare his house and his father's house, who lived across the street from Johns, to mitigate the potential damage, everyone—including Watson—retired for the night as Gilbert spun and moved ever closer with certainty to a collision with East End, Grand Cayman.

In strange surroundings and a strange bed, plus in circumstances he really had no comprehension of, Watson tossed and turned but nonetheless was quickly asleep—not knowing what to expect when and if he awoke the next morning. His last memory was the sound of the wind blowing strongly, and occasionally he would hear branches being broken on trees and odd noises he assumed apparently from items breaking. He wondered how his car would fare, although he had filled the gas tank earlier that day after having been instructed by locals that that was good idea to add weight to the car and should the gas stations be out of order following the storm. The rain was coming in squalls, but it was very heavy tropical and driving rain on odd occasions. Watson was fast asleep, having slept through the night, when Johns woke him about 6:00 a.m. the next morning to tell him that it was very windy outside and was raining heavily. Watson smiled and said, "But if it's a hurricane, isn't that what you would expect?" Nonetheless, Watson quickly got out of bed, put on some clothing, and joined Johns in the carport area of his home. Johns told Watson not to go beyond the coverage of the carport. Although it was light at the time, it was difficult to see beyond the end of his yard, as the air was full of salt and sand, which was being picked up from the nearby seashore and was covering anything and everything. Watson noticed his car was rocking in the wind and some nearby palm trees were being bent almost double in the winds. There was a lot of standing water near the house and roadway, but none of it was coming dangerously near the house. Watson could hear things being blown near the house, but with the winds over one hundred miles per hour, you could not see what they were. Watson later learned that glass, corrugated metal roofing, shingles, tree branches, and all manner of other materials were being picked up and blown by the extraordinarily strong and sustained winds. It was for this reason that Johns ensured Watson did not leave the shelter of the carport at the house. Being hit by any of those items moving at around one hundred miles per hour would most certainly cause serious or even fatal injury. Watson noticed a couple of new but small dings in the bodywork of his Toyota, but nothing else readily appeared out of place.

A few hours later, after the winds had subsided somewhat but strong gusts still prevailed, Johns and Watson were instructed from the Cayman Hurricane Control Center to start some damage assessment exercises in the Bodden Town and south side of George Town to report road obstructions and other potential problems. Johns went out to start the police vehicle, but the battery was as dead as a doornail and showed no sign of starting. Watson stated, "Get the jumper cables from the car, and I will start it from the Toyota." When Watson opened the door to his car, all appeared well until he noticed about an inch of water sitting in the well of the car. The holes on the roof and around the guttering had allowed the vehicle to take on water during the heavy and persistent night rainstorms, when many inches of heavy rain fell. Watson borrowed a hammer and a screwdriver from Johns and carefully selected two places on the car floor to punch two drain holes. Once this had been achieved, the well of the car drained; and when the carpeting was later replaced, that had quickly dried too. When fired up, the car started the first time, and Watson was immensely proud of his inexpensive means of transport. Immediately he was able to cause the police vehicle to also spring to life through the jumper cables. Later that same day, Watson used the Toyota to jump-start a fair number of similarly disabled police vehicles. He was really proud of his car! He would no longer have to listen to friends and colleagues criticize his choice of car and its age and having no air-conditioning, or if he did, he could now recount the Toyota's magnificent response to the storm.

Completing the damage assessments in a number of districts that day showed that in common with one another, a lot of vegetation had suffered extensive damage. Some properties and also a number of paved roads had been destroyed by the roots of trees and power poles being pulled out of the ground. A number of light poles were down, and also a number of electrical wires and posts had been torn down. Each and every finding was reported to the control center so that crews could be dispatched to deal with matters in an appropriate and prioritized order. Experts determined that the damage that had occurred was obviously mitigated by the speed of movement by which Gilbert had come upon and then left the Cayman Islands. Watson thought that all in all, the government and the people of the islands appeared to have handled the occurrence in a most proficient way. What really struck Watson as he journeyed throughout the districts on that day was how calm and beautiful the ocean appeared, compared to the day before when it was raging. It reflected total serenity and beauty, although the vegetation and damage plus some of the buildings illustrated a different story.

After another long and weary day, Watson again returned to Johns's home and had another wonderful evening dinner with the family. Other than a couple of screens damaged, by God's grace, they did not suffer any wind damage, nor did they have any water damage. This night, Watson did not need any encouragement to go to bed and sleep.

The following day was again started early by Watson going to the shelter at East End and duly collecting the lady whom he and Johns had taken to the shelter on Monday. She was delighted to see their return, although she immediately questioned, "Wha 'appened yesterday?" She was obviously asking why Watson had not been there the previous day immediately after the storm. Watson thought she probably spent the day before trying with anyone and everyone to get a ride home! She was not the most patient of people, and she did not suffer fools gladly. Watson explained they had other duties to do first before the residents could go back to ensure their continuing safety and the fact that the homes were safe from all possible continuing dangers to repopulate them. Watson didn't think she heard or cared about the explanation, as she was already making her way independently but with purpose toward the police car. She was driven home, and apart from a few branches and a couple of trees being down around the home, everything looked in reasonably good order. That changed, however, once they reached the rear of the property. The room she had been sitting in had completely lost its exterior wall, and the chair where she had been sitting was now covered with six to eight feet of sand and other debris. She was visibly moved and shocked by the damage she saw, and she also immediately realized that but for Watson and Johns making her leave the property, she might well have been killed or gravely injured that night had she stayed at the house. She broke down in tears and started apologizing profusely for not immediately leaving when she had been asked to do so by Johns and Watson. Watson and Johns tried to comfort her, and they assured her no apologies were necessary and that the home could be renovated in time, whereas they might have been dealing with a far more serious situation if she had stayed at the property. The moment was not lost on the lady who was continually distressed and quietly sobbing. Watson checked the rest of the home for her, which was quite badly water-damaged, and then they took her to a home nearby where some of her close relatives lived. They, too, were most appreciative to the police for the actions they took.

A few months after this event, Watson got an unexpected call and invitation from the family to go back to the house in question in East End. It had been repaired and renovated, and her relatives were now welcoming their relative back into the home. While there, the resident told Watson that no way was she leaving that beautiful home that carried so many memories for her and the family, and she meant it this time. Watson smiled, but it was gratifying to him to see her in good spirits and to be finally returning to her almost brand-new home.

Later that day, Watson and the rest of the CCB staff turned up at the Tower Building to try to clean up the offices there. One office had lost some of its windows, and the papers in that office were strewed all over and saturated. All the other offices, including Watson's, had survived relatively unscathed. After a couple hours of work on the damaged office, the papers had been salvaged as best they could be and were arranged and set out for drying purposes. Now was the time for Watson to go and see how his condo on Seven Mile Beach had fared. He feared, having seen the destruction at East End, that there might not be a lot left of it.

On arrival, a lot of the vegetation was missing or just lying on the ground. A number of the trees were now horizontal, and some were leaning at a forty-five-degree tilt. The vegetation had been severely damaged, but structurally, the condos appeared to be in reasonable order. Both the swimming pools had substantial debris and pool furniture in them, and one of the pools had a family of crabs scooting around in it, along with a couple starfish and some dead fish in the same. Watson's apartment, on the ground floor, looked intact, although all the windows and the siding were covered in a layer of salt and sand caused by spray from the high waves that had attacked the beach. Watson, with some trepidation, opened the door and went inside fearing the worst. Miraculously, everything appeared to be as Watson had left it, with the exception that there was a distinct smell of dampness in the property. The electricity was connected and working, the water was on and flowing, and perhaps more importantly, the air-conditioning—when Watson turned it on to briefly test it—was working. These results were a great relief for him, as he had had views of the place and his belongings being flattened and destroyed in the wrath of the storm.

The readiness of the island for such a storm was illustrated by the fact that within the next forty-eight hours of the storm passing, much of the island was up and running again. Indeed, the very next day, the CCB began their usual duties and were out and about in town doing the usual interviews, serving papers, and other related duties. Clear-up operations and restorations continued island-wide in the days and weeks ahead.

In summary, Watson subsequently learned that Cayman was spared to a degree of the primary and potentially devastating wrath of Gilbert mainly due to the hurricane, which was a fast-moving storm, and damage to the island was further mitigated because the depth of the water surrounding the islands (eight thousand feet in some places) limited the height of the storm surge. There was severe damage to what crops there were in Cayman—also to trees, pastures, roadways, and a number of private homes. A number of boats had been ripped from their moorings and had vanished. A party boat called the Kon Tiki had been ripped from its moorings and was discovered some weeks later washed ashore on a beach in Honduras! Watson wondered how many insurance frauds included claims for sailing yachts and boats. It was further reported that some fifty people were left homeless following the passage of Gilbert. Watson noticed during one trip into town that a piece of two-by-four hardwood had been impaled into the exterior breeze-block wall of the Royal Bank of Canada about thirty feet above street level. Watson found it hard to comprehend the wind force needed to inflict such a result as that that he had been witnessing.

The weekend that followed the storm, Watson noticed that Marguerite and Fred, who professionally managed the condos complex where he was staying, were out in the grounds and were earnestly trying to clear them of tree debris and restore some sort of order to the complex. On Saturday morning, they started about 7:00 a.m. with a couple of noisy chain saws and a crew of about four hired people to help them. Watson therefore quickly got up, drank a mandatory coffee, and went outside to help them. They all worked about fourteen hours that day cutting down trees that were beyond repair and piling them down one side of the car park, which was intended for the residents of the condos. Other trees that could be stood back up and staked to reroot were attended to, and all but one of them, in the fullness of time, did again take root and flourished. Marguerite made some wonderful sandwiches and drinks for lunch. And although it was a hard-physical day, it made it all worthwhile that by the end of the day—although sparser of vegetation—the place was beginning to look like its old self again. Fred and Marguerite were most grateful for the help provided, and after that event, anything Watson needed he was provided with by the managers. The pools were another matter, as those would take some time to drain, clean, and refill. Fred and Marguerite fielded many complaints from residents asking when the pools would be available again. Most of these complaints were from residents who did absolutely nothing to help in the clean-up. Marguerite had become pretty distraught over these complaints since she tried to make the complex so welcoming for guests. The complaints, Watson personally thought, were asinine, bearing in mind the extenuating circumstances the managers had faced following the storm. Consequently, in true Northern England direct and to-the-point style, he advised Marguerite, "Take no bloody notice. Bloody idiots!" This caused her to smile, and Watson never let her forget: "Take no notice. Just do what you can and is reasonable." A favorite saying of Watson to people in such circumstances was "Take no notice of what people may say or do to you. They can only get benefit by seeing your reaction to what they may say or do." This had stood Watson in good stead many times, and Marguerite always remembered the advice.

The next day, Watson borrowed a hosepipe from the management and completely scrubbed clean and washed the outside of his block of condos so he could again see out of the windows. He also thoroughly cleaned off the block of air-conditioning units outside the condos and then attended to the inside of his own condo. The pools were gradually emptied of the garbage and items that were now in the pool, plus some fixtures on the buildings were taken down either for repair or replacement, and other items were once again secured properly. Later that same day, telephone service was restored when the satellite dishes were re-erected by the telephone company, and Watson was finally able to call Sarah in Texas and his relatives in the UK to tell her and them that he had survived his first hurricane with virtually no damage other than a flooded Toyota Corolla! Sarah had been watching the progress of Gilbert through reports on CNN, and at one time, it looked as though Gilbert and its surrounding storm bands had enveloped and engulfed the whole island of Grand Cayman. She had been very worried, and she thought that the whole island had been covered and absorbed by seawater. She was so very relieved to get the message that all was well. Watson smiled, as he was pleased to be back in touch with her too, and it told him that he was beginning to really miss her and feel great affection for her. Sarah did invite Watson to come to Dallas immediately, but the timing was really bad at that moment. So Watson declined, but he did promise to make the trip as soon as the ongoing emergency and associated matters had died down and passed.

In the days and weeks that followed, Watson saw many areas in the island where business and private residences were being repaired. On one such occasion, they had an occasion to visit a private residence on South Church Street where they noticed that a crew next door was replacing a roof on what appeared to be a reasonably modern house there. After Watson left the house he had visited, he walked next door to speak to the men working on the house. There were four of them in total; one man was on the roof working hard replacing felting and shingles, positioning the materials, and duly hammering felting nails in as and when necessary. The other three men were sitting near the foot of a ladder onto the roof, and occasionally, one of them would carry a couple packs of shingles up to the roof for unpacking, positioning, and installation. Watson was wondering to himself why three men were on the ground and just the one man was doing all the work repairing the roof. He introduced himself and asked them what had happened to the home. He was told that over 75 percent of the roof had been basically ripped off during Gilbert. Watson noticed most of it was lying in the bushes at the bottom of the yard. He couldn't help himself but ask the workers why one man was working on the roof and the other three were just taking up shingles as and when needed. The answer floored Watson but equally gave him a moment of sheer joy for the day. It was, "But, man, we only got de one hammer." Watson considered there and then going to the hardware store to buy another felting hammer for them but was acutely aware that they probably didn't have any in the stores so soon after such a catastrophic event. After all, almost everything in Cayman had to be imported. Never could Watson have anticipated that answer to what the guys possibly thought was a stupid question! It was yet another example of what enjoyment Watson was having working in the Cayman Islands and witnessing so many good things in life, notwithstanding the odd hurricane.

CHAPTER 12

A Large-Scale Fraud Committed in Cayman

Watson always ensured his own compliance with a procedure he had previously adopted in the UK, and that was that to look after the needs and food requirements of the secretaries and support staff was always a good thing, both in operational circumstances and also at other times when appropriate. It reflected well when a detective needed help during the normal work hours or even on the odd occasion when he needed assistance into the evening hours or weekends. Watson never had to go too far to find such assistance when needed primarily because of always being concerned for the staff and helping them whenever he could. The secretaries and typists who might have worked four or five days on the trot, sometimes for ten or more hours a day, often liked it when after the initial chaos of the matter had past, Watson would approach them about lunchtime and tell them to go shopping and that he would see them the next morning. This paid so many dividends in the long run, and Watson never had to look too hard for support he might have needed during various cases.

The phone rang, and it was a managing partner from one of the top five international accountancy firms on the island who asked for Watson to come to his office to meet with him and other members of the firm's staff and the firm's attorneys regarding a potential criminal matter for investigation. The matter concerned a condominium complex in a prestigious portion of Seven Mile Beach and the administration of the same by some full-time managers, a man and his wife, a local couple. Watson agreed to visit the next morning and review the facts of which they were complaining and then advise on whatever set of circumstances they might wish to have considered.

Watson duly attended at the accountants' office the next morning along with Detective Sergeant Joey Johns. They met with the partners of the accounting firm in very plush offices of one of the office buildings in George Town together with some employees who had been involved in the audit of the Strata Corporation that oversaw the maintenance and financial aspects of the condominiums in question. The complex of condominiums was ideally situated on Seven Mile Beach—toward the northern end—and consisted of some long-term rentals and other short-term rentals that welcomed vacationers for their stay in the sun. The husband-and-wife team had acted as managers for the Strata Corporation from 1981, and it appeared from the audit inquiries made by the accounting firm that over a period of some four years or so, the managers had misappropriated in excess of $350,000 from the Strata Corporation. The Strata Corporation, through their lawyers, indicated that they wished to make a criminal complaint regarding the same to the police.

The next hour or so was spent with the accountancy firm reviewing a small portion of some of the voluminous documentation they held to ensure that there was prima facie evidence available to Watson of the fraud being committed and the fact that the managers appeared to be both responsible and culpable for the same. Having satisfied himself on that point, Watson then asked for a statement of complaint to be obtained from the lawyer acting for the Strata Corporation. It was agreed that he would provide the same on the Monday following and also that the accounting firm would provide all the assistance needed in the form of documentary evidence plus reviews of the necessary files to support any criminal charges to be brought based on whatever the police inquiries might show.

On the Monday morning following, the lawyer for the Strata Corporation visited the CCB office, and Watson obtained a full statement of complaint from him on behalf of the corporation. Following this, the afternoon was spent at the accountancy firm obtaining substantial evidence of the fraud and all the pertinent documentation required to support the same. This process was repeated many times over the coming weeks as a case was built showing the depth of the fraud, the persons who had committed the fraud and benefitted from it, along with what had happened to much of the monies that had been misappropriated during the term of the fraud.

It was during this inquiry that Watson discovered another idio-syncrasy of working in the Cayman Islands. Detective Sergeant Johns was tentatively scheduled to go to a business meeting with Watson in a nearby business office regarding another potential matter for inves-tigation. The meeting was set for 10:00 a.m. Watson had been busy completing paperwork in the office when he queried with Garnet where Johns was, as he was due to attend the meeting and he didn't appear to be in the office. The answer was clear, succinct, and exact from Garnet: "The sea is flat!" Watson was somewhat taken aback by this response and what that had to do with going to a proposed business meeting. Accordingly, he responded without showing any frustration, "What the heck has the sea being flat got to do with our scheduled business meeting? If it were rough, I could understand it."

The response Watson received from Garnet fully explained the situation: "When the sea is flat, the guys go fishing, and that isn't going to change, not for you or anyone else for that matter." Sure enough, when Johns arrived at the office, it appeared he had been out fishing from around 4:00 a.m. that day; and consequently, that was why he was later than normal arriving at the office. Watson also realized that nothing was going to change this situation and therefore it was best to embrace it. The upside to the situation was that a day later, Watson was invited to dinner at Johns's home and had some of the best tuna he had ever tasted! His only experience of tuna pre-viously was the canned tuna available in the UK. The Caymanians knew how to prepare good and fresh fish that'd melt in your mouth when eaten!

Following the intensive inquiries made in Cayman and abroad, primarily in the USA, and the supporting witness statements and documents obtained, it revealed that the managers had committed numerous offenses of theft and false accounting between January

1983 and May 1987. They stole monies totaling US $355,030.49 from the Strata Corporation, and between January 1982 and October 1986, they also dishonestly, and with a view to cause loss to the Strata Corporation, produced management accounts and documents that omitted items of personal expenditure. Watson wondered why the thefts had not been discovered until the present time, and it was discovered that prior to the current extensive audit, a small local accounting firm had been employed by the managers to review the accounts annually. And those reviews were just simply not done in enough depth, nor were checks made of items, which—to any accountant properly trained and employed—would have been raising numerous red flags all along the process. As an example of the laxity and inadequacy of the reviews, investment monies were placed in certificates of deposit that were supposedly to roll over upon maturity. They were simply altered to show a new amount now on deposit, which was false, along with the interest rates reflected on the CDs. Also, carbon copies of bank pay-in slips were also altered and then proffered to the accounting firm, who obviously never checked the same with the original bank account. As an example, on a deposit for $16,288, on the carbon copy, the 1 was changed to a 9 and another 1 was inserted in front of the new 9, now showing a deposit of $196,288. By this method, on just one document, they hid some $180,000, which had been misappropriated or diverted. A review of the deposit on the original copy of the deposit slip from the bank would have shown the true deposit of just $16,288. Watson mused that their audit procedures were sadly lacking common sense and also not up to generally accepted industry standards. Perhaps this was done purposely, or alternatively, the only answer would be pure and unadulterated incompetence.

Watson and Rowell were out in eastern George Town collecting various items of evidence for this case when a radio call came over the police radio in the vehicle stating that three men had just been found by a home owner in his home which they had illegally entered. The homeowner had unexpectedly found them in his living room when he had returned from visiting a local store. The home was near the rear of Hurley's Supermarket on Walkers Road, and the offenders had briefly assaulted the homeowner before fleeing the scene. It was noted that there had recently been a few daytime burglaries of private residences in that area. The men were described as three young men of color—two with normal height and one noticeably quite a few inches taller. Two were wearing shorts, but the taller one had jeans on. They were all wearing brightly colored T-shirts. Watson asked Rowell, "How far away are we from Hurley's?"

Rowell responded, "About a half mile or so."

Watson told Rowell to drive to Hurley's as fast as he safely could. On arrival there, Rowell radioed in their position to the police control, and Watson got out of the car and told Rowell to drive around the rear of the property and then make his way back through the store searching for the described offenders.

It was less than one minute later that Watson saw three young men, fitting the descriptions given over the radio, walking toward him past some other smaller retail stores near Hurley's. They were in animated conversation, and each was sweating profusely. Watson remained standing where he was, looking in a store window, totally unconcerned as the men were walking toward him. He was not sure what they would do when challenged, but he was certain that at least one of them was going to be arrested! As they got within a yard or so of Watson, he announced himself as a police detective and said he had a nice surprise for them. Simultaneously and surprisingly without waiting to see what the surprise was, they quickly turned and started to run back from where they had come. Having anticipated this, Watson, using his cat-like instincts (well, perhaps a slightly less mobile older cat), took off; and within about three yards, he tackled the taller offender, who was not moving as quickly as the two smaller men, with a classic rugby tackle from behind. He fell to the ground with Watson holding him around the thighs, and Watson then pulled his arms behind his back and secured him by pushing his arms as far as he could up the offender's back. Watson was now considering what to do next. He had neither any handcuffs nor a mobile radio. Perhaps he thought that the customers at the stores in the plaza would notice this unusual event and would call the police. It was at that time that after hearing sirens in the vicinity, Watson saw a police uniform unit

105

arrive, and PC Robert Oaks, a uniform police officer, jumped out of the vehicle and ran across toward Watson and immediately used his handcuffs to secure the prisoner. Watson told him the direction the remaining two suspects had gone, and using his personal radio, PC Oaks conveyed the information to other units who were at that time in the area and who quickly sealed the area, working their way in to find the two missing offenders. Thankfully, the other two alleged offenders were quickly located and placed in custody nearby without incident.

PC Oaks, smiling, curiously looked at Watson and said, "Are you okay, boss?"

Watson retorted, "Yes, thanks."

Oaks said, "I don't know if I should say this, but you shouldn't be rolling around on the ground outside Hurley's arresting a guy who is half your age!"

Watson said, "I know that, but listen, there were three to arrest, and where were you guys when I needed you? I have a thing that comes with age called experience, and I knew at least one was going to be in custody by the time you arrived!" Laughing, he added, "And here he is, exhibit number 1. Now respect your elders."

DC Rowell arrived back at the front of the store and looked at Oaks who was helping Watson to his feet. Rowell, who was looking at Watson in a quizzical way and also quietly laughing to himself, said, "Wha 'appened, Chief?" Watson told him he would explain later and that he had missed some excitement that should be reserved for young men like him! Deep down, Watson had really enjoyed the moment, and Rowell and Oaks both knew he had!

Despite this brief interruption and following the obtaining of the evidence regarding the on-island fraud and compilation of the various aspects of the fraud, including some inquiries in the USA whereby one of the defendants obtained from a large supplier of parts and equipment for watercrafts a substantial amount of marine parts for his personal high-powered boat, Watson liaised with the Legal Department, and it was agreed for the defendants to be interviewed and the case to be submitted for consideration as to further potential criminal actions.

Watson and Detective Sergeant Johns made numerous inquiries on two consecutive days in the West Bay area of Grand Cayman to arrest the two Strata managers for theft and false accounting, but despite these attempts, they were not traced. It was, however, confirmed that they appeared to still be on the island. However, Sergeant Johns, being a Caymanian, was not fazed by the inability to find them initially. He assured Watson that the managers would quickly be told of the police interest in finding them, and of course, as usual, Johns was perfectly on target.

Following one of the days spent making inquiries in the West Bay area, Watson stopped at a little wooden kiosk in a car park near the courthouse where a local lady served up excellent meat dishes daily that were very tasty, served hot, and all at a very reasonable price. Watson became well-known to her over the years, and he never tired of the food she provided. Watson was never able to identify what the food contained, but it was always very tasty and always looked the same. *Why abandon a winning formula?* Watson thought. On this occasion, he ordered an extra serving for the office secretary, Garnet, who also enjoyed the food and particularly so when a staff member provided it for her. Keeping in mind that Garnet always so willingly assisted in providing the necessary clerical support and admin help whenever needed, Watson viewed getting Garnet a meal as a really solid investment for when he needed assistance from her in the office, day or night.

During these on-the-ground inquiries in West Bay, Watson and Johns visited a home to speak to the owners who were known to Johns. The home was surrounded by a sturdy three-and-a-half-foot chain-link fence, and the gates at the driveway were heavily padlocked. This was strange to Watson, but Johns assured him that this person needed security at his home, the cause being a number of his past business dealings that were dubious, to say the least, and involved people of less than good repute. Watson said, "Okay, I understand." Then he added, "Why don't you jump over the fence and go and knock on the door to see if we can rouse him and speak to him?" Johns replied that he would, and being young and athletic, he easily jumped over and cleared the fence. He had not gone above two yards toward the front door of the house, which was probably about forty yards away, when all hell broke loose. A Doberman dog that had been apparently sleeping in the shadow of the house near the front door but was vigilantly watching the movements of Watson and Johns without moving a sinew of his body was now wide awake and moving at a very rapid speed toward Johns who, in the dog's view, was trespassing in the yard, and the dog obviously thought he was some fresh meat delivered. Thankfully, Johns saw the dog approaching; and unaware of the dog's intentions, which Watson found strange when Johns later told him that, Johns took one step back toward the fencing and cleared the fence by more than two feet and ran another two or three yards before diving into the car, where Watson was already both nonchalantly and safely sitting. A second or perhaps two later, the Doberman crashed—there was no other word Watson could think of to describe the happening—at great speed into the chain-link fencing and then continued to be very verbal about the stranger who had been in his yard. *Thank the Lord,* Watson thought, *it is a well-constructed and secure chain-link fence.*

Johns, in a state of shock and with some nervousness, asked Watson, "Did you see the dog?"

"Yes, I saw him lying down in the shade and shadows near the front door," said Watson.

"But you didn't tell me the dog was there," said Johns.

"But you didn't ask me" was the reply. Watson told Johns he was going to enter Johns in the high jump at the Force Sports Day; he would ace it based on what Watson had just seen. The bottom line was that Johns learned another lesson here. Thereafter, following on from this event, anytime Johns visited any property for any purpose, his first job was to look and search for any potential signs of a dog being present there. After he had checked, he then checked again to be totally sure, and he always had his emergency escape routes pre-planned! *Real on-the-job training,* Watson thought.

Following on from the inquiries made in the West Bay area, in midmorning on the following Monday, the condo managers presented themselves at the CCB office along with their local attorney. Watson smiled to himself as he recalled what Sergeant Johns had said regarding it coming to their knowledge of the police interest in speaking to them. More interestingly to Watson, they even came to the right police department in the right building! The island telegraph by word of mouth obviously spread quickly and worked exceedingly well!

In the presence of the attorney, the wife was first interviewed as required by law; but on the advice of her attorney, she declined to answer any questions. And then the husband was interviewed in a similar manner, and he declined to answer any questions also. Watson had no doubt that the husband had been the prime instigator of the fraud. At the conclusion of the interview, they were both bailed to reappear at the CCB a couple months later. Following consideration by the Legal Department, the matter resulted in them being charged with an offense of theft and two charges of false accounting. They pled guilty to the charges in summary court in a case that the magistrate described as one of the biggest private thefts that had come before the court. The magistrate further stated that as Cayman Islands was viewed to be a financial center, the case was viewed very seriously because it involved the reputation and credibility of the country. The magistrate sentenced both the defendants to two years imprisonment on the theft charge and two twelve-month terms on the two charges of false accounting, all sentences to be served concurrently. In the case of the wife, twelve months of the sentence were suspended, meaning she would only serve one year of imprisonment. He also imposed a compensation order of $1,500 per month for twelve years upon their release from prison. This sentence imposed unfortunately left the young children of the marriage to be looked after by their grandparents during the period of incarceration of the parents.

However, less than a month later following the conviction and sentencing, the wife appealed to the chief justice of the Cayman Islands, in the Grand Court, against the sentencing based on the position of the two young children following the same. Upon hearing by the chief justice and the fact that the couple had two children of very young ages, five and eight, the Grand Court agreed because of the total circumstances and the imposition of circumstance forced on the young children and suspended the whole imprisonment sentence relating to the mother, effectively meaning she was released immediately to enable her to continue to properly care for the children. The husband did not appeal his sentence. Normally the hardship suffered by the family of an offender would not be a matter that a court might take into account. However, the QC who represented the wife pointed out three exceptions whereby the degree of hardship was considerably more severe than in normal circumstances. These included where the offender was the mother of young children, where both parents were imprisoned simultaneously, and where other circumstances meant that children were effectively deprived of all parental care. The grandmother was also a working lady, and as a result of that job, on a number of nights each week, the children had to be placed with other relatives. It really was a nightmare for the children, and Watson thought that the judge came to a reasoned and proper decision regarding the mother, in suspending her sentence, while justice was still served.

During this inquiry, Watson came to understand and experience that Sergeant Johns had the attention to detail and analysis of facts and documents, which was so necessary in good and effective fraud investigation. Watson was beginning to understand that there was much good unbridled talent in the CCB that would stand them and the RCIP in good stead both in the present and in the future as the island continued to expand as a world-renowned offshore financial center. It was very pleasing to Watson to be working with such capable and enthusiastic officers who showed an insatiable appetite for knowledge and also for him to personally not be tied to the computer as in the HOLMES training in the UK.

In the course of completing this inquiry, Watson and DS Johns had occasion to visit Boulder and Colorado Springs in the state of Colorado to obtain some statements and documentary exhibits about a further case they were investigating. Colorado really was a beautiful state, and Watson was aware that Johns had not visited there previously. Boulder was a nice university town, and Colorado Springs was near the US Air Force Academy. During the visit, Watson decided to take Johns to Pikes Peak, which was in the southern range of

Rocky Mountains. At 14,115 feet, it was the highest summit in the Southern Rockies. Driving toward the top, even the car was beginning to labor with the lack of oxygen as they got higher in altitude. Watson stopped the car near some deep gullies on the mountainside, which still held snow in them. Watson asked Johns if he had seen snow before, and Johns responded, "Only in pictures and movies."

Watson said, "Let's go and see what it feels like."

Johns was off and quickly got to the edge of a band of deep snow. He bent down and picked some snow up with both hands and then quickly dropped it. He announced, "It's cold!"

Watson laughed and said, "It's snow, Joey. It has to be pretty cold to produce snow." Johns, having seen all pictures of pristine snow, apparently had never considered that the snow itself was cold. They were still laughing as they walked back to the car.

They went further up the mountain to a lodge that was situated toward the summit of Pikes Peak. The views from up there of the surrounding landmass were stunning. Watson parked the car, and he and Johns set off to walk about 150 yards to the main entrance to the lodge. They had not gone twenty yards when a sudden squall brought down snowflakes that were quite large and quickly confirmed to Johns that even fresh snow was indeed cold. Accordingly, Watson and Johns started to jog quite quickly toward the lodge. When they reached the destination, they entered, and both stood inside doubled over and trying to catch their breath. Johns didn't know what was happening, but Watson realized that running a short distance such as they had at fourteen thousand feet was far different to running at sea level. The oxygen available would be far less at a higher altitude, and this had caused both of them to be fighting for their breath. After a few minutes of rest and laughing about the experience, they were both ready to go again. Johns was particularly badly hit in that living at sea level for all his life, he had never experienced such an altitude before; it was another learning experience for him and also a vivid reminder to Watson.

CHAPTER 13

Obeah and Its Presence
in the Islands

One of the young CCB officers, a Cayman islander, Detective Constable Hank Rowell, had been investigating a series of stolen checks and had obtained sufficient prima facie evidence to warrant arresting and interviewing a local female in connection with the same. It was a pretty straightforward matter, and the young lady was arrested and interviewed, and a file was to be submitted to the Legal Department for consideration as to charging her. She was then bailed in her own recognizance to appear back at the CCB for her case and the disposal of the same to be determined. One item of concern that Rowell had was that she seemed to be harboring something, but despite many questions and much probing, the detectives were not able to determine what the problem was. However, over the next few days, it came to their knowledge through friends and associates of the young lady that she was a devotee and believer of obeah and was trying to use the art to spread discourse and negative influence on specific officers of the CCB, presumably—Watson surmised—because they were trying to stop her illegal means of income.

Watson had no idea of what obeah was; they did not have such problems in the North of England. But Detective Rowell was well aware of the art. Watson had heard of voodoo, Santeria, and derivatives of the same, but not obeah. Obeah was a system of spiritual and healing practices developed originally among enslaved West

Africans in the West Indies. To this day, it remained a system of belief among people of black heritage, chiefly of the British West Indies and Guyana, that was characterized by the use of magic ritual to ward off misfortune or to cause harm. It was reportedly first used in 1711. Different Afro-Caribbean communities used their own terminology to describe the practice, such as science among the Jamaican Windward Maroons. Obeah was similar to other Afro-American religions—such as Palo, Haitian Vodou, Santeria, and hoodoo—in that it included communication with ancestors and spirits and healing rituals. Nevertheless, it differed from religions like Vodou and Santeria in that there was no explicit canon of gods or deities that was worshipped, and the practice was generally an individual action rather than part of a collective ceremony or offering. Watson also learned that if you'd have an animal and the animal would begin to act out of character, then obeah might be present in the household. Animals would easily be able to pick up on things that'd be unnatural; Watson thought they had an additional sense to humans. Watson was told by the Caymanian locals never to ignore a barking dog, especially if that dog was yours and there seemed to be no reason why he or she was barking. Also, he was told a cat would become easily afraid or annoyed when obeah would become present in a home or compound and act out of its normal character. Watson got a lot of reassurance from the fact of the cat picking up on the same, as he had previously adopted a beautiful calico kitten named Patch from the local animal sanctuary, and Patch had shown no signs out of her ordinary day, which included eating, sleeping, chasing geckos that ventured inside the house, and also showing annoyance at the local birds who often sat in sight of the veranda outside the home. She certainly showed no signs of doing anything out of the ordinary day-to-day process, and therefore Watson reasoned, with what he believed a solid foundation, that there was no obeah present!

When the young lady returned to the CCB, a decision had already been made by the Legal Department to charge her with some specific criminal charges and then bail her to appear before the summary court in Cayman at a date in the future. However, having been made aware of the fact she was trying to use obeah to spread negative influence on the officers in the CCB, Watson had determined to use a reverse psychology on her to make her aware that there might be others with perhaps more obeah influence than her and thereby show her the error of her ways!

At this time, Watson was assisting officers and lawyers from the UK and the USA who were investigating a large-scale international fraud that had strong ties with Cayman and other Caribbean countries. One of the lawyers was Phillip Williams, an African born in Kenya and educated in the UK. He was also qualified as a barrister in the UK. He was a big and powerful-looking individual (more like an American football linebacker) who spoke the perfect Queen's English, thanks to his upbringing and his Oxford University education in the UK. He was duly recruited by Watson to speak to the suspect about the frailty of trying to use obeah to cause harm and distress to others. Williams joyfully and enthusiastically took on the task. *Finally,* he thought, *my hidden acting talents are being brought to the fore.*

After DC Rowell had completed all the necessary actions with the young lady and before letting her go and bailed to appear before the summary court, Watson asked her why she had been invoking discord on the CCB through her understanding and implementation of obeah. She initially denied doing the same but then admitted it was because she had been terribly upset over being caught and the likelihood of going to court and perhaps to prison. This was extremely unlikely in Watson's view. Watson told her he had someone who needed to speak with her, and then Mr. Williams entered the room, dressed in his beautifully cut Savile Row suit and crisp white shirt and wearing a colorful bow tie. Physically he cut a large and very impressive figure. Williams stood there with his gaze rigidly fixed on the young lady and said nothing! Judging by her body reactions, Watson knew that the suspect was already deeply concerned. You could hear a pin drop in the room, and all eyes were centered on Williams. Watson introduced him as Prince Obegwheni from Kenya, Africa. The lady seemed unsure and nervous and was, to say the least, rather apprehensive. Watson explained to her the connection of obeah and people in Africa and the fact that Prince Obegwheni was well-versed in the whole scenario and proper uses for the invocation and uses of the same when necessary and only when necessary.

Mr. Williams then said to her in perfect Swahili (a native language of Kenya), "Unafanya nini kwa mtu huyu?" (What are you doing to this man?). He then asked, "Kwa nini unatumia obeah kwa madhumuni mabaya na sio nzuri?" (Why are you using obeah for bad purposes and not good?"). She was visibly shaken by his strong manner and bearing—eyeballing her directly—and his perfect English. She obviously thought he had a much higher grasp of the obeah situation than she could ever hope to attain from her humble beginnings in Cayman. He then mumbled further unintelligible words to her without blinking and got closer to her and looked at her directly in the eyes and said loudly and with convincing force, "Res ipsa loquitur" (a well-known Latin legal phrase). He then quickly turned on his heels, and as he left the room, he turned and said to Watson, imitating a good African tribal leader, "If y'am wanting me furder, I'll be down de road." Watson looked across at the young lady, and she was visibly shaking in somewhat a fetal position and sobbing heavily. Williams's speech, appearance, and powerful bearing had obviously had a profound effect on her. When she had calmed down and been provided with some much-needed water, she assured Watson and Rowell that she would never do such a thing again and apologized profusely. Watson was under no doubt that she genuinely believed that Williams was in the higher echelon of the obeah gathering from Africa. In fact, following this meeting and Rowell testifying on her behalf in summary court to indicate to the court her admissions when faced with the circumstances of the case, where she further pled guilty to the offenses, she became a useful informant for the police service in a number of matters that were investigated over the years.

Another offshoot of this inquiry was that Watson, along with Phillip Williams as his guest, was invited for a fish dinner at the home of one of Watson's younger officers, the fish a barracuda caught earlier that morning by the officer, DS Johns. The officer and his wife were perfect and consummate hosts at their lovely family home situated in Bodden Town, a few miles outside George Town.

Upon arrival at their home in Bodden Town, Watson was informed by Johns that the fish was being prepared, and it was noted that a small piece of flesh had been cut from the fish and placed in a distant corner of the sandy front yard. The flesh was left for twenty minutes or so, and then at the behest of the host, they returned to examine it. Naturally, or so Watson thought, numerous ants were all over the flesh devouring the same. Apparently, this was a good sign according to Johns, and therefore the barracuda was duly cooked with tomatoes and onions, and it was served by the hosts. To say the least, it tasted supreme, so fresh and firm. Watson was informed then that if the ants had not been eating the fish, Johns would have disposed it, as it was probably poisoned by toxins. Apparently, some of the barracuda were infected by this in Cayman. After putting his health and welfare in the colony of ants, yet another lesson was learned by Watson from this experience: always listen to the locals and avoid eating what they would not eat. Some toxins in the water accumulated up the food chain, and consequently, knowledge of its dangers accumulated down through the generations of people living in a specified area. This was all good advice for a person from Northern England plus was invaluable knowledge to an Oxford-educated barrister! After a perfect and very relaxing meal and extending most gracious thanks to the hosts, Watson left with Williams to drive him back to his hotel before Watson crashed for the night in his apartment, well-fed and watered. What a most agreeable day Watson had had serving in the RCIP. Great memories that would last him a lifetime.

It was also during this period that Watson, whose relationship with Sarah was getting profoundly serious, had decided to apply for and was granted a two-year extension of his contract. Bearing in mind he loved his Toyota Corolla, but the fact that when Sarah was on the island, she would oftentimes drive it and was not too happy with driving a stick shift or especially the fact that the air-conditioning was not working, Watson decided to take action as he thought another two years for the Corolla to last might be two years too long. Accordingly, Watson advertised the same for sale at $1,000 and sold it very quickly for $900 cash, sight unseen. Watson then visited a local car dealer on Walkers Road and purchased a more modern used Nissan that was fully automatic and also had wonderful air-conditioning, luxury at its finest. This was a wonderful surprise to Sarah the next time he picked her up at the airport; she was incredibly pleased at being treated like a queen. While not having the charm of the Toyota in Watson's eyes, this newer vehicle sure made riding in it far more pleasant; and as an added bonus, it was waterproof. Also, to have the air-conditioning working was wonderful. It also lasted Watson the next four years plus before he sold it when he left the island. His colleagues in the CCB now pulled his leg over the new vehicle, and Watson thought that deep down—although they would never admit it—they, too, missed the character and charisma of the Toyota and the excitement and experiences it had had while in the possession of Watson!

CHAPTER 14

An English and American Wedding in Rural Texas

In mid-1989, Watson was very busy primarily conducting inquiries relating to an alleged trust company fraud, including the execution of a search warrant at a banker's home, and he also had recently conducted an interview, under caution, with a leading attorney on the island who was later to become one of Her Majesty's judges in Cayman.

It was against this continually busy background that an event took place that completely changed Watson's life. His relationship with Sarah had been progressing, and they had met many times and under many different circumstances, including Watson visiting the Dallas area and spending time there with Sarah and her three children. Sarah had also visited Cayman many times, and all her children had visited and stayed with Watson on Seven Mile Beach. On one occasion when her two sons visited, Detective Sergeant Johns took them out one morning fishing in his family's boat. The boys had a great day, and both caught barracuda, along with other species of fish. Watson and Sarah had been engaged for about twelve months but had not made any definitive wedding plans. Bearing in mind the impending wedding, whenever that might be, Sarah had put her house on Carnoustie Drive, Roanoke, Texas, on the market for sale when it was then her intention to move to Cayman and live with Watson along with her youngest son. The other two children were already out of the family home—her daughter was living and working near Dallas, and her eldest son was about to start his criminal justice studies at the Southwest Texas State University in San Marcos, near San Antonio, Texas. Watson had previously written to each of the children separately regarding potentially marrying Sarah at some time in the future, and each of them had responded in a very affirmative way to Watson regarding the plans of their mother and Watson. One of the children responded in a brief yet succinct manner: "Please, please take her." Watson thought that each of the children really appreciated this personal approach from him. During the courtship period, Cable & Wireless, the primary telephone provider company in a large portion of the West Indies, made enormous profits from the continued and ongoing contact between Sarah and Watson both from Cayman to Dallas and also other parts of the world where Sarah was flying internationally. Because of the way the relationship was progressing, Sarah—who had custody of her children from a previous marriage—had been sued by her ex-husband for custody of the youngest child (who was twelve years of age at the time), as he tried to prevent her from taking the child out of the country (i.e., to Cayman). Watson stood by Sarah and told her if she wanted to fight the action, he would stand by her and assist in any way he could. The whole matter was very distressing to Sarah, and it took a few months of court-ordered counseling, various testing, and consulting with lawyers before she finally won sole custody of the child in court and thereby the ability to take him out of the state of Texas and out of the country.

Shortly thereafter, Sarah called Watson one evening, and she was excited yet concerned at the same time. She stated that she had just sold her home in Texas, and according to the contract, she had to be out of the home by the beginning of next month (i.e., August). This gave them about twenty-eight days to decide how to handle the situation. Sarah said that as they were planning to get married, should they do it sooner rather than later? And if they did, should they get married in Texas or Cayman? Sarah stated that they didn't need to rush, but if they were going to live together in Cayman, with her youngest son being there and at school also, she would like to be married before that happened—if Watson was agreeable to that. She also stated that she would prefer to get married in Texas if Watson would further concur with that. Watson was delighted to hear about the house being sold and said he had no problem with getting married earlier and that it was fine if she wanted the ceremony in the USA or wherever she was inclined to get married. Following further discussion, a date in the middle of the month was agreed; and as a result, much work and planning had to be done to bring it to fruition in the next ten to twelve days. All this placed great pressure on Sarah and Watson—but probably more to Sarah.

Watson and Sarah also found a new rental property in Cayman that contained two bedrooms and two bathrooms and was situated on South Church Street—overlooking Eden Rock, which was a popular diving center—and just a bit further down the road was Sunset House, which was an oft frequented bar on the island. These new premises were much better suited to accommodate her young son and also provide accommodation for any guests who'd come to Cayman rather than the one-bedroom apartment on Seven Mile Beach. Right next door was an old Caymanian house that was rented by Superintendent Smithley and his lovely wife, Doreen. This added to Watson's enjoyment on the island in that he and Sarah were often invited to makeshift parties and celebrations of all types. On one occasion, there had been an evening of hard celebration at the house, and the guests had all left about 11:00 p.m. or so. Watson and Sarah had returned home next door when shortly thereafter, they heard a loud sound that sounded like glass breaking. Watson quickly got up, dressed, and went to investigate the same; perhaps a burglar might be there for the taking. He discovered that there was nothing in his block that appeared to have been damaged, and he then decided to call the Smithleys to see if they were okay. The call was quickly answered by Doreen who, when asked by Watson if everything was okay, responded quickly by saying that it was, thanked Watson for calling, and hung up! Watson determined the next morning that Doreen was rather short with him because Mr. Smithley, being somewhat the worse for wear following the evening's libations, had gone into his bedroom, tripped over an area rug near his bed, and accordingly, catapulted headlong into a lovely and old transom exterior glass window, which had then broken into hundreds of pieces. Mr. Smithley, to say the least, was not in Doreen's good books at that stage. Watson imagined that getting such a window repaired on the island would not be an easy thing.

Going back to the marriage preparations in Texas, first and foremost, Sarah had to get a marriage license issued by the local county in Texas; as at any marriage ceremony, this is needed by the minister as his authority to perform the ceremony. This was job number 1 for Sarah. She enrolled the assistance of her daughter Stacey, who was highly organized, and together they worked on matters such as finding a church and minister, a florist, and a photographer and sending out invitations to people locally, all this in the next ten days. Sarah also arranged for a small reception to be held after the service at her home, which was slowly but surely being emptied, in Roanoke. With having sold the house, she would then have to pack everything from the house—some of it to be moved to Cayman, some stuff to her children, some items to her sister in Phoenix, and some to Goodwill. Watson had to get some annual leave from the police, allowing him to take about two to three weeks' vacation to travel to Texas, and also had to arrange for his work colleagues to hold a watching brief on all his ongoing cases during this period of absence. The month was going to be a hard one for both Sarah and Watson, but it'd be a most fulfilling one that would bring each of them great happiness both immediately and in the long term.

The arrangements in Texas went well due to Sarah's daughter and close friends in the area. They were all incredibly happy with the news but concerned that their longtime friend and neighbor, Sarah, would be leaving the area. It was because of the support and help she received from so many people that she was able to stave off a potential minibreakdown!

Sarah picked a hundred-year-old church that was situated on a small hill in Roanoke, Texas, and met with the pastor there. He was most excited to be able to assist, and the wedding was set for a sunset service at the church at 7:30 p.m. The license was secured, and the invitations were sent out to Sarah's close friends. A small hitch occurred when Sarah discovered that her children had invited along their good friends also, but not to worry. Sarah made the necessary trip to Neiman Marcus (Watson always referred to it as Needless Markup) in Downtown Dallas to order two cakes for the day, a wedding cake and also a groom's cake. She was planning on just having champagne and cakes, but at the specific request of her children, she ordered two big trays of sandwiches from the local grocery store. Sarah also had a wedding dress made for the ceremony, which, in Watson's eyes, was spectacular!

Watson arrived in Texas the Sunday afternoon before the planned Wednesday wedding. He found that wedding arrangements were in full swing to say the least. Everything had been attended to, and Sarah had enrolled a pilot friend from the neighborhood to videotape the service, in addition to the professional photographs that had already been ordered. Sarah and Watson met with the pastor on Monday afternoon and went through a quick overview of the ceremony together with the required prayers and hymns. The pastor was a kind and gentle man who made Watson and Sarah feel most welcome. He seemed very pleased for them. The church itself was old but well-maintained, and the pastor stated that at 7:30 p.m. on Wednesday, with the sun streaming through the stained-glass windows from the west, it would look really beautiful. Everything was set for the wedding.

The rest of the day was spent by Sarah packing up parts of the house ready for the sale and other ancillary matters relating to the wedding. Watson spent a great deal of time on the roof of the house replacing some of the broken and missing wooden shingles. In a Texas summer, it was hotter than hell up on the roof!

The wedding party had all been determined at this time. Sarah's daughter was to be the maid of honor, and a friend of her daughter would sing two songs prior to the ceremony at the church. Sarah's eldest son would be Watson's best man, and her youngest son would walk Sarah down the aisle and present her for marriage. One of Sarah's best friends—Anne, who originally hailed from Ireland—would act as a chauffeur to the couple and drove an old Rolls-Royce that she and her husband owned. Anne also borrowed a pilot's cap from an airline friend to enhance her appearance to play the part of the chauffeur. She carried the position off with aplomb. Anne was one of Sarah's most long-standing close friends and that relationship subsisted for many years. Sarah and Watson continued the home sale preparation duties up until about 5:30 p.m. on the day of the wedding.

The day of the wedding arrived, and Sarah found out that same day that the wife of Superintendent Smithley was arriving at DFW International Airport that afternoon from Cayman and needed to be picked up and housed. Also, Elizabeth, Sarah's sister whom Watson met the same day he first met Sarah in Cayman, was arriving from Phoenix for the wedding and would also need accommodation. Luckily, Sarah, unbeknownst to Watson, had planned a honeymoon night at a local luxurious DFW hotel, so that left a number of beds available at Sarah's home. The downside was her two sons had to sleep on the floor, but that was not an unusual experience for them by any means. Two of Sarah's regular flying partners arrived also from Denver to give their support, and they also stayed at the same hotel as Sarah and Watson. Sarah's friend and her cleaning lady stayed at the house after the ceremony to greet all the guests and serve the champagne, sandwiches, and cake.

Watson thought that for having such a short preparation time to plan the wedding, hopefully everything would go off without a hitch. It did. It was about 7:05 p.m. The cakes and flowers were delivered on time, all the guests were at the church, Watson and Sarah's eldest and youngest son had left, and all that was left was for the bride and the matron of honor to make the journey. Anne arrived at Sarah's home driving the Rolls-Royce, and she carefully took Sarah and her maid of honor on board. They set out to drive the two miles or so to the church, but about halfway there, Anne pulled off the side of the road and said, "Brides can't be on time. You have to be about five minutes fashionably late!" Sarah, who was already stressed enough, told her that she did not want to be late, but it fell on deaf ears with Anne. So in her own time, Anne got the Rolls under way again en route to the church. On arrival, the pastor was outside waiting for the bride's arrival. Anne asked the minister to get the cameraman out to video the bride's arrival. The pastor duly responded, and Anne had locked the doors of the Rolls so Sarah could not exit until the cameraman was there. Another five to ten minutes passed, and Sarah was concerned she was fifteen minutes or so late for her wedding, and she genuinely believed that Watson and the boys might think that she had skipped town! They were concerned over the length of time but duly understood later when the circumstances were disclosed to them.

Once Sarah was in the church, the ceremony began, and Sarah's heartbeats slowed down slightly from the elevated position a few minutes earlier. The ceremony went perfectly, and the pastor made a wonderful homily regarding marriage and especially regarding Watson and Sarah, together with their overcoming of a very long-distance relationship and one hurricane. After the ceremony was completed, all the guests at the church went back to Sarah's home for the small reception. That also went off well, although Watson, who had been admiring the groom's cake for so long, found after speaking with most people in the room that Sarah's sons and some of their friends had finished off the whole cake!

After the reception and after the few speeches had been received, the guests began to disperse, and the newly married couple left and went to the hotel for the overnight stay. To say that they were exhausted would be an understatement. Both slept like logs until the following morning. About midday the following day, they returned to Sarah's home, and Sarah visited the refrigerator to recover some goodies she had placed in there the previous evening. They were all gone! Young boys in the house could easily consume anything edible left in the fridge.

Watson mused to himself that these circumstances were like being in an incident room! He recalled that previously in Cayman, during the tenure of running an incident room into a major inquiry, Sarah had often brought in a large slab of Texas chocolate cake or some other delicacy that she had made for the officers to enjoy during the day. She always brought food to the police station, and Watson knew it was always well-received and most appreciated. On this particular occasion, when she brought the food, Watson was out of the office and was at the attorney general's office in the Glass House. Consequently, Sarah left the cake with DS Johns and, after exchanging pleasantries, went on her way. Watson believed that Texas chocolate cake entering a police station could initiate any police officer's smelling buds within an eight-hundred-yard range! When Watson got back to the incident room about fifteen minutes later, the cake tray was empty. Sarah's Texas chocolate cake, as Watson knew full well, was excellent. Watson, who was rather displeased, questioned DS Johns by saying, "Do you enjoy working in the incident rooms, Joey?"

Johns responded, "Yes, sir, very much so. You know I do."

Watson said in a way typical of Garnet, "Now listen here. When Sarah brings any goodies in the future like Texas chocolate cake, or whatever it happens to be, and I don't happen to be here at that specific time, if there are no portions left for me when I return, you will never, never, never ever work an incident room with me again. Do you understand this?"

Johns, without saying anything further, responded quickly and accurately, "Yes, sir, totally. I apologize. You can be sure it won't happen again." Watson recalled that true to his promise, whenever Sarah delivered goodies to the incident room going forward, even if the tray was empty when Watson returned, there were always a couple of the delicacies wrapped in a paper napkin that had been secured in the drawer of the desk that Watson was using. A good man that Johns!

The next day was spent further packing up items from the house and fixing one or two minor problems with the property. Watson and Sarah then went to DFW Airport and first flew on United Airlines to Chicago so that Sarah could show Watson where she had been born and where she grew up, plus a number of other properties she had lived in prior to and following her marriage. Watson really enjoyed Chicago. It was a nice city with lots of beautiful places to visit and full of many interesting areas. They also met with a number of Sarah's relatives who were still living in Chicago. Watson and Sarah then flew on United Airlines from Chicago to San Francisco. San Francisco was one of Sarah's favorite cities that she had visited many times during her career as a flight attendant. Watson concurred; he enjoyed the whole experience there. It was a beautiful city, full of life and many places to experience and visit. Watson enjoyed the trip to Alcatraz Island and the visit to Lombard Street—billed as the crookedest street in the world. They also traversed across the Golden Gate Bridge to a small town called Sausalito—which was like an old quintessential British town, except for the numerous palm trees, which wouldn't do well in the British climate. They enjoyed some great meals while there, one at Scoma's, which had stunning views over the San Francisco Bay looking toward the city on the bay, San Francisco. Watson also discovered a pub or bar there called Pattersons Bar. Inside there were lots of photographs from the UK and Ireland from the time of the Second World War. There was also a picture of the Auchtermuchty football (called soccer in the UK) team from 1811! Auchtermuchty was a town in Fife, Scotland, beside Pitlour Hill and nine miles north of Glenrothes.

During their stay of a few days in San Francisco, which Sarah had visited many times, and during each and every visit, she would put her trainers on and climb some of the many hills that the city possessed. One such climb was up to a monument called Coit Tower. It was a slender white concrete column rising from the top of Telegraph Hill that had been an emblem of San Francisco's skyline since 1933. It was named after Lillie Hitchcock Coit, who was the patron of the city's firefighters, both full-time and volunteers. Just before Sarah's marriage, she had worked a number of trips involving overnight stays in San Francisco. She therefore suggested that she and Watson go walking around some of the areas and hills. They approached one of the steeper roads up to Coit Tower, and she suggested that she'd race Watson to the top of Telegraph Hill. Watson immediately accepted the challenge, although deep down, he was rather concerned about the gradient that had to be scaled for a distance of about six hundred yards. Nonetheless, he allowed Sarah a start ahead of him while he counted off twenty seconds. She was off and running, and then Watson started. It was steep, and Watson wondered if he had bitten off too much. Nonetheless, with his longer stride pattern and after getting into a rhythm, he found he was catching Sarah and then passed her before they had reached the halfway point. He was breathing heavily and must had sounded like a Puffing Billy steam train passing her. Watson reached the end point and turned a little corner to be out of sight while Sarah was still coming up the final incline. Once around the corner, Watson virtually collapsed through exertion and was breathing heavily. He was trying to look in reasonable shape when Sarah arrived. He failed miserably but was reassured when Sarah came around the corner in almost the same state as when Watson had arrived. After this exercise, neither of them wanted to try doing such exercise again during this trip!

Watson and Sarah returned to Dallas after about six days spent in beautiful San Francisco. Packing up her house was completed, and she ended up with three piles of items, including furniture, clothing, dishes, and all manner of other small items. Sarah's children had already acquired the items they wanted to reserve for themselves. One pile was to go to Phoenix for Elizabeth and her home. This was driven there in a rental truck by Sarah's eldest son. One pile was placed into a nearby storage unit, and the final pile was donated to Goodwill. Sarah thought that as she was moving to Cayman for five or six years, she didn't need much of her furniture and the like, purely clothing, and that was what she took. It was all rather topsy-turvy following the hectic time that preceded it and appeared to Watson to be rather confusing, but nonetheless, Sarah obviously knew what she was doing. Watson was deeply in love with this woman.

Following this, one day Sarah was called to the realtor's office, as there were papers and documents for her to sign regarding the sale of the property. Watson had arranged to leave a couple days before this, but due to the work that remained to be done at the house, he stayed to help Sarah finish up the work and items that needed attending to at the house. That decision was proved to be very fortuitous. When they arrived at the realtor's, the lady realtor—who was a friend of Sarah's—informed Watson that he had to sign the papers in order to complete the sale of Sarah's home. Apparently because Watson and Sarah were now man and wife, there was a law on the Texas books stated that because Watson had spent one night in the other person's house, he had become a part owner! This was unbelievable to Watson, and he tried to state that it was Sarah's home, nothing to do with him. Watson was informed that he had to sign the papers as required for the transfer and sale to go ahead. Being obedient, Watson duly signed, but he wondered what might have happened to the sale if Watson had gone back to Cayman as originally planned and not stayed in town. Watson would never know the answer to that question, but he knew that that would probably have thrown a large wrench in the works.

Shocked yet somewhat amused that apparently he was now a Texas landowner, Watson finally caught a flight back to Cayman from Dallas, through Miami, to resume his work duties. He really was exhausted following all that had happened in the last two weeks or so. Sarah had to stay for a few more days in Texas to send her oldest son off to university in San Marcos, and then as she had finished all her vacation time, she had to work a four-day trip for United Airlines. The past three weeks had all been a blur to her, but following her trip, she immediately flew into Cayman for the first time as Mrs. Christopher Watson. Her youngest son was going to stay with his father in Texas for a small duration until the fall school season commenced, and then it was intended he would come to Cayman to be with his mother and Watson.

CHAPTER 15

Cayman's First Armed Bank Robbery

Watson was in the office working diligently to put together some files needed for the prosecution of the on-island fraud that he had inherited—the prosecution aspect—from his predecessor when he noted there was a lot of excitement and officers running here and there in an excited manner. He quickly learned that the first armed robbery experienced in Cayman had just occurred at the National Bank of the Cayman Islands, situated near the port terminal, and apparently, a firearm had been discharged during the incident. It was not immediately known if anyone had been injured during the robbery. It was lunchtime, and the center of George Town was full of tourists who had alighted from the four cruise ships that were visiting Grand Cayman that day. The commissioner, who was aware of Watson's background in the management of major incidents, quickly contacted Watson and instructed him to go to the Central Police Station, a short distance from the CCB office, and help set up a control center or incident room to manage the inquiries being made into the event. Watson quickly recruited Sergeant Johns who eagerly went along with Watson to learn how to manage and run major incidents.

On arrival at Central Police Station, Watson noted large groups of armed uniform officers were being dispatched into the community wearing sidearms that had been usually issued in circumstances such as this. The firearms all seemed rather antiquated to Watson;

they were all the revolver type. The police did not usually carry fire-arms, and Watson later learned that their firearm training involved them firing six bullets a year at a local range to qualify. Obviously, there were cost implications to obtaining the ammunition, and six bullets did not seem a lot to Watson. So how accurate or proficient could these officers be with the firearms, particularly when under the stress of a live-action incident? With all the armed police being out on the street, Watson felt it might be safer to stay in the Central Police Station! However, that decision had been taken out of his hands by the commissioner remembering Watson's background with HOLMES and the major incident management system and ordering the establishment of an incident room. The commissioner had no idea if such an animal were available to the Cayman police, but it only took Watson a couple questions and an analysis of the responses given to understand that the force had not used any major incident procedures in the past. Also, another blow to Watson was that the documentation to establish such, which was readily available in the UK, was not available in any way, shape, or form in Cayman.

In the UK, there were major incident room kits that were read-ily available for such circumstances; and when Watson queried this with the local officers and supervisors at the Central Police Station, everyone looked and shook their heads stating that they had no such kits. Necessity being the mother of invention, Watson put together what he could using normal paper pads, carbon paper, and index cards hurriedly obtained from the local office supply company under a purchase order. The force joiner was recruited and helped greatly by constructing the appropriately sized small wooden boxes designed specifically to hold the card indexes used in the management of major inquiries and so necessary to the long-term goals. Watson also ensured that staff in the police control room who took calls from the public were made aware to ensure that any and all calls received relat-ing to the incident were logged separately and processed in a normal fashion but also passed in a documentary form to the incident room for processing and actioning, if necessary.

A longer term benefit of this process, after the case had been finished, was that Watson obtained various copies of action forms and other documents used in major incidents in the UK and also compiled a local major incident room manual appropriate to the circumstances found in the islands to be used by officers as and when any major inquiry occurred and needed the support of an incident room. A local printing firm in Cayman was recruited and printed all the necessary forms and self-carbonized papers for use in the process following a couple of meetings with Watson. A weeklong course was then held for a cadre of local Caymanian officers to experience and learn the running of a major incident room and all the various actions it entailed. This turned out to be very well received in the island, and later on, at the behest of the British government, all the British dependent territories in the Caribbean sent officers to the Cayman Islands for a week for their training in the use and management of major incident rooms, including the running of a mock incident room. They were all very enthusiastic about this, and following the course, each British dependent territory set up their own in-house training sessions. Many of the officers who attended kept in touch with Watson after completing the basic course in the Cayman Islands, and accordingly, Watson had some good contacts in the other islands as and when he needed such assistance.

The detective branch and scenes of crime officers were already active at the bank, and it was quickly learned that there had been two men in the bank, one of whom had discharged a firearm into the ceiling and demanded money from the tellers at the bank. Thankfully, no one had been injured by this discharge. Another member of the gang had been waiting outside in a vehicle, and following the robbery, the two men who had taken money from the tellers ran out to the car with their ill-gotten gains in black bags and sped off away from town and down South Church Street. The process of getting detectives to the scene paid quick dividends in that when asking questions to the public, most of whom had alighted from the four cruise ships berthed in Cayman for the day, about the robbery and leaving the scene, one detective found an elderly tourist from the USA who offered the information that the getaway vehicle was a 1976 brown-colored Chevrolet Monte Carlo. When asked how he could be so certain, the tourist responded by saying that he had an identical vehicle from 1976 at home in the USA. He was most adamant that the Monte Carlo was the type of vehicle used. He had heard the commotion at the bank and then saw two people run from the bank carrying some bags and jump into the Monte Carlo parked outside with the engine running, which then sped off, and he indicated the direction of travel down South Church Street. "Just like a scene from a movie," he stated, but this was real life!

Based on this specific information, detectives were immediately dispatched to the local Cayman Islands Department of Motor Vehicles where details of all motor vehicles (*Well, perhaps most of them,* Watson thought) on the island and also the registered owners' details were to be found. Very quickly it was learned from these inquiries that there was only a total of six Chevrolet Monte Carlos on the island. Of those six, four were owned and operated by local people of apparently good repute whom the detectives believed would not be involved in such an act, and two were owned by a rental car company whose operations were based very adjacent to the Owen Roberts Airport. The rental cars thus became items of intense interest to the detectives.

Detectives were immediately dispatched to the car rental company and quickly found from the inquiries made there that one of the Monte Carlos was currently off the road receiving some major engine repairs at a local garage and the other one was out on a rental. This became interesting for two reasons. The car involved in the robbery had been seen moving by another local witness at high speed on South Church Street just after the robbery had taken place and was seen turning left onto Walkers Road. In making the turn, the driver had lost some control of the same and sideswiped a chain-link metal fence for some twenty-five feet or so, leaving brown paintwork from the car all over the fence. Also, the vehicle had been hired by a local man the day before the robbery using his own Cayman Islands driving license! Watson thought you'd sometimes have to love criminals and also be thankful on occasions for their idiotic decisions! It was also noted by local officers—again the advantage of intimate local knowledge—that this person's stepfather in Cayman owned a garage near the airport. The stepfather lived in a property near Walkers Road toward the Catholic church.

Watson thought that this was getting very interesting. Subsequently, the car was found by PC Webster at the stepfather's property near the airport with a damaged left-hand side. A touch of the hood showed that the vehicle had just recently been driven extremely hard, as the hood was still hot, and the brake pads exuded heat. Armed police and detectives were dispatched to the home of the stepfather. Upon entering the residential property, the detectives were told the stepfather was having a nap and, accordingly, duly raised him from his sleep. When asked about the car in his garage, he stated he did not know how it got there; but when shown the rental agreement for the same and a copy of the driving license used in renting the vehicle, he did admit to knowing of his stepson renting it, and the car keys were also found in his possession.

Another lesson was also learned here by Watson. Many criminals in the islands buried ill-gotten gains in their yards, or if it involved paperwork (as in many frauds), they burned the same to ashes at the bottom of the yard. Some of the local Caymanian officers at the house noted this and saw two freshly turned over and distinct areas of sand and soil in the backyard. Using a spade from the scenes of crime vehicle, a few shovels of dirt removed from each area revealed a number of separate black plastic bags, and each bag contained numerous US dollar bills of varying amounts, all bundled with the bank denominations slips on them. A firearm used in the robbery was also found. These items were all preserved and seized and, along with the stepfather and also the motor vehicle, were taken to the Central Police Station for processing and further scenes of crime examination.

Following interviews by the local detectives, the stepson was quickly arrested, and it was established who the two other accomplices in the robbery were. Consequently, they were arrested shortly thereafter and thankfully without incident.

Watson then worked with a member of the senior staff from the National Bank of the Cayman Islands, and following their review of the happenings and also the monies involved, the bank came to the decision that the money stolen totaled US $360,000, all in current US dollar banknotes. Concerned for the safety and security of keeping that amount of money in a police evidence room, Watson—along with the senior official from the bank—arranged to count the money in each and every bundle that had been recovered. The bank also agreed that the police could preserve each wrapper from the bundles, along with the top and bottom US dollar note from each bundle, thereby allowing that should it be necessary in the future to forensically examine each for fingerprints and other purposes, they would be available. This was an onerous task that took quite a few hours to complete, but it was made somewhat easier by using money-counting machines provided by and borrowed from the bank. However, at the end of the same, the police and the banking official determined that the police had recovered a total US $370,000 in the two bags! This was a cause of much consternation to the bank official, although Watson tried to convince him it was a positive thing, at least better than the alternative. However, the police department sat more comfortably knowing that the bulk of the money recovered was now back in the safe custody of the bank's vault while the remaining money kept for evidentiary purposes and possible forensic examination was kept in a police safe with very limited access. In subsequent dealings Watson had with the bank official, he always raised concerns over how they had reported one amount while an additional $10,000 had been recovered. Watson held the view that it was never satisfactorily resolved to the official's satisfaction, but that was the bank's problem, not his.

Subsequently, two of the men involved in the bank robbery were found guilty at the Cayman Islands Grand Court and sentenced to varying terms of imprisonment at Her Majesty's prison at Northward, Grand Cayman. One of the robbers was acquitted. Two of them, interestingly enough, had—at various times in the past—worked for the bank that they then robbed.

Albeit early on during Watson's attachment in the Cayman Islands, it was an inquiry that reflected well on the officers involved and showed what could be achieved when all the police would come together with a tenacity and objectivity of purpose. It also illustrated to Watson that working in an island with nineteen thousand population, the police force of two hundred or so officers, plus civilian staff, had enormous value in the contacts they made through being born and living there all their lives, together with working as police officers in the community. If only the same were true in the UK and other large principalities, it would make the mission of crime prevention and solving much easier.

While this incident was ongoing, Watson had occasion to leave the incident room at the Central Police Station to return to his office in the Tower Building to prepare some documents that were needed in a court case, shortly to be heard in court. He arrived at his office, passed the usual pleasantries with Garnet, and noted one of the detective sergeants in his office interviewing a young Caymanian offender regarding some petty theft matters. Watson excused himself and asked the detective if he could sit in while the interview was being conducted. The detective responded, "Of course, sir." In accordance with good practice, Watson drew up a chair and sat where he could observe the actions of the young Caymanian from the top of his head down to his feet. Watson always told his young detectives that 75 to 80 percent of communication would be nonverbal. Only 20 percent was what the person might say. Other actions—including sweating, hand movements, eye movements, leg movements, fidgeting, swallowing, and other indicators—oftentimes would answer a question for an experienced detective before he'd hear any verbal answer. Watson immediately noticed that the interviewee had an air of total disdain about him for the process and was being most disrespectful toward the detective. Watson let the interview continue, but as the time went on, the alleged offender displayed more bravado and started telling the detective that the detective knew nothing and was basically worthless as an investigator. He was becoming most insolent. Watson was growing more frustrated over the way the interview was being allowed to progress, and he stared intently at the Caymanian offender. The interviewee also became aware of Watson's riveting glare at him and started to shift uneasily. He knew or, at the very least, suspected that Watson would not accept his indifference much longer, but that didn't stop him!

135

Watson was wondering why the detective was not doing something to bring the interview back on track and add discipline to the same. Suddenly the offender pushed his chair back and stood up. Watson was now concerned on what the suspect was doing, and he started to move toward Watson and the door. Watson reacted immediately and stood up, fixated on the suspect, and moved toward him. The suspect now looked concerned as Watson took hold of him under each arm, lifted him away from his chair, and pushed him firmly against the wall of the office; both of the suspect's feet were some six inches off the floor. It should be noted that in the office next door was Superintendent Smithley who was at the time interviewing a potential new recruit for the RCIP in his office. The wall was purely metal frames covered each side with Sheetrock, so there was virtually no soundproofing, and the wall would actually shake when hit! Smithley sat with his back to the adjoining wall, and hanging on the wall behind him were commemorative plaques from other forces, memorial plates and pennants received over the years, and most importantly, a pegboard that contained the names of all the RCIP officers on staff and denoted by various pegs, what courses they had attended, current posting, and other indicators. When Watson lifted and pushed the offender against the wall, he was immediately aware something had happened in the office next door. There was one crashing sound as the plates and other items left the wall and then another sound as a number of the plates, plaques, and also the pegboard hit the floor. The really bad part was that the numerous pegs, hundreds probably, that had been in the pegboard were now all over the floor, and the records recorded had been basically wiped out by that one action! Watson, however, knew something had happened but did not know the actual circumstances until some fifteen or twenty minutes later. Watson continued to hold the offender against the wall, his feet dangling in the air, and explained to him the need to show proper respect for a police officer and also the benefits of telling the truth to police officers as opposed to lying and being cynical and insolent. The young man obviously got the message being imparted to him by Watson, as his whole attitude changed, and immediately he decided to show respect to the interviewer by calling him sir! Watson told the detective to continue the interview and take a voluntary statement from the young man regarding the circumstances alleged. Watson told the detective that he must visit with Superintendent Smithley to speak with him but he would be back shortly should he be needed! There was no doubt that the offender didn't want to see Watson again.

Watson left the office, and immediately Garnet asked what had happened. She had been spooked by the sound of the interviewee being pushed into the wall! Watson told her, and she laughed away to herself. It certainly made her day, and then Watson went to see Superintendent Smithley. When he entered the superintendent's office, the superintendent was on his hands and knees picking up plaques, plates, pegs, and pennants! The superintendent rose and exchanged pleasantries. Watson asked him what had happened. Smithley explained he had been interviewing a potential recruit when all hell broke loose. First there was a loud bang on the wall, and then his plaques, plates, pennants, and pegboard came off the wall. Smithley said he was startled, but the young recruit was more so; he came some two feet off his chair, clearly spooked by what was happening. Watson asked him how he explained it to the recruit. Smithley said he calmly and nonchalantly said to the recruit, "Nothing to worry about. It is Detective Chief Inspector Watson's interview techniques."

Watson smiled and said, "Well, it doesn't always happen, does it?" In an attempt to show remorse and concern, Watson himself got on his hands and knees and started to recover items from the floor, including hundreds of pegs that, a few minutes earlier, had been ensconced on the pegboard.

Going forward, Watson did notice that on future visits he made to Smithley's office, there was nothing on the wall behind Smithley, just one small picture. On the wall opposite him, the plates (that survived), the plaques, and more importantly, the pegboard had all been placed on the wall farthest from Watson's adjoining wall. Watson smiled to himself at this wise decision made by Smithley. Watson was also amazed at the time and effort that must had gone into reconstructing the details reflected by the pegboard. Watson, in an effort to bring some normality to the situation, apologetically asked Smithley if he wanted to go for a beer after work on Watson's tab, an offer that Smithley quickly accepted. After a few Miller Lites for Watson and a few Beck's for Smithley, all seemed well and calm, perhaps temporarily, between the two Tower Building neighbors!

A few days after the completion of this inquiry, Watson found himself suffering from a heavy cold. He went into the office and tried to keep to himself while he loaded himself up with vitamin C to fight off the cold. Garnet immediately seized on Watson's apparent ill-health and told him first and foremost that he shouldn't be at work and that the panacea for the cold was well-known in Cayman. She instructed Watson to go home and then immerse himself in the sea and said the salt water would take care of the rest. Apparently, there were not many ailments in Cayman that couldn't be cured by a dip in the sea. Watson went home as instructed and went in the sea twice that day. He felt better the next day but was still suffering slightly, so he took the morning off work and again went in the sea twice. By midafternoon, he was feeling like an almost new man, so he repeated the treatment in the afternoon; and by the following day, he was fully clear of all his symptoms and went back to work as usual. Garnet was delighted to see that Watson had recovered and, more importantly, through the panacea suggested by her. Garnet told Watson with a broad smile on her face, "Now listen here. We know some things, you know." Watson called her Dr. Garnet after that!

CHAPTER 16

A Gold and Jewelry Store Robbery

Just a stone's throw from the cruise ship landing in George Town, a prime spot for tourists to visit, on Goring Avenue was a small strip mall of various types of shops offering all things Cayman. In the row of these shops was a small store bearing the words "Cayman Gold and Jewelry" over the front windows. The store was owned by a local who took great pride in providing valued gold and jewelry to the tourists at what he stated to be reasonable prices. It was a midafternoon in March 1990, and the streets were busy but not overcrowded. An elderly man was working in the store doing his usual daily tasks of cleaning the display cabinets, balancing the till, and when necessary, serving and assisting customers. There was the usual foot traffic of tourists wanting to buy something before they left the island to travel on a tender back to their cruise ship. It was just another normal day in paradise! Watson was busy preparing a case for court that had been worked on by members of the CCB for quite a few months. It was finally coming to fruition! The detective chief superintendent called Watson and informed him that there had been a murder during a robbery at Cayman Gold and Jewelry and that detectives and the scenes of crime officers had been dispatched there. Watson was requested to attend Central Police Station and, with colleagues, establish a major incident room for the crime. Watson immediately again recruited Detective Sergeant Johns and set off on the way to the Central Police Station. A pleasant surprise was that Detective

Inspector John Wickerson of the Special Branch also offered assistance in the major incident room, having had a little experience of the same from his time as an officer in the English police prior to joining the Cayman police.

The task was now not as daunting as it originally had been because major incident room cases had previously been made and stored for such an eventuality. Consequently, it was just a case of retrieving one of the boxes that contained all the documents, index cards, action forms, and other needed items and commencing the work. Once the boxes had been miraculously found (much to Watson's relief) after a rather lengthy search, a room was allocated, and the work began. As in all major crimes' statements were recorded by detectives from potential witnesses in and around the scene while the scenes of crime detectives continued their examinations at and adjacent to the scene. All the incoming phone calls and information—including documentary items—was logged, indexed, and actioned if necessary. It was quickly apparent that the person in the store had been shot and had died almost immediately. There were signs of a struggle, and it was obvious that the elderly shop assistant had resisted his attacker(s). Further, some of the display cases were broken and had some jewelry missing. Until the owners were allowed into the scene following processing, there was no way of actually knowing what the stolen jewelry comprised of.

Statements began to flow into the incident room as they were taken and then processed and indexed in there. They were read by at least two people in the room, plus the senior investigating officer, and marked up with any additional queries that should be addressed, plus any further actions that needed to be taken based on their contents were raised by the incident room staff. Of specific interest was the fact that two young men of West Indian descent had been seen immediately before the occurrence riding their motor scooters at higher than normal speed in and around the area of the crime. A number of witnesses had seen them and remarked on the fact that it seemed rather odd and certainly was out of the ordinary. The good information was that they recognized these two young men as being of local descent, and more importantly, some of the witnesses actually named them. The witnesses further described the clothing that they were wearing when seen on the scooters and also gave a general description of the scooters. Everybody knew nearly everybody in those days in Cayman! All the details were indexed, and of course, every item that was indexed showed where that information had originated from. Much incident room work involved cross-referencing details and ensuring that the same or similar facts appeared in each and every statement when witnesses referred to a certain happening.

Appeals were made through the press and local radio and TV for anyone with information pertaining to this murder, and several snippets of information from the public were provided, all of which were duly actioned and prioritized for detectives to undertake the necessary inquiries. Another advantage of the incident room system that was established was when an action was issued to a detective, if a person or witness in that action was already indexed and in the system from previous documents or actions, then the detective who was to undertake the inquiry was provided with copies of documents already pertaining to the subject he was about to interview.

Following the appeals made to the public and additionally evidence being developed from other sources, a number of witnesses were identified and interviewed who, after the offense had been committed, saw two young West Indian males riding motor scooters at a fast pace, going generally away from the scene. One of the witnesses knew the names of the two young men seen, and he described them, including their clothing. The difference was that this description of their clothing, in both cases, was totally different from that that they were reportedly wearing prior to the crime. Other witnesses described the same event but, not knowing their names, also described different clothing from what the offenders were seen wearing prior to the crime. It was significant that the scooters they were seen on by the witnesses were of the same description as those described prior to the incident taking place.

By examination of the statements and other documents in the incident room, this noteworthy discrepancy was immediately brought to the attention of the senior investigating officer. Based on this and on the assumption that they had probably stripped off a layer of clothing following the crime being committed, the inquiries were now being directed primarily on these two suspects. Inquiries regarding their actions on the day in question were followed, and efforts were also made based on the potential route or routes they took to flee the scene to recover the clothing that they had probably disposed of. Information coming in from the scene of the murder from the scenes of crimes officer also began to show what had happened at the scene and the suspects' potential involvement in the same. Based on their suspected routes of escape from the store, detectives searched various yards and gardens along the potential routes and were delighted to find some discarded clothing in bushes remarkably close to the scene of the murder. Also, some of the pieces of clothing had traces of blood splatter on them.

During the ongoing inquiries being made in this matter, Watson was approached by Detective Sergeant Rixon who complained regarding a government fraud he had been investigating; a local building company owner named Tony Hancock had been approached by Rixon to provide some business documents that were imperative for Rixon to build a fraud case against the miscreant. Hancock, who was known to Watson, had apparently refused to produce the documents requested, as he was terribly busy building a new set of condominiums and stated that he could not spare the time necessary for the same. Without these documents being made available, it would be impossible to put together the evidence necessary to sustain a potential prosecution in the case. Watson said to Rixon, "Get the car and let's go have a word with Mr. Hancock." Together they traveled to the construction site where four blocks of condos, four stories in height, were being constructed. The scaffolding around each block had a number of workers—probably around forty in total, mainly Jamaican nationals—swarming all over the sites completing various construction jobs, and in the far corner of the site was a temporary hut that the whole operation of building the condos was being run out of.

Upon entry, Watson found three people in the administration hut: Hancock, another worker, and a secretary. Hancock immediately recognized Watson and shook his hand. Watson introduced DS

Rixon to Hancock and said, "My officer, Detective Sergeant Rixon, tells me you or your company hold some important evidence relating to a fraud case he is investigating and that despite polite and very necessary requests from him on three separate occasions, you have offered excuses for not being able to produce the same, and in fact, last time you told him outright that you couldn't provide them. I am asking you to kindly cooperate in this matter and produce the same as soon as possible. DS Rixon has been more than reasonable in his requests to you. I do not want to think you are withholding the documents for any nefarious or personal reason."

Hancock said, "I am sorry, but I am overwhelmed with business at the moment. And with construction deadlines fast approaching on this project, the last thing I can do is take time out to prepare the documents for you. I just don't have the time. I am sorry, but that's how it is."

Watson realized that more than the normal courses of action, which sometimes could be rather lengthy, was required in this case and would probably quickly resolve the impasse. Watson believed from information previously received by him that Hancock was flaunting the government regulations regarding a number of his Jamaican workers not holding the necessary documentation and work permits to allow them to engage in employment in Cayman. Accordingly, he went to the door of the administration unit, opened it, stepped outside, and bellowed at the top of his voice, "IMMIGRATION!" The response was both immediate and dramatic. Workers on the fourth floor of some of the units were down on the ground before the echoes of immigration ceased around the site. Of the forty or so who were there initially, probably only about fifteen to twenty remained on the site. Watson turned back into the unit where Hancock was holding his head and saying, "No, no. Did you have to do that?"

Watson then said in a calm and measured way, "Now let us talk sensibly about when we can get the documents that Sergeant Rixon has been asking for, for quite some time now." Hancock immediately promised, without any hesitation, that he would bring the documents to the Commercial Crime Branch office in the next twenty-four hours, and Watson responded by saying, "Don't make me have to come back again!"

Hancock responded, "I won't. I won't. I fully understand now."

About five hours later that same day, Hancock arrived at the Commercial Crime Branch office and handed over a large bundle of papers containing the documents and information that Sergeant Rixon had been seeking. Watson duly thanked him for his cooperation. It'd be worth noting that following this intervention, Hancock never did see some of his employees again, and the number of work permits he secured from the Immigration Department rose exponentially, thereby making more money available for the government coffers. Also, every time Hancock met Watson on the streets of George Town following this intervention, he queried whether or not Sergeant Rixon needed any further evidence and said that if so, he would provide the same immediately thereafter. Certainly, the whole episode seemed to concentrate Hancock's mind and ability on proper and reasonable requests that were made to him going forward. In the years that followed, Hancock and Watson became particularly good friends and shared many a story over a beer or two.

The inquiries concerning the murder were still ongoing, and after about ten days or so into the occurrence at the jewelry store, the two young men who had been identified had been fully investigated and researched, culminating in their being arrested and charged. They admitted to the offense resulting in the death of the elderly shopkeeper. One offender was charged with murder and the other with manslaughter, and both received substantial prison sentences for the same.

Again, this showed to Watson the value of operating in the island and the results that could be achieved by the local officers working together in a structured and effective way. Great credit was due to all the officers involved in the inquiry. It was a good result, and perhaps more importantly, the local public was pleased with the results achieved by their police department. Perhaps even more importantly, the officers investigating the same were beginning to see the advantages that the major incident room system was giving regarding the receipt, analysis, and organization of information from all sources. Watson knew that if the detectives with boots on the ground supported the system, then that'd make presenting the case for it so much easier.

Also, the senior investigating officer appreciated the support of a major incident room in that at the conclusion of a case, it helped him substantially identify material and statements of value to the case, plus it could help him assemble the case file and also other unused material. The officer running a major incident room could usually further contribute fully at case management meetings, having read all the material and the like as it passed through the incident room process. The system was a necessary evil, but one that showed its value time after time. Following on from the successful result of the murder inquiries, a debriefing session was held with all the staff to review the complete circumstances of the inquiry and reactions to each and every aspect of the same; and then as was a detective's want, they adjourned to CB's for a refreshing beer or three!

CHAPTER 17

USA-Based Large-Scale Fraud and Making Beautiful Cayman Home?

It was late one January afternoon when Watson received a phone call from HM Immigration Officer Banks regarding four people who had just entered the jurisdiction aboard a private jet. One was an elderly gentleman, Joseph Serrano (forty-four years old), and his wife. Their daughter and her boyfriend, Joseph Lenscombe (twenty-three years old), were also present. They were from the New York area and were scheduled to stay at the Hyatt Hotel condominiums according to the information they had written on their Cayman Islands entry card. Officer Banks was interested in them in that the boyfriend had been rather "mouthy and insolent" and stated they were coming to live in the Cayman Islands. Also, they stated that back in the USA, they had a couple of pet dogs, namely pit bulls, whom they would eventually bring to the islands. Immigration Officer Banks tried to explain to them that that would not happen, as the pit bulls were a breed of dog, due to its checkered history, that was specifically prohibited at that time from entering the Cayman Islands. Lenscombe had become rather loud and slightly objectionable, stating that they had lots of money and that in the end, the dogs would be coming to Cayman no matter what anyone said. Officer Banks, who had many years of service as an immigration officer and was well-known to Watson as a very sound and perceptive officer, was seeing red flags popping up everywhere regarding these people, especially the young man, and he wanted to notify the police to allow a check to be made into their backgrounds to see if anything was noticeably amiss that was not at that time readily apparent. They certainly did not, according to Officer Bank's records, have any permission to reside in the Cayman Islands and duly gave them a visitors' authorization.

Accordingly, Watson and Detective Constable Rowell went to the Immigration Department and obtained copies of the immigration cards from Immigration Officer Banks completed by persons as they entered the Cayman Islands. Officer Banks was still upset about the attitude that they displayed to him and kept telling Watson there was something not quite right about the younger man. These immigration cards contained full personal details of the people entering the islands, along with details of their address in their country of domicile. They also included details of how the people entered the island and where they were planning to stay during their time in the islands. Each of these cards bore its own unique number that, although of no use in this particular case, was often very useful when people entered by commercial jet, as the cards each bore a consecutive number would often be used to identify who sat alongside who on a particular aircraft. The individuals in this case had entered by private jet, so there was no need to group them together as in a large commercial jet. Watson thought this was a great investigative tool that could be most useful in some inquiries and indeed often proved particularly useful in establishing certain facts in other cases.

Watson and Rowell returned to the CCB and began efforts to check out who these individuals were and the real reasons for their entering the jurisdiction of the Cayman Islands. A telephone call was made by Watson to the FBI field office in North Miami to speak with the FBI officer with responsibility for liaison with the Cayman Islands. He was not in the office, and Watson thought he had either left early to go and play a round of golf or perhaps gone home early for an important family event. Watson then contacted officers at the US Customs Service in Miami, with whom various operations were conducted from time to time. He spoke to his newer contact, Dave Domenico. In their usual customs exemplary manner, he agreed to run the two names of Serrano and Lenscombe through the law enforcement systems and see what they could find out. Watson knew this wouldn't take them too long and knew that if there was anything to be found out, they most certainly would. While waiting for their return call, Watson and Rowell decided to visit Britannia Villas, near the Hyatt Hotel where Serrano and Lenscombe were apparently staying. These condominiums were among the most expensive to rent on the island, and the going monthly rate was around $4,500 to $5,000 per month—about five times of what Watson was paying for his humble abode! Watson thought perhaps he was in the wrong business. Having checked the position and situation of the condo in question—together with entrance and exit points, should that knowledge be needed in the future—Watson and Rowell returned to the CCB. On return, Garnet quickly and excitingly informed them that Dave from the US Customs had called back and wanted to speak with Watson as soon as possible.

Watson immediately called the customs agent, Dave Domenico, in Miami and was informed that both the male subjects were wanted on warrants in the USA for a large-scale fraud committed on a major computer conglomerate in the New York area. The amount involved in the fraud was in many millions of dollars—it was suggested about $30 million—and the warrants were showing as current and of high importance. The agent provided Watson with the phone number of the FBI office in New York holding the warrants and suggested that Watson should speak directly with them. This was now becoming remarkably interesting, and it seemed as though Cayman Islands Immigration Officer Banks's instincts were yet again spot on. Watson thought, *You just can't beat experience in some jobs.* After profusely thanking their US Customs friend and undertaking to buy him a beer on the next occasion his business brought him to the Cayman Islands, Watson called the New York number provided, although it was now past normal business hours. The phone was quickly answered by an agent who stated that he was working the FBI service desk for that office. Watson introduced himself and told the agent that he understood from contact with a US Customs agent in Miami that the FBI in New York had high-priority arrest warrants out for two individuals namely Joseph Serrano and Joseph

Lenscombe. Watson provided personal identifiers regarding the two persons to the agent and also said that they were currently domiciled in Grand Cayman, having arrived by private aircraft. The agent asked Watson to hold for a moment, and within a few seconds, he came back on the line to say that the information was correct and the warrants were being held by FBI Special Agent Rosemary Kartaka. Agent Kartaka had left the office for the day, but an urgent request had been put out for her to contact her office, and then she would be directed to call Watson. Apparently, the FBI had been searching for these people for quite a few weeks but without success. The duty agent mentioned that Kartaka would be delighted to hear the news.

Based on what they knew thus far, Watson and Rowell immediately spoke with Cayman Crown Counsel Adam Robinson to put him on notice of the possibility that there might be a case that could lead to extradition proceedings based on what Watson might learn from contact with FBI Special Agent Kartaka. Crown Counsel Robinson was somewhat excited, and Watson was sure he would begin researching the procedure for extradition from the Cayman Islands to the USA. Robinson had dealt with members of the CCB on many occasions regarding many different criminal matters, and he was totally aware that if the CCB said something might happen, it was more than likely going to.

About thirty minutes after Watson had spoken to the FBI office in New York, Special Agent Kartaka called Watson in his office. After exchanging pleasantries, Kartaka provided personal identifiers of Serrano and Lenscombe to ensure they were one and the same people who had just entered the islands. They were, and she was delighted to hear the same. She confirmed that the FBI held arrest warrants for the two relating to a large fraud perpetrated against a computer company. Watson updated Kartaka on their current standing in the island and also the fact that two females were present who had entered Cayman with them. Kartaka was also informed of the documentation that was needed initially to allow Watson to obtain provisional warrants to arrest both men and also an overview of the facts in issue in the case to ensure that those facts would be similar to such a case if it occurred in the Cayman Islands. Kartaka agreed to send the request for the men to be arrested together with an overview of the facts in issue. She also agreed that within the time allowed, the FBI—through the US Department of Justice Office of International Affairs—would send the full formal request for extradition of the two individuals for consideration by the honorable attorney general along with the Cayman courts.

One important fact that was made known to Watson by the FBI was that they had reasonable cause to suspect that either Serrano or Lenscombe was in possession of a firearm. This did not seem likely to Watson, but nonetheless, he made a note of the same and would be sure to let all officers involved in the arrests aware of the same. This all seemed fine to Watson, and consequently, he and Rowell informed Crown Counsel Adam Robinson of the same. And then they commenced work to put together the necessary documents for the obtaining of the Cayman Islands provisional warrants of arrest. Later that same evening, faxes were received from the FBI in New York attaching a copy of their warrants of arrest plus details of the crime that had occurred causing them to be issued; the offenses alleged were similar to such offenses that prevailed in the Caymans. Another piece of information was further received from Immigration Officer Banks that Serrano and Lenscombe were likely to be at the Department of Motor Vehicles the next morning to acquire the registration of a motor vehicle they were intending to purchase. In those days, a party buying a vehicle in Cayman from a resident had to appear at the DMV along with the resident for the transfer of the vehicle and its associated title to take place. An advantage to this location, rather than the Britannia Villas condominium in which they were residing, was the fact that it was immediately next door to the Central Police Station, the main operational police station in George Town, Grand Cayman. It appeared, according to Kartaka, that the two men had set up a company styled Computer-Techs in New York and established an account with the computer company. They had systematically ordered parts and equipment from the company and sold it to companies in the US at large discounts, which they could afford to do when not paying the supplier and then disappearing.

The following morning, which was a Friday, Watson and Rowell were in the CCB early working on the paperwork required to obtain local warrants to arrest these two miscreants. All the paperwork was initiated, and Detective Rowell and Detective Sergeant David Rixon, also from the CCB, were sent to the Central Police Station by DCI Watson to recruit two uniform officers. Rowell and Rixon duly recruited Police Constable Young and Police Constable Luke to assist the CCB officers in the apprehension of the two wanted persons.

DCI Watson went to the magistrate court, and there before the senior magistrate in chambers, he submitted a sworn information, along with copies of the arrest warrants issued in the USA, seeking Cayman Islands provisional warrants for the arrest of both Serrano and Lenscombe. Based on the information sworn and documents submitted relating to it, the senior magistrate quickly approved and signed the Cayman Islands provisional warrants of arrest and handed them to DCI Watson while at the same time wishing him luck in arresting these men.

Watson, with the warrants in hand, then continued to the Central Police Station where Rowell, Rixon, and PCs Luke and Young were waiting in a briefing room. Watson briefed them on the operation and the venue at the DMV, which was usually a terribly busy and bustling place. He reminded all concerned of the fact that the FBI suspected that one of the two men might have a firearm in their possession, although this had not been confirmed by anyone.

At about 10:15 a.m. that day, Watson, together with Rowell and PC Young, saw Serrano outside the DMV. Lenscombe was still inside the premises. Watson introduced himself to Serrano, cautioned him, and told him that he was in possession of a warrant for his arrest concerning a matter in New York. Serrano was instantly searched for a weapon, and none being found, he was taken by PC Young to the Central Police Station for processing. Shortly thereafter, Lenscombe ran from inside the DMV and was making his way toward the waterfront. Watson immediately suspected that he might have seen Serrano being arrested. Lenscombe made the mistake of running near one of the unmarked police cars while looking back toward the DMV building. The passenger door was opened at the appropriate time by Watson, and Lenscombe's escape was quickly halted when he ran into the car door while looking back to see what was happening to Serrano. Lenscombe fell to the ground. He was quickly detained by Rowell, DS Rixon, and PC Luke. The downside to this was the fact that Watson had to submit a report in due course explaining how the passenger door had been damaged slightly! It seemed to Watson in the days ahead that he submitted more paperwork over the damaged government car door than he did to obtain the two arrest warrants! Watson introduced himself to Lenscombe, cautioned him, and as before with Serrano, told him that he was in possession of a warrant for his arrest concerning a criminal matter in New York. Lenscombe was also instantly searched for a weapon, and none being found, he was escorted by Rowell and PC Luke to the Central Police Station for processing.

At the Central Police Station, in company with DC Rowell, Watson again interviewed Serrano under caution. Serrano was informed that he had been arrested on a Cayman Islands provisional warrant because there was an arrest warrant in existence in New York for him relating to criminal matters. Watson showed both the Cayman Islands and the New York warrants to him. Watson then said to Serrano, "The case in New York concerns your conducting business with a computer company using a company styled Computer-Techs and ordering various parts. Do you want to say anything about this?"

Serrano replied, "No. I don't understand all this."

Watson said, "The allegation concerns ordering parts from the company without paying for the same and your disposal of those goods."

Serrano responded, "I don't want to be obstructive, but I ought to speak to my lawyer."

At this stage, Serrano was documented and placed into a holding cell to await further determination regarding the matter. Watson also took the brief opportunity to speak with Crown Counsel Robinson to update him on the position and the fact that Watson now wanted to obtain a search warrant to search the suspects' rented home at Britannia Villas. Robinson was in agreement with the request and suggested that based on the information received from the FBI regarding the suspects potentially having a firearm, the application should be made under the Cayman Islands Firearms Act. Watson agreed to obtain the search warrant as suggested later that day and execute the same.

Watson and PC Luke then interviewed Lenscombe under caution in the detention room at the Central Police Station. He was asked questions about his identity to confirm he was the same Joseph Lenscombe identified in the New York warrant, and this was quickly confirmed. Watson told him why he had been arrested and showed him copies of both the warrants. Watson then said, "The case in New York concerns your conducting business with a computer company using a company styled Computer-Techs and ordering various parts. Do you wish to say anything about this?"

Lenscombe quickly responded, "I am saying nothing until I've a lawyer."

Watson said, "That is your prerogative. However, you will remain in custody pending a court appearance here, possibly later today."

"With a view to what?" Lenscombe asked.

Watson responded, "Your extradition to the USA."

Lenscombe got angry and responded, "That's all right. I'll get the best lawyer that money can buy, get bail, and I'll go again." Lenscombe was then to be moved to a holding cell, but before leaving the room, he went into something of a diatribe and tirade saying that he was going to cause the earth to come crashing down on Watson and his cohorts, the Cayman police department, the Cayman Immigration Office, the Cayman government, and anybody else he could think of. He continued, almost without drawing breath, to say Watson would be hearing in the near future from the US Supreme Court, the US Department of Justice, the Court of Human Rights, the Civil Liberties Union, the UK Privy Council, the Amnesty International, his US lawyers, and civil rights groups. He said his liberties and rights had been grossly and unfairly infringed, and actions that Watson should have taken had been ignored unfairly and to his detriment. He stated that these positions were all supported by the US Constitution and the president of the USA, Mr. Clinton. Watson let him continue for about ten minutes before Lenscombe seemed to pause to take a prolonged breath. Watson thought he must be thinking of other groups to protest to. Taking advantage of the pause in Lenscombe's diatribe, Watson—in a quiet manner—asked, "Have you finished now?" There was no audible reply. Watson, in a gruff voice, said, "Stand up!" And surprisingly, Lenscombe complied quickly and immediately. Watson then took Lenscombe securely by the arm and led him to the wall at the end of the detention room. Lenscombe was visibly getting more anxious with each step. Hanging in the center of the wall there, as in most government buildings in the islands, was a four-by-three portrait of Her Majesty Queen Elizabeth II in her ceremonial regalia and with one of her ceremonial maces in hand.

Watson pointed out the portrait to Lenscombe and said, "See this lady here? She is in charge in Cayman, not Mr. Clinton, and she says I can do everything that we have done today!" Lenscombe's head dropped, and there was a big sigh as if he were now becoming resigned to his fate!

Lenscombe was put in a holding cell, and just as Watson was leaving, Detective Sergeant Mel Greene of the Drug Squad, whom Watson knew well from various operations they had taken part in together, was walking into the cell block with four local young junkies well-known to the police. The junkies all seemed rather high from their overenthusiastic use of opioids or some other substance. Watson thought that this was serendipitous and immediately took the opportunity to ask Greene what he was planning to do with the prisoners and was told that he was detaining them pending further inquiries. Watson asked Greene if he would lodge them in the same cell as Lenscombe was in, knowing that they would not be in there too long. Sergeant Greene responded, "Yes, sir, certainly."

Accordingly, Watson watched with some amusement as Greene placed them in the same cell as Lenscombe, thinking that this would be a whole new experience for this young verbose and insolent man from New York. Watson also spoke to the duty inspector in the cells and stated that neither Serrano nor Lenscombe should have any visitors until after the search of their premises by the CCB team had occurred. He would let the officers know when the search had been completed. Watson did not want to risk any firearm or other evidence at the apartment being moved before the police could search and possibly seize the same.

Watson went back to the senior magistrate in the local courts and this time offered another sworn information, based on the FBI information, regarding the two suspects having a firearm, seeking a warrant to search their apartment at Britannia Villas. Again, the magistrate willingly signed the same under the Firearms Act and expressed hope that luck would again be with Watson and his team. He was pleased to hear about the arrests earlier that day from the warrants issued in the morning and said he would look forward to seeing the two arrested men in court at some time in the future. He did not know at that time that it would be later that day.

Watson and his search team of Rowell, Rixon, and PC Luke plus one officer duly armed, together with solely Joseph Serrano (who was handcuffed and not at all verbose or insolent), went to the apartment at Britannia Villas where Serrano's wife and daughter were waiting. They were shocked to see Serrano in handcuffs but were shown the search warrant for the premises, and Watson explained to them what the process had been earlier that day and now would be in executing the same. The search team began a comprehensive search of the apartment. Every room was systematically searched and recorded. No firearm was found, but two boxes containing documents apparently highly pertinent to the fraud were found along with a substantial amount of cash. All items recovered were, as was usual procedure in Cayman, entered on search forms designed for that purpose, and at the end of the search, after about two and a half hours, the forms were signed by the exhibits officer, and each page was signed by Mr. Serrano. The evidence seized and Mr. Serrano were then returned to the Central Police Station for further processing. The two ladies were left in the apartment having been updated on the process regarding the two men. Watson had briefed them on the process going forward and warned that the men might be kept in custody prior to potential extradition proceedings.

Crown Counsel Robinson had been remarkably busy in the interim and had hastily arranged with the magistrate court for a hearing before the senior magistrate late on Friday afternoon following the arrests of Serrano and Lenscombe. The application was made under the Extradition Act of 1870, and the application was for them to be remanded in prison custody until the following Wednesday when another appearance would be made in the magistrates court in George Town. The reason for the request was to keep the suspects in custody, allowing the FBI the time and opportunity to file the necessary mandatory paperwork for their extradition and also allowing the Cayman police to review the documentation seized in the search to be examined. This was needed in order to determine whether or not any criminal offenses had been committed in Cayman during their nefarious dealings. The magistrate quickly granted the application, and Serrano and Lenscombe were off to Northward Prison the following morning, as it was too late to transport them to the prison that Friday afternoon. It should be added that Lenscombe told Watson he was adding the harassment in the holding cells with the four young junkies to his list of complaints to anyone who would listen! Through their Caymanian attorney who had been engaged in the interim, both men indicated that they would not be fighting extradition. Perhaps they both had enough time in Caymanian custody and the reception that they had been given!

On the following day, a beautiful sunny Saturday, Watson, Rowell, and Rixon spent the day going through the seized documents and realized that it was more or less a blueprint of the fraud that had occurred and would be most useful to the FBI and US authorities. It was all indexed and logged by Rowell and Rixon, ready for onward transmission to the FBI. The examination revealed no specific offenses of any gravity committed by the suspects in the Cayman Islands, and consequently, Watson would, with the authority of the Cayman courts, hand the seized property and money over to the FBI at some point in the future. It was also discovered that the documents also identified a number of financial institutions that had been utilized by the suspects in running their fraud, vital information for the FBI for both their inquiry and the ultimate recovery of the misappropriated monies.

Watson later updated Agent Kartaka on the arrests and the results of the search at the villa on West Bay Road. Kartaka was delighted with the results and agreed to work with a district attorney from the Southern District of New York to prepare the necessary papers and evidence required in Cayman for the extradition to be agreed and completed.

The suspects were again before the court on the Wednesday following and once again remanded to Northward Prison to await extradition to the USA. When they appeared before the court, Lenscombe reminded Watson that all hell was going to descend upon the Caymanian police once Lenscombe had got his act together and in order in the USA. Watson politely responded, "Thank you, sir. I await the same with bated breath and much interest." Watson knew Lenscombe would have much more to worry about than him and the Cayman police once he arrived back in the USA.

All the necessary papers were subsequently received and submitted. Extradition had been authorized. Crown Counsel Robinson stated that arrangements could now be prepared for the two arrested men to be extradited back to the USA. Agent Kartaka was informed, and through Watson and the US Department of Justice's Office of International Affairs, three US marshals were later flown from New York direct on Cayman Airways to escort the prisoners back to the USA. Prior to their arrival, Watson told them he would meet them at the airport and hand over Serrano and Lenscombe to them and they could return to New York on the same flight. This didn't go down too well with the US Marshals, as they stated they would have to discuss the case at length with the Caymanian authorities. Consequently, other arrangements were made! Upon arrival, the US Marshals did indeed have a number of discussions with Watson regarding the case, the prisoners, and the extradition; but they were usually held at beach side bars or in restaurants around dinnertime!

The marshals arrived in Cayman on a Wednesday lunchtime and were met by Watson and Rowell at the airport and taken to a hotel on Seven Mile Beach where reservations had been made for them. They appeared to be most agreeable with the arrangements and the hotel. After checking in at the hotel, Watson took them to a rental car service situated on the main road, not far from the hotel. They were quickly provided with a rental car for the duration of their stay. While they were outside the rental car premises speaking with Watson and Rowell, an old bedraggled car was passing by, and the engine backfired, quite loudly. The reactions of the three US marshals were instantaneous. They each dropped on one knee to the ground, looking toward the source of the noise, and were fumbling around trying to draw their service weapons from near their waists. The problem was that they had left their firearms in New York! Rowell and Watson stood there unconcerned and laughing at them, but it starkly illustrated how life was in Cayman for law enforcement officers compared to their day-to-day problems in New York.

The following day, the two prisoners were back in court, and their extradition was formally confirmed. Accordingly, next day, Watson and his officers took Serrano and Lenscombe to the Cayman Airport where they were formally handed over to the US marshals to be taken back to New York aboard a Cayman Airways direct flight. The marshals seemed very happy with their stay in Cayman and also with the fact that they were returning with two wanted fugitives for the FBI in New York. When Watson returned to the CCB from the airport, he updated Agent Kartaka, and to say she sounded happy would be an understatement. She assured Watson that she and her colleagues would provide a welcoming party reception for Serrano and Lenscombe. Watson completed all the necessary paperwork before retiring for the evening to CB's for a well-earned beer or two.

During the follow-up to many aspects of this case, Watson was at North Side on the island completing some inquiries regarding the papers taken from Lenscombe to determine if there was any local involvement or fraud in their scheme that might warrant police involvement when he heard on the police radio that a man who was being sought for the wounding of a police officer—who had a nasty wound inflicted above the eye when he was trying to arrest the offender—was holed up in a small property he was associated with on North Side and was threatening to attack any police officer who'd enter the house with a machete. Watson immediately diverted to the scene to see if he could be of any assistance to the officers; in

Watson's world, it was an opportunity not to be missed. Once there, he spoke with the uniform inspector already there and found out that the offender was a well-known local person and a petty criminal who occasionally resorted to violence. The inspector was reasonably certain that there was no one else in the house. The offender was responsive to calls for him to come out of the property by saying that he would attack any police officer who'd come in with a machete. He was known to a small degree by Watson, and accordingly, Watson therefore offered to help the inspector, if he so wished. Watson's offer of help was gladly and quickly received. Before going further, Watson asked for two of the officers there who were the tallest officers in attendance, both six feet four in height and really powerfully built, to come with him, and he asked the inspector to get another two or three officers to station at the rear exit door of the property. Watson explained that if the offender were to come out of the rear door, they should immediately engage him and disarm him—no questions were to be asked, and there should be no messing around to ensure he was restrained and put in custody without any further injury to any police officer. He told the two officers who were to enter the house with him to follow him and that he would confront the offender in the house. They were to be behind him on each shoulder, and if Watson walked slowly or stopped, they were to do likewise. Equally, if Watson rushed the offender, they were to follow immediately and remain in close contact. They both confirmed that they knew what they had to do. Watson went through the scenario once again with the two officers and also confirmed that the objective was to take the suspect down without harm to anyone. If needed, they must act swiftly and decisively. Watson then confirmed that the officers were at the rear of the house already in position and would act decisively if needed.

Watson rattled on the louvered screen door, and it appeared locked. He thought a good kick in the area of the flimsy lock would break it and allow entry to the main door. He asked the offender one last time to allow them access, but again he refused. Watson said, "Okay. The police will enter your house." With that, Watson kicked near the lock and was surprised by the result. The louver-type door, which was old and very dried out, collapsed like an accordion from the top louver down to the very bottom—just like Watson had seen in some cartoon movies! Watson and the officers just stared in disbelief at the door. Watson then decided to employ a new tactic for the main door and shoulder-charged it in the lock area. That was not as much fun. It was only partly hinged, and the door flew wide open. Watson went into the house, quickly followed by the two officers whom he could hear breathing right next to him. Inside the house, the main passageway turned to the right, and Watson was followed by his two wingmen. Down the end of quite a long passageway, the offender was standing holding a machete in his right hand. Watson was laser-focused on the man's right arm and the machete. He started walking slowly toward the man, telling him to lay the machete down so that no one else would be injured. The man didn't respond, but Watson noticed he was breathing heavily and sweating profusely. Watson stopped and told the man to drop the machete and give himself up. There was no response, so Watson began to walk more quickly toward him and then broke into a trot. By now, the offender must have appreciated the force that was coming toward him rapidly and looked really apprehensive, if not frightened. Watson took one more step, and the offender threw the machete to the ground just a couple seconds before Watson tackled him with a classic face-to-face rugby tackle that was taking Watson and the offender backward and to the ground. Watson didn't expect what happened next, almost instantaneously. The two officers who were with him also tackled Watson and the offender, and their combined body weight of about five hundred pounds landed on Watson and, by natural progression, on the offender. With about seven hundred pounds in total of manhood on top of the offender, Watson was concerned whether or not the offender could move easily; Watson certainly could not move, nor did he even attempt to.

Quickly, thank goodness, the officers got off Watson and then stood the offender up and handcuffed him. They then helped Watson up and asked if he was okay. Apart from ribs that would be very sore in the next few days, Watson was fine. The offender, who had been at the bottom of the pile, was also slightly bruised and somewhat battered, but nothing worse had happened to him. He was taken outside and handed over to the officer in charge, and scenes of crime officers were called to examine the scene and also the machete involved. The inspector at the scene was delighted with the result and duly arranged a time and date to meet with Watson and fulfill the police obligation of buying him a couple drinks. Once Watson got back to the CCB, he was duly called in by the police commissioner. As always, Watson was wondering what had happened now! The commissioner asked him about the incident on North Side that he had been involved in earlier that day. Watson immediately thought of the door that had been ruined and started to apologize, saying that it was very dry and rotten. The commissioner said he was not worried about that and that he just wondered why the police on the scene had not taken action immediately. Watson said they had only just got there when he arrived, and he harped back to his experiences in Bilberry. He said if a person in Bilberry injured or drew blood from a police officer, his colleagues in the CID would take a house apart, brick by brick if necessary, to get at the offender, and that was purely what happened in this case.

Watson, on quite a few occasions after this incident with the offender, met him in and around town following his release from prison. He would always apologize for having threatened Watson and the other officers with the machete but would always say that he was still having traumatic nightmares about having seven hundred pounds lying on top of him and being unable to do anything. Watson would always remind him that that was of his own making and that it wasn't easy for Watson either. Watson told him, "In the future, do what the police tell you, and there would be no repeat." Watson never knew of the man coming into contact with the police again other than socially on the street or around various bars on the island after the incident.

This was not the end of the Lenscombe and Serrano story, however. Some days after the extradition of the two men, Agent Kartaka and an assistant USA attorney from the Southern District of New York arrived in Cayman to follow up on the arrests of the men and the papers that were recovered regarding the same. Watson and

Rowell duly met them at the airport on their arrival and took them to their hotel on West Bay Road. A meeting was then held, with Crown Counsel Robinson also included, and then the documents recovered in the search from Britannia Villas were formally handed over to the agent and the US attorney, against signature. Watson also arranged for visits to be made by the agent to the premises where the family had been staying and also to various financial institutions that had been utilized by the suspects. This was all good information, and it provided an overview and background of the suspects' activities and the prearrangements that had been made by the criminals in Grand Cayman prior to committing the fraud in its entirety. After just a couple days, they left Cayman with the vital evidence that had been seized. They surely were grateful to the Cayman police for assisting them in detaining their fugitives and the added bonus of the documentation seized. They concurred that it basically provided a complete overview of the fraud perpetrated and a road map of the actions taken by the two individuals, plus, of course, an amount of cash recovered, which was a bonus.

Even this was not the end of the matter from the Caymanian perspective. Agent Kartaka had subsequently informed Watson that the pair of fugitives were currently appearing in the court in New York and had, in fact, pleaded not guilty to the numerous charges that had been laid against them. Apparently, as the trial was starting, the defense attorneys had lodged an objection to the admission into evidence of the documentation that had been seized from Britannia Villas in Cayman during Watson's execution of the search warrant at that address. These papers formed a critical part of the case against the two defendants, and to lose that evidence could have had a dramatic effect on the case from the prosecution's perspective. As Watson thought initially, it basically formed a road map of the fraud in question, their intent and involvement in the same, and the disposition and hiding of the ill-gotten gains.

Kartaka and the US assistant DA spoke with Watson and queried, "If the Cayman police had executed a warrant granted under the Firearms Act in Cayman and took evidence of the criminal fraud but found no firearm, under Caymanian law, would that seizure be valid? And further, would the documents seized be handed over in accordance with the law and therefore be admissible?" Apparently, the judge in New York, at the request of the defense attorneys, had adjourned the matter for a day to allow this question to be researched with the Caymanian authorities and for an affidavit to be provided so that the judge could answer the objection over the standing of the documents and determine one way or another. It appeared that if they had been unlawfully seized, then they might well be eliminated from the evidence to be adduced against the two accused men. This could have had a fatal blow to the prosecution's case mounted against them.

As Watson understood the position, he believed that the case with warrants executed by American Police was that the police may only search the particular area mentioned in the warrant and seize the specific items called for in the warrant. Police may search outside the scope of the warrant only if they'd be protecting their safety or the safety of others or if they'd be acting to prevent the destruction of evidence. Police may also only seize objects not specified in the warrant only if they were in plain view during the course of the search. The position, in relationship to warrants issued to the British police and, by extension, to the police in the Cayman Islands, was that only the premises mentioned in the warrants may be searched, but if during the execution of a warrant evidence was found pertaining to other criminal offenses that had been committed, it could be seized under the terms of the warrant and used in proceedings that may emanate from the findings during the lawful execution of the search warrant. Consequently, since Watson, although he found no firearm during the search, found evidence of the underlying fraud committed by the two men and thus seized the same and then—with the authority of the Cayman courts—handed it over to the FBI and the US assistant DA, it was deemed as a legal procedure.

Kartaka asked Watson if, as a matter of urgency, he could obtain from a senior law officer on the island an affidavit setting out the circumstances of obtaining a warrant under the law of the Cayman Islands and explaining how evidence of other criminal matters could be seized and used in any hearing pertinent to the same under that warrant. Also, she asked that the affidavit explain how property properly recovered under a warrant would then be notified to the court and handed over to an investigative authority. Watson promptly spoke with Crown Counsel Robinson and subsequently to the honorable attorney general of the Cayman Islands, the chief law officer of the islands. The AG duly and expeditiously completed and swore an affidavit setting out the circumstances under which the Cayman police, following a proper request from the US authorities, had obtained the search warrant albeit under the Firearms Law, how it had been executed, and also how documents pertinent to the criminal enterprise in question was found. He concluded by stating that the documents had been properly seized under Cayman Islands law and protocol and, following notification to the Cayman court of jurisdiction, had then been properly handed over to the American authorities following all protocols necessary to preserve the chain of custody of the evidence from the time and place of seizure to the handing over of the same. Following the execution of this affidavit, it was faxed, and the original of the same was couriered to the assistant US attorney in New York for his use and for submission to the judge in the New York court.

Watson was subsequently notified by Kartaka that the judge, upon receipt of the affidavit, had read the same in open court and then accordingly determined that all the evidence seized had been properly obtained by the Caymanian police and then handed over to the US authorities under the purview and instruction of the Cayman court of jurisdiction. Finally, the judge determined and ruled against the defense motion to exclude the evidence. Following this decision, the lawyers acting for Lenscombe and Serrano asked for a short adjournment; and following the same, they quickly changed their pleas to one of guilty and were subsequently sentenced to varying substantial terms of imprisonment.

As an aside, Watson was still waiting to hear from the various entities that Lenscombe would be complaining to when he returned to the USA. The constant worry and concern over being approached by these entities on behalf of Lenscombe would continue to drive Watson to many a beer at CB's or Sunset House!

CHAPTER 18

Security (or Lack Thereof) at the Tower Building

When Watson first arrived in Cayman, it was a relatively crime-free island, and security was seldom rarely seen or even less practiced. At the Tower Building, which was surrounded on all four sides by car parking for people who worked in the building and also by visitors to the building, security was not a large priority in those days. The Commercial Crime Branch's motor vehicle, which was now a newer Nissan saloon (the Chevrolet Caprice had long been sent to the scrap heap), was usually left at weekends, duly locked and secured, in the car park area outside the Tower Building. Watson didn't like this idea, but it had been so for a number of years, and consequently, there was seen no reasonable need or basis to change the same. Following a weekend when none of the CCB staff had had to work, Watson arrived on Monday morning and needed the vehicle to go on some inquiries in the East End area of Cayman. Consequently, Watson and DS Johns took one set of the vehicle keys from the office and left the Tower Building to get the vehicle to drive to East End. They diligently checked all four sides of the Tower Building car park but had no success in locating the force vehicle. They checked again to ensure that their findings were correct! Neither thought for a minute at that time that the vehicle had been taken by any nefarious person or act.

They returned to the office and called the Central Police Station to see if the vehicle had been taken for some operational purposes and called the force garage to see if the vehicle had been taken in for a service, but all inquiries were met with a negative response. Accordingly, they treated the vehicle as missing and put out a circulation to police and government to try to locate where the vehicle was. Everyone seemed to believe another branch of the force or perhaps government had borrowed it. All the inquiries placed came back with a negative result, and it was then that it had been confirmed that the vehicle had apparently been stolen or just taken from the Tower Building. Consequently, a circulation was made to all police officers notifying them of the theft of the vehicle and to be on the lookout for the same. If it were to be located, they should stop the same and arrest the driver and any passengers. At the same time, checks were made to try to determine where the vehicle had been throughout the weekend. It was last seen on the previous Friday evening after having been parked following its operational use that day.

The days came and went, but there was no sign or any sightings of the vehicle. On Wednesday afternoon, Watson and Johns were again leaving the Tower Building through the rear doors into the car park when Johns grabbed Watson's arm and, in an excited manner, said, "Look, there is our car." It certainly was the missing car, and it was being reversed into a parking spot at the Tower Building by a young Caymanian driver. There was no one else in the vehicle. Johns started to run toward the car, but Watson urged him to walk slowly and not look at the car. As Watson got near the car, he reached through the open window and grabbed hold of the young Caymanian driver. At the same time, as Watson was beginning to pull him out of the car through the window, Johns was reaching into the car through the same window and trying to get hold of the keys that were still in the ignition. Watson told Johns he had a secure hold of the young man and would pull him out the window if Johns would get out of the way! Johns did so, and the youngster exited the vehicle through the window, greatly assisted by Watson. Johns got the keys, while Watson cautioned the young man and told him he was being arrested on suspicion of taking and driving away a motor vehicle. He was then taken into the Tower Building and up to the CCB office after being told by Watson, in no uncertain terms and in a forcible manner, not to try to run away from their custody or he would be severely dealt with. In the CCB office, the young man was asked why he took the car and was now returning it. He said he didn't know it was a police vehicle, which was highly unlikely in Watson's humble view, bearing in mind the police radio setup that was in the vehicle, along with a logbook that was updated anytime a police officer used the vehicle. Also, most Caymanians knew every police vehicle on the island, even the ones utilized for undercover cases. The fact that he was now returning it as it was extremely low on gas did not escape Johns's attention, and Johns suggested to him that after they had refilled the gas tank, he would be taking it again! Watson smiled at this direct yet very much to the point suggestion by Johns.

As in all matters concerning the unauthorized taking of motor vehicles, Watson called the RCIP Traffic Department officers to come to the CCB where Watson would hand the offender over to them for them to complete the inquiries and file the necessary charges for a criminal court case to be pursued against the youngster. The Traffic Department officers came and took him back to the Central Police Station, but it was not without mishap. Unfortunately, they did not properly attend to the securing of the youngster while in their custody, and they allowed him an opportunity to run away from the officers as he got out of the car just before they entered the Central Police Station. Despite their best efforts, the Traffic Department officers were unable to initially catch him. Of course, his time was limited; as in Cayman, where was he going to run?

As in all such cases with the escape of a prisoner from lawful custody, a police disciplinary inquiry was initiated by the Complaints and Discipline Department into how the officers had failed to secure the continued apprehension of the offender. The disciplinary officer's job was to put together a file and statements regarding the happening, and then the deputy commissioner would make a decision on what disciplinary action or otherwise should be taken regarding the occurrence against the officers in question. The offender, not being one of Cayman's more successful offenders, was eventually recaptured a few days later, and the necessary court action was taken, including his escape from lawful custody.

A week or so later, following the submission of the disciplinary inquiry to the deputy commissioner, Watson was summoned to come and see the commissioner. As was always the case, Watson's mind was racing to determine what he had done to warrant such an intervention. The commissioner told him it was regarding the arrest of the youngster related to the taking of the CCB police vehicle. The commissioner now had the disciplinary file and had read the file, including the formal interview with the youngster by the disciplinary inspector. The commissioner asked Watson what had happened when the youngster was found in the police car, and Watson told him that he had been removed from the car through the window and was then told not to try to run away or he would be in serious trouble! The commissioner smiled and said, "Through the window?" Watson replied in the affirmative and added that the window was open! The commissioner then said, "I am going to read a part of the inspector's interview with the offender after he was rearrested."

> *Disciplinary inspector to offender*—"You ran away and escaped from the Traffic Department officers before you were taken into the Central Police Station, but why didn't you try and escape from the Commercial Crime officers who arrested you initially near the Tower Building?"

> *Offender to disciplinary inspector*—"Well, while I was being taken into the Tower Building, that big guy, the DCI, who pulled me out of the car window had a strong hold of me then threatened me that he would kill me if I tried to run. He said if I did run, I would not get away and I would just die trying—and be very tired."

Watson immediately told the commissioner that he did not recall using those exact words but that he had told the offender not to try to escape or run and that there would be profoundly serious consequences if he did. Obviously, Watson added with a smile, the offender got the gist of the message. He didn't run from the Commercial Crime Branch. The commissioner, who was now smiling, agreed that the offender had certainly got the message.

CHAPTER 19

Formation of the Royal Cayman Islands Police Association

During the late 1980s and early 1990s, some of the officers of varying ranks within the RCIP were somewhat disgruntled over various actions being taken by both the government and the police hierarchy regarding their working conditions and also their pay structures and other allowances. Their main cause for concern was that they felt they had no real avenue to raise these concerns and a number of other items of importance to them in an appropriate, structured, or meaningful way. Consequently, a number of the persons involved with these concerns called an informal meeting to be held by police officers who were inclined to the same view, and they invited Watson along to the initial meeting. Watson heard them protest about various matters and concerns that they had, and to a degree, Watson felt that they had reasonable cause for complaint over a number of the items. When such items had been brought up to the government or the police hierarchy, they felt that scant regard or appropriate consideration had been given to their concerns. They were getting very discontented and, to some degree, frustrated over what they viewed as items of genuine concern to many members of the RCIP. From his experiences in the UK, Watson believed a formal police federation could properly mitigate a number of the circumstances that was concerning them.

Watson spoke to them about the Police Federation of England and Wales that he had lived with during his twenty-four years of service in England. It was a statutory staff association for officers from the rank of constable to chief inspectors in the police forces of England and Wales. Under UK labor laws, the police were prohibited from joining ordinary trade unions to defend pay and working conditions. The federation was originally formed in 1919, after two UK police strikes in 1918 and 1919, to represent staff where disputes could be resolved through arbitration so long as all parties negotiated in good faith. The government at the time, and rightly so, was frightened by the prospect of police officers going on strike. It was widely anticipated that anarchy would prevail. The federation would now negotiate with the government on all matters involving its membership pay, allowances, hours of duty, annual leave, pensions, and all manner of conditions of service. The federation was controlled purely by serving police officers, had no political affiliation, and most importantly, had no powers by which to call a strike of its members. Having said that, the federation—by virtue of its stance and, on occasions, actions—was still able to exert some political pressure as and when appropriate. The federation's membership slowly but surely rose to more than one hundred thousand members. Small dues were paid by its members, and if some officers did not want to be paying members, they could elect not to pay the subscription but still be a member of the federation by virtue of their position. The downside to this was a personal one to those members in that they could not receive legal representation from the federation when needed and other ancillary benefits that paying members might receive.

Watson suggested to the officers present that having listened to their complaints, perhaps the time had come for them to have proper and organized representation that would be made on behalf of all officers from the rank of constable up to and including chief inspector. In very general terms, all the officers present agreed. Watson told them of the history of the police federation in the UK and said he saw no reason why such an organization in Cayman could not endure and survive. Watson agreed to speak with former colleagues of his in the UK police who had, for many years, acted as officers of the police federation in their particular areas and get advice from them and perhaps also some copies of their charter and organizational documents, plus the areas in which they specifically had rights to negotiate on behalf of their members. This was done, and based on the documents he received, Watson extracted the sections pertinent to the circumstances in Cayman and drafted an organizational document for the Cayman police, along with addendums covering what areas of police work they should be allowed to negotiate with the hierarchy and the government.

This was well-received, and following another two meetings, wherein certain local officers were stepping forward to take on responsibility for initiating a police association, Watson then withdrew himself from the meetings, feeling that it was only fit and proper for the local officers to take the concept and run with it. Of course, he remained available to them to answer any and all questions they might have. Occasionally, because he was not a thoroughbred federation officer, Watson would not know the answer, so he again called his police federation colleagues in the UK and invariably got well-planned, cogent, and persuasive arguments to answer each and every question that had been posed.

Following on from its inception, the police officers continued to build and construct the association, and it was duly recognized in 1994 as a voluntary service organization representing its members to advance the legal, professional, and welfare interest within the Cayman police service. It was also duly registered as a nonprofit limited liability company under the Cayman Islands laws. Since this time, the association had been involved in many matters covering all aspects of police service and administration, acting on behalf of their members.

As an aside, a considerable time later, Watson noticed that the Police Federation of England and Wales—following numerous suggestions that the police be allowed to strike in certain circumstances—duly balloted their members in 2013 but failed to get enough signatures in favor of that right to attempt to change the law. Watson never thought for a minute that the police should have the right to withdraw their labor; it could have a catastrophic effect on the public at large in many differing and consequential ways.

CHAPTER 20

A Missing Four-Year-Old Child from Canada

Watson was unavoidably trapped in his office on a lovely March day in 1990 catching up on paperwork and planning additional inquiries to be made in a number of ongoing cases when he received a call from John Wickerson, the detective inspector of the RCIP Special Branch. The Special Branch was a name customarily used to identify units responsible for matters of national security and intelligence in British Commonwealth police forces as well as in Ireland. They acquired and developed intelligence, usually of a political or sensitive nature, and conducted investigations to protect the country from perceived threats of subversion, particularly terrorism and other extremist political activity. Wickerson had also, on a couple occasions, helped Watson in the management of major incident rooms that had been established in Cayman relating to serious crimes. Wickerson told Watson that he had a private investigator in his office from Toronto, Canada, who was asking questions regarding a financial matter that Wickerson knew would be better suited of being asked to Watson. Accordingly, Wickerson asked if he could send the investigator, Mike Kingsbury, over to see Watson. Watson agreed upon being offered a beer or two at some time in the future by Wickerson—the usual currency for detectives receiving help from other detectives. In this instance though, Watson never recalled collecting on the promise, a fact he recounted many times to Wickerson during their numer-

173

ous interactions, unfortunately without engendering the appropriate response from Wickerson!

About twenty minutes later, Mike Kingsbury had wended his way from the Central Police Station across town to Watson's office in the Tower Building. Having first been met by Garnet, the receptionist (along with numerous other titles, including gatekeeper), he was cross-examined by her as to his purpose for being there. No one got past Garnet easily! Having satisfied herself of his bona fides, she let Watson know that he was here and duly ushered him into Watson's office. The usual pleasantries took place, and Watson determined that Kingsbury was a former British police officer with the City of London Police and that he was now living and working in the Toronto area of Canada. On a part-time basis, when he was not at his daytime job, he worked for a well-known Canadian private investigation firm that was duly licensed and owned and operated by a former Canadian senior law enforcement individual. Watson's path crossed somewhat with Kingsbury in that Watson had completed substantial work for officers of the City of London Police when their inquiries and those of the Metropolitan Police in London regularly touched on the Cayman Islands. Kingsbury's licensee had been formally engaged by a group of investigators who were acting on behalf of a lady named Anna whose young daughter, aged four years in 1982, was apparently abducted from her grandmother's home in Etobicoke, Canada, by the biological father and immediately covertly removed from the jurisdiction. The investigators had happened upon information that tended to show that the father of the girl was being financed by his mother primarily through a bank in Florida. The father had apparently said that he was taking her for a walk and would return in two hours or so. He never did, and the child was not seen or heard from again. Watson could not imagine the heartache that the mother, Anna, had gone through. This had happened some eight years previously in 1982, and still the mother had no idea where her daughter or ex-husband were. The local police in Toronto had been engaged in the ongoing search for the same as had the national police, the Royal Canadian Mounted Police, and also the American FBI; but all were without any idea where the father and child were—or even the ability to confirm whether or not they were still alive.

Kingsbury explained that they had received what they viewed as reliable information that the father's mother was sending money abroad to help support the father and his abducted daughter, wherever they might be. Kingsbury mentioned a bank in South Florida that was initiating the wire transfers, and they also suspected that a bank in the Cayman Islands was the final destination before the money was sent to the stated beneficiary (i.e., the father). Kingsbury mentioned a Caymanian bank that was well-known to Watson, and the suspicion that it was interacting with the bank in Florida was well-placed, as Watson had completed other inquiries that showed the banking connections and transactions undertaken fairly regularly between the two banks. Kingsbury asked if Watson would be able to determine where the money, if it were being directed to or through the bank in Cayman, was being ultimately sent and if there could possibly be any further clues or information to positively identify where the father was, along with the abducted child. Watson explained to Kingsbury regarding the confidentiality laws that applied in Cayman and the responsibilities of banks to adhere to those laws regarding the identity of investors. Kingsbury said he understood but that anything that could be determined would be welcomed by the authorities in Canada investigating the case. Apparently, they and the US authorities at that time held and had held for a substantial period a warrant of arrest for the father on abduction charges. Watson agreed to see what could possibly be determined, albeit on an unofficial basis. Kingsbury left the office and thanked Watson for any potential help he might be able to provide.

Nothing happened for a week or two due to other more pressing matters being conducted by Watson regarding an armed robbery and murder that had occurred in George Town and the establishment of a major incident room to cover the administration and control of the same. However, something happened about two weeks later when Watson had to visit one of the 583 banks in the Cayman Islands in relation to a formal matter to serve a Mutual Legal Assistance Treaty notice on the same, requiring production of documents in an ongoing criminal matter being investigated in the USA. Watson had called the bank and made an appointment to meet with the senior bank manager to serve the MLAT notice and mentioned he also wanted to discuss another matter that was of concern to the authorities in the USA and Canada. Upon meeting the manager, along with DS Johns, and serving the manager with the usual MLAT notice, Watson and Johns then had to listen to the usual perfunctory objections regarding what the bankers saw as a nuisance matter to take both time and effort to research and then produce the documents. Watson acknowledged the same, apologized, told the manager he would look forward to receiving them and then, without missing a breath, turned to the matter regarding the abducted child from Canada.

Watson then explained to the manager the facts of the matter regarding the young four-year-old girl abducted from Canada by her father who then took her unlawfully out of the jurisdiction of the Canadian courts that were overseeing the mother's divorce and child custody together with other related matters. Watson explained that there was no compunction on the manager to do anything but that the mother who had been searching for seven or eight years, through numerous resources, but without success was consequently very distraught and wanted to find her child and get her back home to Canada. Watson reiterated that there was at that time no compulsion on the manager to do anything. Watson told the banker that the mother, for nearly eight years, had contacted various organizations and police forces about the child's disappearance, but each and every lead and the costs associated with some of them had come to nothing. Watson then explained that he believed the father and abductor of the child was being funded by his mother through a bank in South Florida whom Watson knew from past experience held a relationship with the Caymanian bank. Watson then asked if the manager could, in any way, let them know if there was a relationship with the father maintained at the bank and, if they were able to confirm that, whether or not they had any knowledge or information that would lead to the current location of the father and possibly the missing child. The manager, sitting behind his ornate wooden desk, which did not have one piece of paper on it (unlike Watson's), thought and then stood up, asking Watson and Johns to remain seated. He left the office and returned about five minutes later. The manager was carrying a brown manila folder, which he placed on the center of his desk, saying, "I am going to leave the office for five or ten minutes, and I don't want you, Mr. Watson, to touch that file," indicating the manila folder on his desk. He then left the office. Based on the specific instruction given, DS Johns picked up the file and reviewed the same. It was readily apparent that the father had been receiving money from the bank over a few years, and it was primarily instigated from the bank in Florida by the father's mother. Just a few days earlier than Watson's visit to the Cayman bank, the bank had, in fact, sent the father a letter and a draft for some monies by courier to an address in Santiago, Chile. The manager duly returned and asked if DCI Watson had touched the file, and he was duly assured by Watson that he had not touched the file.

Once back at the office in the Tower Building, Watson continued making some inquiries through Chilean law enforcement resources regarding the address shown as an address of contact for the father as recently as a few days prior. Watson, having updated the commissioner, then contacted the RCMP in Toronto and spoke with officers who were aware of the abduction case. Watson made them aware of the address and knowledge of the same that he had determined regarding his meeting with Kingsbury and also from other inquiries made. They were most grateful to receive the information and stated that they would follow up on the same. Kingsbury was also made aware of that contact and to whom the details had been passed by Watson. A result of the information was that in May 1990, the child's mother flew to Chile and—interacting with the Canadian Embassy in Santiago, Chile, and also the Chilean police—the child was finally recovered from her foster parents and flown home to Canada.

Based on all that came to Watson's knowledge, it appeared that the child had been taken from her grandmother's home in Canada by her father in total and abject defiance of a duly issued court order. It was discovered that she was initially taken to Florida, where she was hidden in a large community of Jehovah's Witnesses, before being moved out of the country to Chile by her father. Watson was surprised to learn there was a substantial number of reasonably large communities in Florida where Jehovah's Witnesses resided. Over the years, various police agencies, the RCMP, and the FBI tried diligently—without success—to find her. It was following this action that the private investigators happened upon a snippet of information that they believed might have led them to an offshore connection and potential tie with the Cayman Islands. Once Watson had contacted and spoken with the RCMP in March 1990 regarding his findings, things happened quickly, and the child was positively located in Santiago, Chile, and equally quickly reunited with her mother. She had been living with her father but, according to persons nearby, was being treated terribly and was also neglected by her father. There was a reliable information she had been placed in an orphanage but then taken into the home of a respectable Jehovah's Witness family who had seen and heard of the abuse she was suffering, took great pity on her, and tried to rescue her from all the harm that was befalling her. In this same period, it was learned that she had been visited by her father on only five or six occasions in three years. There was also a suggestion that when she was found by the Chilean police, she was on the verge of being further relocated by her father to Argentina because he feared she might yet be found and returned to Canada. It appeared from what Watson learned from various sources that her father wanted her for himself to spite her loving mother but really did not want anything to do with her. Thankfully, she was found and quickly reunited with her mother and repatriated to Canada, where Watson understood she continued to be living a good and healthy life. Watson's respect for the young girl progressed even further over the years, as after being reunited with her mother and living a settled life in Canada, she did well both academically and socially. She eventually married and became the mother of a son. In her own personal business life, she also was doing well and became a dress designer of some repute and was excelling in the fashion world. Great credit, according to Watson, was due to her following the terrible start she had in life.

It was most refreshing for the commissioner, Watson, and all the different people involved in the search for the young girl, where the police work and international cooperation among many persons of different skill sets and abilities had had such positive and humanitarian results.

CHAPTER 21

Royal Cayman Islands Police—a Cricket Tour to the UK

Over the first two years of his tenure in Cayman, Watson had become deeply involved in cricket that was played on the island, and the police cricket team was an integral part of the local league, the Cayman Islands Cricket Association. Watson was, shortly after his arrival in Cayman, elected as the secretary of the league and further held some training courses teaching some of the players how to umpire cricket games under the Laws of Cricket, of which there were forty-two laws. Watson knew that better umpires invariably led to better and more disciplined cricket. Watson learned that many years previously, the Police CC had visited Barbados on a short tour that had been beneficial to them in improving their game in Cayman. Consequently, during a meeting of the Police Cricket Club Committee, Watson suggested to them about possibly organizing a tour to the UK to give them an opportunity to play on some grass pitches rather than the artificial pitch that was in Cayman and also to allow them to further develop their skills, whether it be batting, bowling, or fielding. They would also be exposed to some other police sides in the United Kingdom plus a number of good club sides comprising mainly of civilians there. Watson explained that he would select the teams and games they should play, but his first criteria was that the grounds would be ideal, including from a small picturesque village cricket ground to a couple of grounds where county cricket was played, the highest form of professional cricket in the UK, including the legendary Trent Bridge cricket ground in Nottinghamshire where county cricket had been played since the early 1830s and Test match cricket (international matches) since 1899 when the first Test match was held there between England and Australia. It had long been considered by many cricket afficionados as one of the best grounds in the world to watch cricket.

The idea received very favorable reaction from the members, and about fifteen months before the date of the proposed tour, numerous and varied actions were commenced by Watson and the committee to raise money for the tour and also plan the whole itinerary—including games, venues, accommodations, transport, and clothing (including caps, blazers, sweaters, etc.). Certain members were given various tasks, and they all set about enthusiastically to complete their tasks. There was a chairman of the Tour Committee, a secretary, a treasurer, a captain, two committee members, an advertising representative, and also Garnet—who now had a new title as police tour administration and secretarial officer, plus anything else (unpaid)—who assisted with all the typing and the like. She undertook the task with her usual good humor, verve, and commitment.

To raise money for the tour, the committee arranged for a dance to be held—which would be open to the public—and one of the things to be covered at the dance would be a raffle for which the first prize would be a brand-new motor vehicle, a Nissan family car, which had been kindly donated to the committee by a local garage at their wholesale cost. Tickets were printed, and all the cricket team members, plus other supporters, were given books of tickets for the raffle to sell to people on the island. Also, tickets were printed for attendance at the dance when the draw would be made for the car. There were another couple of prizes available but of far less value than the new car. The chance to win a new car for just a few dollars captured the public's interest, and almost all the tickets that had been printed were sold. The dance was also well-attended, and everyone had a great time. A brochure was being prepared and printed showing the persons involved in the tour, messages of goodwill from people in authority on the island, messages from the hosts in the UK, and an itinerary of the matches planned, and it also contained a number of adverts from local businesses who willingly supported the tour by paying various prices for a full-page and half-page advert and also a premium for an advert on the back cover of the brochure. By the time all these things came together, in excess of $100,000 had been raised to pay for the tour.

The airfares and transport were on Cayman Airways from Cayman connecting in Miami to British Airways to Heathrow and then return some twenty days later. Booking en bloc for the trip, Watson found Cayman Airways and British Airways allowed one free ticket both ways. The cost for the round-trip flights was about $20,000. The accommodation was at a police training center in the UK, and it was unbelievably cheap. Bed-and-breakfast for the nineteen nights for twenty-one tourists totaled about $6,700. The car was purchased at cost from the local garage, and that was about $15,000. The adverts and payments from the advertisers added further to the money available for the tour. Ford Motor Company in England, after being approached by a colleague from the Essex Police, had very kindly allowed the party to use—free of any charge—two Ford Granada motorcars and one minibus, which held fifteen or sixteen players plus had adequate room to carry all the luggage and cricket equipment that they had with them. Watson was pleased with the response of the committee members, and the tour was indeed coming to fruition. A request was made by Watson to the commissioner for the tour to be undertaken, and he and the governor willingly gave their authority and best wishes for the success of the same. The police members of the party were also fortunate in that the commissioner allowed them to take one week of the tour as paid time off from work so that they did not have to lose their normal vacation time for at least one week of the tour. On the days that no cricket was scheduled, tours were organized to various local industries and also sporting events to give the tourists a more complete view of what happened in the UK in summertime. All the visits were well-received and enjoyed by one and all. Some of the tour members took time on their days off to visit with family and friends elsewhere in the UK.

Knowing to a degree the problems that could arise in dealing with certain things in the Caribbean, Watson called for a meeting of the tourists at CB's about three months before the tour was scheduled to commence. The objectives were twofold. First he wanted to let them know that as they were traveling as representatives of the Cayman Islands and the police in particular, certain standards of behavior were expected from them and that no matter what'd happen or who would be involved, they must—at all times—adhere to those standards expected and demanded. To do otherwise, they might be asked by the tour managers to go home early; their conduct must be beyond reproach was Watson's message. Second, Watson instructed them to bring their passports with them to the pre-tour meeting. He wanted to ensure that they all had passports and that the passports were all current and there was no reason why they might encounter entry problems either at Miami or Heathrow. This was a good decision by Watson, as one of the people turned up at the meeting and proudly presented his Barbadian passport that was about six months out of date. It had expired. After being told by Watson that no current passport, no travel, the player got his passport renewed by going back to Barbados and, about two weeks later, brought the new passport into the CCB for Watson to check on the same. All was now fine, but Watson was so pleased he had the meeting when he did and not have the problem at Miami Airport or elsewhere. Watson had been put on notice of this possible eventuality by another expat who had taken a touring team to Canada—only for one of their number to not be allowed to enter the USA due to a long-expired passport. Watson subsequently bought that expat a beer or two for the great and sound advice!

The day following their arrival in the UK, the police touring party, accompanied by some senior members of the UK police, was invited to the local county council offices for a meeting with the chairman and other senior members of the local county government to welcome them to the UK. Refreshments were served, and finger foods were provided. Watson was totally impressed when during the proceedings, the county council chairman entered the meeting room wearing his large gold chain of office (livery collar) around his neck.

It was a large gold medallion, about four inches in diameter, bearing the coat of arms of the county and lots of other gold decorations and the like. Watson noticed the tourists had all gone quiet and were staring intently at the chairman. Bearing in mind that a lot of drug pushers in the Caribbean wore big gold necklaces and rings as a sign of their importance and affluence, Watson was fairly sure that the tourists thought that the world's largest drug dealer had just walked in the room! Watson mentioned this to the chairman who laughed long and hard over it! Speeches were made, and all the dignitaries wished the police team the best of luck and much enjoyment during the tour. That same day, Watson had arranged for the groundsman at the police training center to prepare a grass cricket pitch for the tourists to practice bowling and batting on. It was a far different proposition to batting on an artificial pitch, which they were used to in Cayman. Suffice to say, some of the tourists had played on grass before and knew the adaptations they had to make, while the other players learned quickly.

The schedule that Watson organized was demanding in that thirteen games were scheduled in the twenty days available in the UK. Watson presumed they might lose one or two fixtures due to the usual English rain during the summer precluding play, but it only rained about thirty minutes one day during the tour, and that was on a day that there was no game scheduled! The vagaries of the English weather still reigned supreme. The dates were mid-August to early September, as that was the best time for cricket clubs in England to host visiting teams. When complete, the fixture list featured some excellent teams who played on excellent grounds and also very picturesque arenas. Each match included an after-the-match social or a luncheon during the game. It was the considered view of the tourists that the tour was above and beyond what they had anticipated or expected. All the games, bar perhaps one, were played in the traditional spirit of the game with no quarter given or asked by either side. Of the thirteen games played, the RCIP won ten and lost three.

There were some tremendous efforts by the Cayman players, but one player, Christopher Wight, was in devastating form throughout with the bat scoring a total of 589 runs at an average of 53.54

scored per game he played. In the game against Nottinghamshire Police, played at the world-famous Trent Bridge cricket ground near Nottingham, Notts—batting first—scored 272 runs in their allotted forty overs. Notts was a strong side and included two former first-class players and a number of others who had played county Second XI cricket or Combined Services cricket. Watson, speaking to them during the tea break between innings, said they were fairly confident they could defend that total; but Watson, while admitting they should be able to defend the total, cautioned that if the Cayman lads get going, they might not have enough. Watson knew full well what the Cayman team was capable of. Suffice to say that on that day, Christopher Wight, who opened the batting for Cayman, scored 165 runs before he was out, and the Cayman police passed the 272 total of Notts in the thirty-seventh over with the loss of just four wickets. Suffice to say that every member of the touring party enjoyed their entire day spent at the Trent Bridge ground or, as Watson described it, hallowed turf. Watson had a lot of fun speaking with the Notts players following the game in the incredibly old pavilion that had hosted many world-class players over the years.

Other team members excelled with the bat and others with the ball, but one remaining memory concerned tourist Lascelles Johnson and a game against the Lincolnshire Police at a lovely ground in the shadows of the impressive and old Lincoln Cathedral, which was situated on the high point of the city of Lincoln. Lascelles loved cricket and always gave 100 percent of himself during games. In the game at Lincoln, his acrobatic catches in the slips belied his girth and certainly engendered the mirth of amazed spectators who witnessed three unbelievable catches by him in that game. In the process of taking the three catches, one while he was horizontal to the green grass, he clutched the ball at extended length with one hand. The spectators gave him the Disneyesque nickname of Dumbo, which did not leave him the rest of the tour. After the game, all the spectators wanted to meet and greet Dumbo at a very pleasant after-match social in the cricket club bar!

At the end of the tour, everyone was pretty tired, but they all left the United Kingdom with indelible memories of the events of the twenty days and many new friends they had added to their lists. It was a great tour and certainly one of the best that Watson had ever partaken in, and he had been on quite a few with rugby, cricket, and athletics. When all the expenses and ancillary matters were reconciled at the end of the tour, there was still enough money left to sponsor a further Police Cricket Club tour two years later to Grenada and Barbados. The police cricket team was getting the taste for touring and all that that entails, together with the multitude of benefits to be obtained from the same!

CHAPTER 22

A Cruise Ship, Caribbean Wanderer, Mystery—Part One

A cruise ship styled the *Caribbean Wanderer* maneuvered to an anchoring spot just off Hog Sty Bay in Grand Cayman. It looked resplendent in its white livery, sitting in the azure-blue waters of Grand Cayman. The ship had been plying its trade in the Caribbean basin for almost twelve years and carried, when fully loaded, a maximum of 1,500 passengers and about 420 officers and crew. It had been idling some two hours or so about three miles offshore of Grand Cayman because it arrived early from its last port of call at Montego Bay in Jamaica. It moored in Hog Sty Bay about 6:30 a.m., and passengers who wished to go ashore, by tenders, would start disembarking at 8:00 a.m. In Cayman, all passengers ashore were transferred from the anchoring point by tenders that scurried back and forth from the ship to the port terminal dockside where the passengers would then pick up tours by minibus or taxis to varying parts of the island and other notable spots to be visited in Cayman (e.g., the interesting hands-on Turtle Farm, the Blow Holes, beautiful Rum Point, North Sound, enchanting Stingray City, or the splendid Pirate's Caves in Bodden Town). Some enjoyed just strolling around George Town for a few hours and visiting the old library, which was built in 1939, and having some of the best air-conditioning in town!

Heinrich Willenbrock, a German national born in Hamburg, was in his mid to late thirties and had been working on the ship as a server in a number of the restaurants on board for almost four years, and his girlfriend of three years, Anneka ten Velden, who came from the Netherlands originally, was also working as a server in the restaurants and dining rooms. They always tend to work on cruise routes that cover various permutations of the Caribbean islands, and they especially seemed to enjoy visiting the Caymans and Jamaica. The crew members were allowed to leave the ship in any ports they visited, especially on any days off they might have. On this day in Cayman, Heinrich had twelve hours off duty and had announced that he wanted to visit the stingrays at Stingray City in Cayman. Unfortunately, Anneka had to work; therefore, Heinrich would visit with some other crew members who had time off. They all were expected to be back on board in time for the last dinner service at 7:00 p.m., so they were planning to catch the last scheduled tender out to the ship, which was at 5:30 p.m. The ship was not due to depart from Cayman until 7:00 p.m., and its next port of call was scheduled to be Cancun in Mexico, about fifteen hours sailing to the west.

Anneka was off duty that day at 5:30 p.m., and immediately after work, she anxiously waited to welcome Heinrich back on board to see what surprise he had bought for her in Cayman, as he always brought her a nice gift every time he went ashore alone. She knew he should have been back at the ship on the 5:00 p.m. or 5:30 p.m. ferry, but he did not, and she didn't believe he might have come back any earlier than those times. If he had, he would surely have contacted her to let her know. Also, that would have been totally out of character for him; he always enjoyed his full allotment of time ashore. She spoke to mutual friends of both of them, but equally, none of them had seen Heinrich since he left the ship in the morning. She also checked with the security officers on board the ship who kept a tally of when people leave the ship and when they return, including crew. They found that Heinrich had swiped his identification card when he left the ship, but despite an extensive search, there was no record of him coming back on board. Now she was getting genuinely concerned; this was totally out of character for Heinrich. He was described by people who knew him as somewhat arrogant but very punctual, and whenever he did a job, he always did it to the best of his capabilities. Some of his passengers on board viewed him as slightly standoffish. But the majority loved him, and on return cruises they booked, they would even ask for him as their server.

As a last-ditch effort, Anneka made an emergency call to the maître d'—who basically ran the servers' operations and those in the kitchen—to see if he knew where Heinrich might be. He had not seen or heard from Heinrich, and despite issuing a bulletin to all staff members, there was not any response regarding Heinrich. The senior officers on board the ship then decided to notify the Cayman port authorities and also the local police department to see if Heinrich had been hurt in a road traffic or other type of accident while onshore or perhaps, God forbid, had been arrested. All the inquiries made came back with negative responses, and it was at this time that the ship's officers, after some discussion regarding the same, made a formal complaint to the police regarding the missing Heinrich.

The two-crew people that Heinrich had left the ship with were identified by the crew records, and they were subsequently interviewed at length by the police. They said that they had missed Heinrich from the moment they landed ashore at the terminal in the morning, and then they visited the Turtle Farm (traveling by mini-bus) and had a bite to eat at one of the many restaurants on Seven Mile Beach during their return to the ship. They stated that since leaving the ship, they had not seen or heard from Heinrich. During the interviews with them, there was no evidence of any injuries to their bodies, and also the scenes of crime officer examined in depth their clothing and cabin contents, but again, nothing of any value was found. They had described Heinrich to be wearing some blue embroidered fashion jeans, a Polo sports shirt, and some Nike trainers when he went ashore that day. He was carrying a blue rucksack also, which, according to them, was a piece of equipment that Heinrich always took with him when he went ashore. The crew people said Heinrich was enormously proud of the new jeans, as Anneka had recently purchased them for him while they were docked in either Miami or Fort Lauderdale—they couldn't remember which port.

The detective branch was duly called to start efforts to trace the missing crewman, as were a number of uniform police officers and traffic officers, plus DCI Watson—with a couple CCB officers—was also involved due to the pressing time constraints regarding keeping the ship at anchor. Passengers were sometimes late back to a ship but not usually the crew. Timing was of the essence, as the ship was scheduled to depart at 7:00 p.m.—some fifty minutes after the first notification was given to the police. The police and scenes of crime officers were allowed on board, and they thoroughly checked Heinrich's cabin, but nothing of any value or anything out of place was found. Two different phone chargers were discovered and taken possession of. Watson suggested that the scenes of crime officers retrieve perhaps a hairbrush or other personal items of Heinrich that might bear a DNA profile, which was in its infancy in its use in criminal matters at that time. The uniform police coordinated with the ship's staff and officers to complete a thorough search of the ship and all its little nooks and crannies on each and every deck, but again, after an extensive search, all turned up with a negative result. All this was being done working against the clock, and with the authority and assistance of the captain, the ship was detained from departing for at least four hours, meaning a possible 11:00 p.m. departure from Cayman en route to Mexico. Watson and other detectives contacted tour companies who had operated that day out of the port to see if there was any way to identify what had happened to Heinrich after he had departed on a ferry to the port and ashore. An appeal was made on the radio and TV stations in Cayman for any and all information pertaining to the whereabouts of Heinrich. Usually such an appeal would generate a few leads of potential interest, but initially nothing of any value was brought forward or discovered following the appeal. Inquiries were also made with rental car and motor scooter rental agencies at the port and also in Cayman to see if Heinrich had rented a vehicle and perhaps been involved in a road traffic accident that had not yet been discovered. Inquiries made at the local hospital and various doctors' offices also met with negative responses. It was as though Heinrich had dropped off the face of the earth after landing in the port terminal. Watson did not like how this inquiry was going and was getting extremely concerned for the safety of Heinrich.

Senior police officers were considering what alternatives might have happened to Heinrich, and a woman detective was dispatched to interview Anneka at length on board the ship and discover the depth of her relationship with Heinrich plus get an idea of how Heinrich lived and what sort of income he had access to over and above what the police knew by then that he received from the cruise line and also tips left by passengers at the end of each cruise. Anneka stated that she only knew about Heinrich's income from his employment on the cruise ship. During this interview, Anneka was asked about Heinrich's cell phone and the place of issue. She knew of one that he used for ship purposes and general purposes but then also mentioned nonchalantly that he had another cell phone that he always kept with him, but she had no idea of that number or where it was obtained. She had been told by Heinrich it was extremely high-tech; it was a sputnik phone or something like that. She was pressed extensively for what purpose he had two phones, but she professed she had no idea and, in Watson's eyes and experience, seemed to be truthful. These circumstances, however, attracted Watson's interest as to why a server on a cruise ship would need and pay for what he believed Anneka was describing a satellite phone. In some countries, possession of a satellite phone was illegal. Their signals would usually bypass local telecoms systems, hindering censorship and wiretapping efforts, which led some intelligence agencies to believe that satellite phones aided terrorist activity, perhaps along with other nefarious acts. Watson also knew that it was pretty common for restrictions to be in place in countries that were run by oppressive government regimes as a way to both expose subversive agents within their country and maximize the control of the information that made it past their borders. There just was no easy answer as to why Heinrich would have or indeed require a satellite phone. This was causing great concern to the investigators regarding Heinrich's present position and whether or not he was involved in some unlawful business or otherwise.

As the time drew closer for the ship to depart, the police were no further forward in finding what had happened to Heinrich; so sitting down around a table in the Central Police Station, the management team came up with a list of potential possibilities:

1. Heinrich had rented a car or scooter and had been in an accident and had not yet been found. This was a long shot, as the rental agencies had no such record of a rental by Heinrich.

2. Heinrich was separated from his two crew friends and had met with a local person for some nefarious purpose. Port Authority security tapes might help here and was actioned by Watson for completion early the next day.

3. Heinrich had met with some locals and delivered some contraband or drugs to them that he had acquired in Jamaica, or alternatively, the Cayman operators were providing him with drugs for resale on board. Perhaps there had been a dispute between them?

4. Heinrich did not personally use drugs according to results from all the inquiries being made, but he did always seem to be short of money, and perhaps the Jamaica and Cayman link he consistently worked was a catalyst to the current problem.

5. Heinrich got in an argument with the two crew members he traveled with and had been left for dead somewhere in Cayman, and the two crew mates were lying about not knowing where he was.

By the time 11:00 p.m. came around, the captain anxiously wanted to up-anchor and proceed to the next port of call. With some 1,500 passengers on board, plus crew, the ship could not reasonably be detained any longer. The captain did assure the police and the authorities that whatever they needed as the case went forward, he would make everything required available to them, including crew members who might need to be interrogated again in the future. That also would include helping the police reconstruct the financial well-being or otherwise of any crew members of interest. Watson did ask for a full accounting of Heinrich's earnings from the cruise line over the past three years and where the money was deposited by the cruise line. Also, Watson requested an accounting of the cruises and routes Heinrich had worked during that same period and, if possible, how many of those cruises had stopped at both Jamaica and Cayman and when Heinrich had been ashore at the two. The captain stated that that would be provided as soon as possible, but it would take some time, as he would have to get those details reconstructed from the cruise line's corporate offices in Miami. The captain and his senior officers also had their own questions and concerns regarding the crew member's disappearance and were eager for the matter to be resolved. Watson made a note to ask the Cayman immigration services if it were possible to reconstruct how many times Heinrich had come ashore in Cayman out of all the times he might have visited. This was actioned for an inquiry to be made the following day.

While it was difficult for the police to see the ship depart, it was also very reassuring that the cooperation that had been given thus far would be continued. After all, at this time, the inquiry was basically a missing person inquiry; and but for the fact that the actions of Heinrich were somewhat a departure from his norm, there was no available evidence at this stage to think of it or argue persuasively otherwise. Following the events of the evening, Watson recruited some of the CCB officers to set up a mini-incident room to keep track of the inquiries being made and the results therefrom. Also, the objective was to ensure that any details given or discovered were cross-referenced and researched to discover any irregularities and, if necessary, to seek corroboration of any matters. Watson and his team worked well into the night.

About 7:00 a.m. the next morning, after an all-too-brief night, Watson sent a team to the Port Authority to search tapes from their security cameras to try to determine what had happened to Heinrich following his landing ashore. Watson also sent teams to the minibus operators and taxicabs to see if they could find any further evidence regarding Heinrich or the two persons whom he was known to have left the ship with. Later during that morning, he got a call from the officers completing the inquiry at the Port Authority stating that they had found some evidence in the various security cameras searched.

On arrival at the Port Authority, Watson was shown evidence of the two crew members landing and then leaving the area on a minibus, which the local police knew took passengers to the Turtle Farm. Also, around 4:30 p.m., the cameras showed the two crew members returning to the ferry docking station and taking a 4:30 p.m. ferry back to the ship, which was also corroborated by the security check on the ship when they returned. Watson said, "That's all good, but what about Heinrich?" The officers told him to be patient! A few minutes later, they produced a security video showing Heinrich carrying a blue backpack on his shoulder in the morning while landing at the terminal with his two friends, and Heinrich then visited a restroom in the terminal. About five minutes later, he was again seen in the grounds of the terminal, and he eventually got in line for a taxicab. He waited for about ten minutes and could be seen speaking to other people in line around him. He then got into a cab by himself, and the cab left the area. Watson asked his colleagues, "Can we find out who the cab driver is?"

Immediately he was told by one of the officers, "It is Jordan Ebanks. He has been driving cabs for years. I recognize both him and his cab. He has worked the cruise terminal for quite a few years."

Watson said, "I suppose you can tell me what he is doing today," silently marveling at the amount of local knowledge that some of the police officers had.

The officer's response surprised him even more: "He will be working the airport today, as there are no cruise ships until just after lunch."

Watson was speechless, and he asked if they had seen Heinrich returning. They said they hadn't but would recheck the same. Accordingly, he asked the officers to be sure to secure and preserve all the videotape evidence pertaining to the terminal during that day, which they said was already being processed and completed. They knew Watson and that that would be his request!

Watson instructed a local member of the inquiry team, together with his partner, to go the airport and find Jordan Ebanks and bring him to the Central Police Station to be asked some questions regarding his actions at the terminal the previous day. Watson felt that at least the inquiry was getting somewhere. Heinrich had been seen leaving the port terminal but had not been seen returning. Now it became important to find out what had happened to him and where and when. The chances of him having been involved in an accident were lowering considerably, while the chances of something bad having happened to him were rising exponentially.

An hour or so later, Watson was sitting with Jordan Ebanks in the interview room at the Central Police Station. Jordan, in true taxi-driver style, wanted to know how long he would be there, as he was losing money not being at the airport, and then around lunchtime, he had to be at the cruise terminal for more cruise passengers. The taxi drivers in Cayman zealously guarded their regular pickup points for passengers. Watson recounted to him the interactions with Heinrich the previous day and showed Jordan a picture from the security video of Heinrich getting in the cab. He told Jordan all he wanted was honest answers and where he took Heinrich after collecting him at the terminal. Jordan said Heinrich told him that he was a crew member on the ship, the *Caribbean Wanderer*, and he wanted a taxi ride to West Bay via the Kirk Freeport store in town. Jordan took him there first and waited in the nearby car park for him to return. Heinrich went into the Kirk Freeport store, exiting about ten minutes later sporting a Kirk Freeport bag that he was carrying and said he had bought a diamond tennis bracelet for his girlfriend (Anneka) who was also working on the ship. Jordan said he told Heinrich that it must have cost a pretty penny and Heinrich said $3,500. Watson asked why he would carry Heinrich about three hundred yards from the terminal and let him go in the store without collecting any fare; it was very trusting of him. Jordan told him that was because Heinrich had often called him in the past prior to his scheduled arrival in Grand Cayman and that he used to be available to him to carry him around various places but usually to West Bay where he nearly always dropped him off.

After Heinrich had got back in the cab, they carried on out of town and down the West Bay Road and into West Bay itself. On arrival, as always, he left Heinrich in the area near the public beach in West Bay. Jordan mentioned that although he had often carried him from George Town to West Bay, Heinrich had never once had a ride back from West Bay to the port terminal. All this was vital information to Watson, and accordingly, he arranged for Jordan to come back to the police station about 6:00 p.m. (after he had finished transporting the cruise ship passengers) for a more comprehensive interview and for a witness statement to be obtained from him regarding his dealings with Heinrich. Jordan agreed but again protested to ensure Watson didn't forget that he was losing money at this time being stuck with the police. Watson then gave him a peace offering in the form of a twenty-five dollar bill for his time to date and suggested he go and get a nice lunch at Champion House or somewhere before the cruise ship would come into port, which seemed to make Watson one of Jordan's best friends. Watson asked if Jordan had seen the TV or heard the radio programs the day before regarding Heinrich, but Jordan said he hadn't. Apparently, after finishing work, he had gone to a local bar on Shedden Road and relaxed with some friends by drinking a few Red Stripe beers; so by the time he arrived home, he hit his bed until the following morning.

Jordan did return that evening to the Central Police Station as arranged and, after about two and a half hours, had been fully interviewed. And he provided a full and very comprehensive witness statement of the time spent with Heinrich the previous day. Watson noted that all the times he had taken Heinrich, he never saw or met anyone with Heinrich in the West Bay area. Heinrich had spoken at length with Jordan, but it was all small talk. Never once did Heinrich mention what he was doing or who he was meeting in West Bay. One important point Watson noted that Jordan had not told him when he first interviewed him was the fact that prior to going into Kirk Freeport to buy the tennis bracelet, Heinrich had called in a bank next door for about four minutes then gone immediately thereafter into the jewelry store where he apparently bought the bracelet for Anneka. This was some vital information for Watson, and he made an action note to call the bank the following day and meet with the manager.

Heinrich was still missing, his backpack was still missing, and all Watson knew was that he had been dropped in and around the area of West Bay Public Beach. Watson believed that based on what they knew thus far, some harm had befallen him, possibly in West Bay. It was vital for the police to find out what had occurred in West Bay and who was involved in the same.

Watson and the CID staff therefore set out a plan to complete some extensive house-to-house inquiries in the West Bay area, stretching from the public beach area further west and also toward the north. There was an extensive area to be covered, but it was marked with grid lines on a map of the area, and teams of detectives and uniform constables started the necessary trawl of the area. It was a boring matter but was essential to discovering what had happened. A prepared questionnaire was given to each officer to be used in respect of each and every person interviewed, and the teams were fully briefed by Watson and the CID senior officers on what ground should be covered and also what facts should not be disclosed to the people being interviewed. House-to-house inquiries could take time to ensure that everyone who should be seen and questioned was. Having said that, Watson knew that on occasions, it could yield much useful information. Watson did not know what to expect from the house-to-house inquiries in West Bay; he had never experienced such actions in the Caribbean before.

Having sent the house-to-house teams out, Watson called the bank identified by Jordan and arranged to go and see the manager. Watson was well-received by the manager, and the manager listened intently to what had occurred involving Heinrich the day before. A search of account holders at the bank revealed that an account in the name of an exempt Cayman corporation styled Munich Enterprises Ltd. had been established some five years previously and was showing as current in all respects. A signatory to the account was named Heinrich Willenbrock. There had been some action on the account the day before, when a withdrawal of $9,000 had been made from the account. Watson asked if the withdrawal slip could be recovered. The manager left the room and came back in some ten minutes later with a copy of the withdrawal slip and also a current copy of the statement of the account held. Watson smiled as he thought that the signature of Heinrich that he had seen in documents on board the ship was almost identical to the signature on the bank withdrawal slip. Heinrich had obtained the money and probably paid cash for the bracelet a few minutes later at Kirk Freeport. The statement also shocked Watson. It was clearly showing that after the withdrawal had been made from the account, the balance remaining therein was $42,850,900. *Where the hell*, thought Watson, *did a guy serving meals on a cruise ship obtain this sort of money?* Watson asked the manager for a full copy of the account from inception and also documents supporting every deposit to the account and also any withdrawals from the same, again since inception. The manager was quite happy to supply these items and then asked, "Who will pay for them?"

Watson told him that it was a formal police inquiry into, at the very least, a missing person. But he said that if he wanted to try to get paid for the same, "Send your invoice to the chief inspector of administration at police headquarters and see what he says." Surprisingly to Watson, this seemed to placate the manager. Watson didn't think he had a chance in hell getting the fees for the production of the same without some additional effort, but nonetheless, Watson did make a note to speak with the chief inspector and try to cajole some money out of him for the production process. Asked when he could expect to obtain the copies he required, Watson was told it'd take seventy-two to ninety-six hours of a normal business day. That was acceptable to Watson, and he left the bank with a copy of the withdrawal slip and also the current page of the bank account. Watson did ask—and the manager agreed—to keep the notice of his visit to the bank purely between them two for the current time. The manager stated he would notify Watson immediately of any further actions being made or requested on the account before they were processed. An inquiry subsequently initiated at Kirk Freeport by Watson regarding the bracelet purchased by Heinrich was completed and Heinrich could be clearly seen on security tape there buying the bracelet and paying for the same by cash.

Watson returned to the police headquarters and called a meeting of the senior staff involved. He outlined details of what Heinrich had done on the day he went missing, the evidence obtained from the cab driver, the result of the meeting with the banking official, and the fact that the house-to-house inquiries were being set up and processed in the West Bay area. "The bottom line," he explained, "is that Heinrich—with almost $43 million in a bank account and in possession of a satellite phone, which isn't a cheap item to possess—is obviously involved in some nefarious dealings in which he is using his employment with the cruise line as both a potential cover and to facilitate the same." He also explained that having interviewed Anneka, he did not think that she had a clue about Heinrich's extra-curricular activities, nor did probably anyone else on the cruise ship. With the bank account controlled solely by Heinrich being in the Cayman Islands, it was obvious, Watson believed, that Cayman played an integral part in the whole scheme—whatever and wherever it might be based. As the officers discussed further ongoing actions, Watson said he was going to contact some colleagues whom he knew in the Federal Criminal Police Office, a central police agency known in Germany as the Bundeskriminalamt. They operated from head-quarters in Wiesbaden and had over two thousand agents attached to them. They were a clearing house for criminal intelligence records and helped State Criminal Police Offices in forensic matters, research, and also criminal investigations. It was also the national point of contact for the International Criminal Police Organization (INTERPOL) and inquiries that arise from other member countries. As Cayman was a member country of INTERPOL, Watson had dealt with them on a number of occasions and therefore reached out to friends at INTERPOL and was finally referred to the Federal Criminal Police Office.

He reached an agent in Germany, and thankfully, the agent spoke surprisingly good English. Watson explained the circumstances regarding Heinrich and all that had happened in Cayman. He asked what the German authorities could perhaps do to assist in unraveling what was happening in Cayman, including—purely at this stage—a missing person. The agent asked for a few days to find out what he could and promised to revert to Watson as soon as he could. Watson, knowing the German police, knew that they were very thorough and that he would undoubtedly hear back from them, hopefully sooner rather than later. He was already considering traveling to Germany to dig into Heinrich and the source of his wealth but must wait first while the Germans did their initial inquiries and see what transpired from them. Watson had plenty to keep him busy in the interim and accordingly dealt with the same, but Heinrich was never far from Watson's thoughts. And time and again, Watson checked and rechecked to ensure that all that could be done in Cayman regarding the mystery was being done. He also visited regularly with the local detectives still making inquiries and researching tips regarding the same to ensure that each and every lead was being given the attention it deserved and that it was properly being finalized based on whatever evidence or results were found. Watson knew that this case could be properly solved in the fullness of time, but he was not sure how and when!

CHAPTER 23

Closure of a Worldwide Bank—Initial Actions

When the Bank of England moved at 1:00 p.m. Greenwich Mean Time on Friday, July 5, 1991, and closed down a big international bank's global operations, a pioneering financial citadel built on Pakistani and Indian entrepreneurship and—to a great degree—Arab money, it crashed as quickly as a house made of cards. It was undoubtedly one of the world's worst financial disasters. The operations of the same was special. It first penetrated jealously guarded European and American financial strongholds and then competed with more established Western banks, eventually owning some of them. It also became one of the world's largest private banks, operating in excess of four hundred branches in more than seventy countries with total assets estimated around $20 billion.

Unfortunately, the bank's motives and banking practices had always been suspect to both regulators and law enforcement in various parts of the world. Its assets raced ahead from a mere $10 million at its September 1972 founding to a massive $20 billion frozen worldwide nineteen years later. However, its viability always caused considerable concern among many countries and their regulators and other individuals associated with finances in many forms. As a result, it came under the scrutiny of regulators and various intelligence agencies in the 1980s due to concerns that it was poorly regulated and being used for nefarious schemes. Subsequent investigations revealed that it was involved in massive money laundering efforts together with other financial crimes and had illegally gained the controlling interest in a major American bank. As a natural progression, it became the focus of a huge regulatory battle in the early 1990s; and accordingly, on July 5, 1991, customs, law enforcement, accountants, and bank regulators in a number of countries raided and simultaneously locked down records of its many branch offices and subsidiaries.

The fallout of the closure was many and varied. In India, the country's solitary branch in Bombay closed shop along with others in over sixty countries. In Britain alone, twenty-five branches were closed, and 120,000 accounts were frozen. These were worth £250 million. Another £500 million was apparently held by overseas depositors. Thousands of South Asian businesses were crippled. What caught Watson's eye and was particularly unsettling to him was that being a staunch supporter of Indian restaurants wherever he traveled, it became apparent that following these actions, they did not have the money available to continue to buy provisions! This was potentially a major disaster of great magnitude to Watson!

The closure took everyone in various parts of the world by surprise. Staff in Britain returned from lunch to find their bank had shut, their jobs disappeared, and the building about to be padlocked. In the Caribbean, staff arrived to work and found the offices had already been secured and were duly protected. In Bahrain and Oman, the bank suspended operations too. Unsurprisingly, however, the three branches in Pakistan were kept open on orders of the government anxious not to disturb their day-to-day banking operations!

The whole operation, which culminated on July 5, came to the notice of DCI Watson a few days before its execution but was held in a very tight-knit circle of knowledge for obvious reasons: to ensure its successful execution and completion of the same on the assigned date and time. The effort was intricately coordinated on a worldwide basis to close branches simultaneously and thereby preserve evidence and assets as far as possible. The actions that day were primarily to take control of the various premises together with any and all documents relating to their business and also seize control of their assets.

The bank and two of its subsidiaries had a reasonably large operation in Cayman, based at two distinct and separate buildings. On the day prior to the implementation of the procedures, Watson spent time with the attorney general of the Cayman Islands, the commissioner of police, and other senior personnel regarding the procedures and policies to be followed the next day, along with receipt of the necessary documents of authorization for the actions to be taken. Watson also liaised with accountants from the firm (one of the big five accountancy firms in the world) nominated to act as the liquidators in the ongoing procedures relating to the bank. Once the premises in question were secured, they would be placed into the hands of and become the responsibility of the liquidators and their staff. A locksmith on the island was also contacted by Watson and put on notice of the potential for some work to be done on business premises in Cayman following the seizure procedures being completed the following day.

On the day of execution, Watson and the teams who were informed the day previously met at 5:40 a.m. for a further briefing by the commissioner of police and then departed to the bank's two physical premises in George Town. Watson and his team went to a building on North Church Street, while the other team went to a bank building on Mary Street. Watson's team arrived about 7:20 a.m., but the premises were still secure. Consideration was given to getting the police control room to contact a key holder to come and unlock the premises for the police, but on checking, it appeared there had been no key holder listed with the police. Most business premises had a key holder or two listed with the police department so that they could be contacted by the police in the event of an emergency. Fortuitously, while Watson was considering entering the building by breaching the nice glass doors at the entrance of the same, one of the assistant managers at the branch appeared, apparently totally unaware of the events that were unfolding. The position was explained to him by Watson, and accordingly, he unlocked the building and also was allowed by Watson to disable the security alarm having entered the building. He was then instructed to remain outside the premises while Watson and his team did an initial check of the same and a listing of what offices and any other noticeable items of importance were contained in the building was made. Watson had previously arranged for some officials from the big accounting firm to be present, as they were to take over the liquidation, administration of the building and its contents. Watson also arranged for the alarm system to be reset by an alarm installer and locksmith with new codes and also for all the locks on the doors to the building to be replaced. It was a coincidence that the locksmith knew the system in place pretty well, as a few years previously, he had supplied and fitted the system to meet the bank's requirements plus done yearly maintenance on the same. By 3:30 p.m. that same day, the building and its contents had been totally secured and handed over to the accountancy firm for their liquidation inquiries and the preservation of the documents and computerized records plus assets. Similar actions were also taken at the bank's other premises situated on Mary Street.

Investigators in the United States and the UK subsequently revealed that the bank had been set up deliberately to avoid centralized regulatory review and operated extensively in bank secrecy jurisdictions, including those such as Cayman. Its affairs were extraordinarily complex. Its officers were sophisticated international bankers whose apparent objective was to keep their affairs as secret as possible to commit fraud on a massive scale and to avoid detection.

By the end of July 1991, Watson learned that forty-four countries had totally closed down branches of the bank in question.

Over the next days, weeks, and months, a lot of time was spent by Watson and other law enforcement personnel interacting with the liquidators regarding the ongoing inquiries and additional inquiries arising therefrom. The work never seemed to slow down, and over a period of the next two years, Watson and his fellow officers were invariably concerned in numerous additional inquiries regarding the bank and its subsidiaries emanating from the Caymanian liquidators of the bank, the Cayman attorney general's office, the UK Serious Fraud Office, the UK City of London Police, and also the US Department of Justice Office of International Affairs and other US district attorney's offices. Hardly a week went by without some inquiry or disclosure measure being made and an answer required.

The files kept and maintained by Watson grew exponentially over the years and were creating a substantial drain on the force's budgets and expenditures in the form of purchasing and maintaining sequential binders and other required items of all the requests for assistance sought and the responses to the same. Nonetheless, the inquiries continued, and prosecutions of all manner of individuals were mounted in various parts of the world, much of which was dependent on some of the evidence determined and seized in Cayman and reflected in documents held by and being processed by the liquidators.

CHAPTER 24

Closure of a Worldwide Bank—Further Actions Regarding the Liquidation and Criminal Concerns

It was a fact that the inquiries conducted thus far had confirmed beyond any doubt that the bank had committed numerous serious criminal offenses in Cayman, the UK, the USA, and elsewhere. The inquiries also revealed that individuals auditing the bank over the years had knowingly passed and approved items in the accounts that were patently false. Almost from the inception of the bank, the accounts included loans and income from loans that did not exist, and they also recorded liabilities and expenditure in a manner that deceptively concealed them. It was transparently apparent that the frauds had been going on for a number of years, but the fact that the bank had divided its activities between a number of countries, no bank regulator in any one of the jurisdictions in which they operated had been able to get a full picture or grasp of what had actually been going on. It was also believed that certain inducements were received by the accountants to approve the accounts in the manner that they did.

From Watson's knowledge of the ongoing inquiries, he believed that the accountancy firm and some of its officers were criminally culpable. Also, the relevant audit papers used by the accountants were suspected to have been transferred to its solicitors and lawyers who were acting for them. Due to a variety of reasons and concerns, plus the fact that the solicitors acted in a number of capacities for officers of the accountancy firm, after consultations with the attorney general of the Cayman Islands and other deeply interested parties (like the DOJ in the USA and the Serious Fraud Office in London), it was determined that Watson would obtain search warrants for both the accountancy firm and the solicitors, plus a couple of individuals connected with the primary accountancy firm.

Watson then commenced inquiries involving the UK authorities and the Cayman attorney general to procure the evidence necessary to justify obtaining search warrants on the four entities and individuals identified. This was almost one year after the actions taken in July 1991 to obtain access and seizure of the bank and its subsequent management by the liquidators. A sworn information was prepared by Watson and taken on a Wednesday morning to the court to swear out the warrants before the chief magistrate to be used to effect entry to the various places and take possession of documents relating to the same and responsive to those items set out in the search warrants. That same afternoon, Watson held a briefing with a team brought together regarding the execution of the warrants the following day. Eleven officers were at the meeting, and an outline of the actions to be taken the following day was provided to them. They were all told that the matter was extremely sensitive and not to be discussed with anyone. A member of the UK Serious Fraud Office who happened to be on island was also present during the briefing. The US Department of Justice was also put on notice regarding the same. Watson had split the personnel into the appropriate teams and highlighted the searches and in what order they should be made. Leaders were assigned to each group, and the search documents to record the collection of documents were also provided to the teams. They were all told by Watson to report for duty the following morning at 5:40 a.m. and collect radios to enable contact between the groups and also provision of police vehicles to be used. One officer, PC Robert Oaks, was loaned from the uniform police department, and he was instructed by Watson to establish a command post in the Tower Building CCB offices and to log all calls, phone messages, and others he'd receive contemporaneously regarding the ongoing actions. That same officer was also to be responsible for the ultimate safe custody and control of any and all documents seized—a vital job where thousands of documents might be seized. A provisional arrangement was also made for a medium-sized van to be available if necessary for the conveyance of documents seized, as Watson suspected there could be many documents that would be seized and conveyed in police custody, which would require a van rather than the usual police cars that might be totally inadequate.

During the preparation period and bearing in mind that one of the most prestigious law firms, and the most expensive, on the island was being slated to be searched, Watson—along with other top members of the inquiry team—decided to put together a draft affidavit for Watson to swear out in the event that upon execution of the warrants at the law firm and also the accountancy firm, either of them went to court in the Cayman Islands in an effort to obtain an injunction to try to stop the warrants being executed. Watson's and the team's suspicions that this might happen were not misplaced as could be seen upon their arrival at the law firm. The affidavit drafted contained a lot of evidence and supporting theories to indicate the potential criminal misdoings of the accountancy firm and, in specific circumstances, misdeeds involving two of the persons primarily responsible for the audits. During inquiries in the London area, it was discovered that two auditors who had given the bank a clean bill of health before its collapse had been provided with prostitutes paid for by certain officers of the bank during some of their business visits to London. At the time, the two accountants were in charge of auditing one of the bank's primary subsidiaries, its Cayman Islands operations.

At 5:40 a.m. the next day, the teams met at the Tower Building; and following a further short briefing, together with the establishment of the control room by PC Oaks, and radio checks made, the teams went on their way. The two teams went to the private homes of the two individuals and completed searches there. A few documents and photographs were recovered at the property Watson and his team searched but not the amount of evidence that Watson had been expecting. Following on from this, Watson went to the other house that was being searched; and as in his case, not much of evidentiary value had been found there. Subsequent to these two searches, the teams went back to the Tower Building and logged in the evidence recovered from the two addresses before embarking on their further searches of the two targeted business premises. Timing was of the essence now because the parties being searched would now know that the police had already executed two of the search warrants at private residences.

Watson and his team went on their way to the solicitor's offices situated on two complete floors in a local business office in downtown George Town. The other search team went to the accountancy firm in another part of George Town a stone's throw away. At the solicitor's office, Watson, after introducing himself, was escorted into a conference room, while the other team members protected the doors to stop anyone or anything leaving. One or two minutes later, some of the senior lawyers at the firm entered along with a lady. Watson showed them the search warrant and told them the matters it referred to and how it would be executed. The lawyers, led by one member who was a senior member of the staff and would later become a QC (Queen's Counsel), expressed severe concern over the same, and following a discussion, the lawyers left the room. They had told Watson that they vehemently opposed the warrant and would not allow him to search. Watson explained that if that were the case, he would have all the staff removed from the office and search the offices until sundown, a peculiar part of the Caymanian law at that time. If the police were not finished by that time, Watson explained that they would padlock the doors, leave a police officer on guard overnight, and come back at sunrise the following day to continue the search. This would continue until the search was completed, and no one would be there to answer any or all phone calls that the firm constantly received on a daily basis. Watson explained that they should also consider that aspect, being out of touch with their clients while the search continued.

Watson's fellow officers were still positioned so that they could observe the primary lawyer's office, as Watson had received hard and corroborated information indicating that the bulk of the documents Watson was searching for were all held in cabinets in that primary lawyer's office. Consequently, Watson wanted to ensure that they were protected prior to and before any seizure. While the lawyers were out of the office, Watson learned that some of the junior lawyers had been sent to the court's office, which was directly across the road from the lawyers' offices in an attempt—he suspected—to obtain an injunction to curtail the search. Watson did not know at the time whether an injunction had been obtained. The lawyers duly returned and stated that they had agreed to provide the documents being sought and as set out in the search warrant. They then added that they wanted Watson to know that he would be searching against their will and taking the documents without their authority. Watson smiled to himself at this statement before responding, "Well, I have a search warrant issued by a court of jurisdiction to search for and seize these specified documents. I am sorry, but I really don't think I need your will to search or authority to seize documents responsive to the warrant!" Watson noted that this did not seem to go down too well with the lawyers, but perhaps these high-priced commercial lawyers did not understand the more mundane and simple meanings of a search warrant obtained in pursuance of criminal matters. Watson felt quite sure that they had never had a search warrant executed at their offices before. They seemed rather offended by the process.

The team then commenced a full search of the offices in the presence, at all times, of one of the less-senior lawyers. Apparently, Watson confirmed that the junior lawyers had also been across at the courthouse trying to get an injunction to stop the search. A copy of the injunction sought was duly provided to Watson, but it was never enforced. Watson never knew the reason or understood why it hadn't but suspected that it might have been that the opposing lawyers had been given a copy of the draft affidavit that was prepared in possible response, and Watson knew that that contained some very damning and possibly embarrassing information. That might have exercised the lawyers' minds and determined them not to enforce the injunction. The search was duly completed some four hours or so later, and the search team had filled by that time thirty-seven large Bankers

Boxes with documents applicable to those specified in the search warrant. The van that had been called into action during the search was loaded by the search team and taken back to the Tower Building, where the documents were duly unloaded, logged, and secured.

Early on during the search at the lawyers' office, Watson had a radio call from the team leader searching the accountancy office to state that the person in charge there was refusing to let them in. Watson stated to the team leader, "But you have a search warrant. Use the strength of it to enter and execute upon it." The response was that notwithstanding the warrant, the person in charge was refusing them access. Watson asked if the person in charge at the accountancy firm was within earshot of the radio, which was shortly thereafter answered in the affirmative. Watson then said, "Tell the kind gentleman that you have a search warrant and to let you in. If not, I will immediately come over to the premises and force entry as permitted by the warrant. I would, if necessary, break their lovely large glass doors to gain entrance and execute the search warrant. Do you need me to come over?"

There was a slight pause in the conversation, and the search team leader at the accountants' responded by saying, "Okay, sir. We are in now and will proceed accordingly." The accountant in charge had had obvious concerns as to how he was going to explain to his senior partners the glass entrance doors—and large and expensive ones at that—being broken and off their hinges!

Following completion of the search at the law offices, Watson's search team then visited an off-site storage unit held by the lawyers that was used for the accountants' documents, but nothing in there was found to be relevant to the current inquiry. It was at this time that Watson was informed that another area had been rented quite recently by the lawyers to secure documents specifically relating to the accountancy firm and the actions being taken. This information was passed to the search team at the accountants' office, and it was received from an accountant that Watson trusted, and the information was previously unknown to the search teams. The premises being used were an older bank building in George Town; the former occupant, a banking corporation, had previously been placed into liquidation. Watson immediately made his way there and again met, on-site, the primary lawyer and a colleague of his in the case. Watson's intention in going there was to secure all those documents under the terms of the search warrant. Watson confronted the primary lawyer and asked him why he had not disclosed the existence of this store of documents to him during the duration of the search at the lawyer's office. The lawyer responded that it was not for him to tell Watson where to search. Watson said the accountancy firm had felt obliged to disclose this to the police, bearing in mind how the search warrant was worded, and that it should have been disclosed immediately so that there could be no allegations or suggestions of documents being tampered with. Watson told the lawyer he regarded the circumstances as very suspicious. Another two four-drawer filing cabinets full of relevant documents and a number of Bankers Boxes were removed from this building and taken back to the Tower Building over the next seventy minutes or so. Watson was not very pleased over the primary lawyer's stance and wondered whether or not an allegation of obstructing the police in the lawful execution of their duty could be laid against him. He thought perhaps he should arrest the lawyer. However, as the fourteen hours plus grueling day worked by the detectives was coming to an end, Watson decided to allow discretion to be the better part of valor and retained this thought to ferment in the back of his mind for the current time.

The following day, Watson spent most of his time in meetings with the attorney general together with the lawyers acting for the accountancy firm and also members of the Cayman government Crown Counsel's office. The concerns revolved around the issue of legal privilege concerning the documents taken from the possession of the lawyers, an issue that had originally been raised at the time of seizure of the documents. To satisfy this claim, Watson had originally agreed during the search that when the documents were seized and privilege issues were raised, he had ordered that the police officers secure the appropriate boxes with police evidence tape and the documents would not be reviewed further until such time as the issue had been determined by a court or an agreement between the parties mentioned in the case. These primary concerns were overcome in the next few days following welcomed cooperation between the involved parties.

Following the meeting with the attorney general, the lawyers from the law firm that Watson searched asked for a private meeting with Watson to go over some administrative matters. Watson agreed, and the AG's secretary, who was a lovely and most pleasant and capable Caymanian lady who always tried to accommodate Watson in any action or help he needed, immediately made an adjacent conference room available to him. Once in the room, the primary lawyer, without hesitation and in a brusque manner, told Watson that they considered it very unreasonable for the police to search a lawyer's office. Watson was not the least impressed by this and reminded them that that was predicated upon actions they themselves had taken over the preceding twelve months or so and that the law of the country allowed for the police to seek and obtain search warrants in such circumstances as and when necessary. They then complained that Watson had not acted reasonably because the police had searched their client's office, the accountancy firm, simultaneously. Watson reminded the lawyer that following his request during their initial meeting prior to the searches, Watson had delayed the accountancy office search by some thirty minutes, which had then been extended to one hour to facilitate legal representation to be available at the accountancy offices. Watson informed the lawyers that generally in such cases in the UK, all the searches would have been completed simultaneously. Having regard to representation of their client, Watson stated and again reminded them he had been sympathetic to their request in delaying the search by thirty minutes, which had, in fact, stretched to almost an hour. The lawyers then asked for Watson to return the documents taken from the liquidated bank building, as they were purely a reflection of the originals taken from the law firm. Watson said that could not happen until the privilege claims had been first resolved and the documents then compared to ensure that they were copies, as they had intimated. He also stated that far more documents had been recovered from the law offices than the bank building. The lawyer then asked Watson if he would accept his word as a lawyer that they were a reflection, to which Watson responded by saying yes but that he wanted to satisfy himself. The other lawyer then argued that Watson should accept his word as a lawyer, but Watson understandably maintained his ground but was becoming somewhat irritated. Finally, the lawyers argued that they should have a person present at any time the documents were examined, but Watson did not agree to this point. The primary lawyer became quite irate and stated they had these rights, as they were their documents. Watson was becoming quite frustrated ***but remained*** very placid on the exterior, having come to the meeting on the grounds of wanting to discuss administrative matters and yet he was being berated with this nonsense. He stated to them that he could not understand why they had not brought these matters up during the meeting with the attorney general, as the points they raised were far more than just normal run-of-the-mill administrative matters. Neither of the lawyers responded to that comment, and each of the parties went their separate ways, Watson immensely more satisfied than the lawyers. Watson spent further time that day with the attorney general, updating him on the ambush held of himself by the lawyers. Even the AG could not understand why those matters had not been raised during the prior meeting with the AG.

Another matter of utmost concern to Watson was related to the safe storage of the voluminous documents seized during the execution of the search warrants, and accordingly, the police secured a separate vacant office in a nearby building where metal storage racks were installed, and the room was duly protected with a most secure burglar alarm system. It was only by entering a security code accessible solely to Watson and PC Oaks, who was the officer designated to have the primary custody and control of the same. The documents totaled easily in excess of six hundred thousand, and the usual evidentiary systems that were used in the police, especially in Cayman, were not structured for anywhere near that number of documents. Watson knew it was imperative in this case to document the evidence from the point of seizure and on and above until such time as any and all trials and inquiries were completed and the documents could be properly returned to the owners. PC Oaks also had to control who had access to the documents for examination purposes and log both the times and dates they had access to the documents and what documents they reviewed. Watson knew that custody and control of the same were paramount together with showing a full chain of custody throughout the time the police had possession of them, from seizure to whenever. PC Oaks devised a system that he maintained on a day-to-day basis that showed everything that had happened to the documents and who had access to the same and when. Watson gave much credit to Oaks for the system he implemented and the way in which he meticulously and, with no small amount of good humor, recorded everything pertaining to the same. It truly stood the test of time during the period in which it was used, and never did any valid problem arise regarding the custody and control of any of the documents.

Following this execution of search warrants in the matter and especially executing them on the prestigious law firm, Watson was often stopped in the street or in the courthouse by other lawyers from large island practices and sometimes single-person practices and con-gratulated on the job the CCB did. The other lawyers thought that the prestigious law firm regarded themselves as above the law, and consequently, the actions taken engendered—as the locals would say—"much street cred" for Watson and his team. Not much love was apparently lost for the law firm from other practitioners on the island. Up until Watson's retirement from the police department in Cayman and the UK, other lawyers would often stop him, some-times in the streets or at a local hostelry, and speak to him about the day "he rattled the cages" of the prestigious law firm! It was some time after the raids had taken place on the law firm that they moved slightly out of town to some brand-new offices. Watson, who met one of the partners at a social function not long after they moved offices, was invited to come along and see their new offices so he could make a plan of the new accommodation and thereby save time next time he executed any warrants there! Watson did visit at some time shortly thereafter, and the new offices were indeed sumptuous. But during his tenure, Watson, unfortunately in his mind, never had to execute another search warrant at that law firm!

One further matter involving Watson particularly came to mind during the inquiries conducted by various offshore authorities in the Cayman Islands into the bank in question. The matter in question involved teams from the Department of Justice in the USA and other agencies, usually consisting of eight to ten people, who came to Cayman for extended periods gathering evidence for the various cases being pursued in the USA and the UK, using the documents retrieved from the searches in 1992 and also those obtained and held by the liquidators when the bank was closed in July 1991 as their main source.

Watson was greeted by some of the visiting staff one morning during his usual daily visits to their workspace, for one reason or another. A senior member of the team took Watson to one side and reported that a laptop computer they had been using to compile various information and spreadsheets had been stolen the previous evening from their hotel on Seven Mile Beach while they were out of the hotel getting sustenance from one of the excellent Caymanian restaurants. The details and information contained on the laptop was obviously extremely sensitive information, although they assured Watson that it was all highly secured by passwords. Watson, at their request, immediately agreed to make pertinent inquiries regarding the same and recruited DC Rowell to help him. DC Rowell was an enthusiastic, good-on-the-ground young investigator who, by being born in Cayman, had numerous sources he could tap into in an effort to identify and recover the stolen laptop. He was the ideal type of detective to assist in such a matter. Watson briefed Rowell on the same and the need for everything to be completed on a strictly confidential basis. Inquiries made by Rowell and Watson at the hotel used by the officials and research through the electronic key door opening system utilized there showed that the room in question had been opened when the staff returned from work for the day and then locked again a short while later while they went to dinner. It was not opened again until such time when the occupants returned later that evening and they opened the door with their electronic key. This raised a big question in Watson's mind regarding the scene of the theft previously described to him, but he said nothing at this time.

DC Rowell then went out into the community and started asking questions of a number of good sources and informants that he had, including a number of well-known opportunistic criminals, to try to identify who had taken the laptop. *This is just how it used to be in the UK,* Watson thought—pounding the pavements and wearing out shoe leather in an attempt to surface leads and useful evidence. Within a matter of a few hours, Rowell informed Watson that the following day, one of his informants would be coming to the office to meet with Watson. In the interim, Watson met with the head of the party from offshore and informed them that there might be a break in the search for the missing laptop. They were delighted, but Watson still did not mention the alleged scene of the theft—he still remembered that problem!

The following day, Watson and Rowell met with the informant who indicated that he knew where the missing laptop might be. However, he was somewhat confused by the fact that the missing laptop had been allegedly stolen from the hotel and wondered whether or not he was speaking about the correct laptop. Watson's interest peaked upon hearing this information. The informant suggested that his information indicated that it was stolen from a rented Jeep Wrangler that had been parked near a restaurant on the night in question. It had been on open view in the rear of the Jeep. He believed that he could recover the same but wanted to know what might happen to the offenders. Watson informed him that the primary objective was to recover the laptop and the police would listen to anything the owners decided regarding a prosecution. The leader of the team had already suggested that all they wanted was to recover the laptop; they did not want any sort of prosecution possibly because of the embarrassment of having the laptop stolen. The informant did state that the thieves had been having great difficulty in gaining access to the computer, which was refreshing and, to a degree, gratifying for Watson and Rowell to hear. Suffice to say, the very next day, DC Rowell and Watson went to meet the informant, and the missing laptop was handed over to them. It was wrapped in cloth and obviously had been very well-cleaned! The informant stated and confirmed that the laptop had been stolen from the back of a Jeep Wrangler truck that was parked outside the restaurant where the team members had been for dinner. It certainly had not been stolen from the hotel.

Now armed with the laptop, Watson and Rowell subsequently handed the same over to the leader of the team, and to say that they were relieved that it had been found and effectively none of the information thereon had been seen or compromised would be an understatement. They were not so happy when Watson stated and scolded them that he believed they had misled the police and especially Watson and Rowell over the actual scene of the crime, and after some thought, the staff apologized most profusely and wanted to keep the incident as confined to themselves as possible. Watson duly arranged through the commissioner of police for a payment to be made to the informant for his assistance in the recovery of the same. His actions certainly prevented an extremely critical release of highly confidential information. Yet again, Watson saw through the actions of Rowell the benefits of operating in such a confined and small community as the Cayman Islands. Relationships were built and maintained over many years that could prove useful in the pursuit of justice for any and all matters in the fullness of time.

Watson, even after retirement from the police service, continued to regularly receive information regarding the liquidation of the bank. The liquidators sued the bank's auditors, and after a few years, the case was settled for a sum of $175,000,000 in favor of the liquidators. It was also reported that the liquidators recovered about seventy-five cents on the dollar for the creditors and account holders who had lost money. Also, in 1993, the liquidators had sued the Bank of England following evidence that had been received and also a report that had been compiled regarding the target bank. The amount they sued for was £1 billion. The grounds alleged for the action was that the Bank of England failed in its regulatory duties to protect investors. The Bank of England denied it had been willfully negligent in its supervisory duties. The case became notorious for the length of the same, the large number of witnesses who were called, and also the extraordinarily complex arguments that were proffered from both sides. Watson had a wry smile in November 2005 when the liquidators dropped the £1 billion lawsuit, and the final sting in the tail came in June 2006 when the Bank of England were awarded £73 million in legal costs against the liquidators. From the beginning, the case had been branded by some well-informed individuals as a farce, and the Bank of England had always denied it had been willfully negligent in the supervisory duties that were assigned to it.

CHAPTER 25

A Cruise Ship, Caribbean Wanderer, Mystery—Part Two

While faced with all the matters that came to light and emanated from the sudden closure of the international bank, Watson had never lost sight of the missing crew member from the *Caribbean Wanderer*. As serious as the dealings involving the bank were, Watson viewed the missing crewman as much more serious, on a personal level. During the inquiries with the bank, the matter concerning Heinrich had now come to a head, and it required some decisive actions taking place. Consequently, Watson worked extensively on the missing person inquiry while also balancing the matters of importance in the ongoing banking inquiry. His colleagues in the CCB helped in a most professional way to carry on with some of the never-ceasing bank inquiry workload.

Watson had now heard back from the German authorities regarding their trawl for information, and it was decided that Watson should travel to Germany and work with the police to see how Heinrich could be connected to Cayman and for what purpose. Heinrich Willenbrock apparently was not his correct name; it was an alias used by a native German named Heinrich Muller. Muller had been involved in a number of scams and drug-related offenses in Germany and was also thought to be heavily involved in supporting a large national drug ring that obtained its wares from South America and also through the Caribbean. Having said that, the German police had lost track of Heinrich, and he had dropped off their radar about six years previously. While the German police were still very interested in the drug cartel, Heinrich had fallen off their scope of inquiries; but if, as Watson was suggesting to them, he had amassed a fortune in the Caymans, this might explain a branch of the drug cartel that was previously unknown to them. Usually drug cartels would range from a very loose association of a few individuals to large and formalized criminal enterprises. This was what the German police were dealing with. Watson knew that a cartel would normally involve a hierarchal structure, beginning with the drug lords, responsible for every aspect of the industry, including appointing territorial leaders along with financiers and money launderers. Then came lieutenants who were responsible for ensuring the smooth operations in their area of distribution, followed by the hit men who were an armed group responsible for organizing hits, thefts, extortion and also operating protection rackets, followed finally by the falcons who were the eyes and ears of the streets and who ran various operations in specific areas. This final group was the lowest on the cartel totem pole but of great importance to the cartel. Other persons associated with any cartel, although not considered as part of the basic structure but more as subcontractors, would be the financiers, money launderers, together with drug producers and suppliers. Obviously, as a cartel business would rise, the business to these links of the drug chain would increase exponentially.

Watson, after briefing the detectives continuing to work on the bank fraud to ensure that they kept him up to date with any developments, duly traveled to Hamburg through Miami and Frankfurt before finally arriving to work with two Drug Squad detectives from the Hamburg State Police. They were first-class officers, and their knowledge of the various drug cartels operating in Hamburg, which was something of an epicenter for the drug trade in Europe, was second to none. When Watson met them, they had already positively identified Heinrich and also the fact that he maintained a number of bank accounts in different parts of Germany and possibly France. Watson had no doubt that when the Cayman bank records were provided to him, a number of the accounts in Germany would have been used to fund his Cayman account. Watson also discovered that Heinrich had been working for the drug cartel in the years before he joined the cruise lines, and one of his main jobs was dealing with the various in-country people who were supplied with drugs for distribution, and he was a main wheel in the financing of the same, along with bonuses paid to them for increased sales and the like. *He certainly seemed to fall into the description of a lieutenant,* Watson thought. It was just like a proper corporation and probably would explain the flush Cayman account that Watson knew he held. Heinrich had gone missing after law enforcement in Eastern Europe put pressure on the cartel there, and certain key members were duly spirited out of Germany as the screws tightened on the cartel. The German detectives originally strongly suspected that Heinrich had been eliminated by the cartel at that stage. Based on what the German police were now learning, the two detectives set up a meeting with a deep undercover officer who was working at a reasonably high level within the cartel. For added protection for the UC Officer, Watson was not invited to the meeting, but the local detectives fully briefed the UC on the affair in Cayman, and the UC officer said he would use the information to try to corroborate that Heinrich was still connected with and working for the cartel, albeit under a different surname and in the guise of a server on a cruise ship. He would also, as far as he could research the Cayman-registered entity Munich Enterprises Ltd., and attempt to discover if there was any documentary connection with that, but he did caution that that might not be possible with the sort of access he had. Lastly, he was also tasked to see if there was any way in which he could identify the individuals in Cayman, if such existed, who were facilitating and driving the business there. All the officers felt that this might be an opportunity, if handled correctly and in a timely manner, to destroy a big part of the cartel and thereby the supply chain in Germany and other parts of the world. Watson felt the complete trip had been well worth the visit in trying to put together an overall picture of what was happening.

The next day, Watson met with the officers and some of their colleagues and then had a tasty lunch at a local bierkeller! The officers stated that they had a surprise for Watson, and they asked the question, "Have you ever flown in a police helicopter before?" Watson stated that he had not, and in the Caymans, he hadn't even seen one! After lunch, they drove him to a local *flughafen* (airport). They went out onto the tarmac where a four-seater helicopter, emblazoned with police insignia, was waiting. The pilot, wearing a police flight uniform, and the copilot were waiting for Watson. Watson was introduced to them, and he discovered that the pilot had originally served in the Luftwaffe for twenty-eight years before he joined the police and now served as a helicopter pilot. The second officer was rather younger but had been trained initially also in the Luftwaffe. This gave Watson some degree of comfort. Apparently, they told their colleagues they would be back in about one hour. Watson was seated in the rear seats, behind the pilot and the copilot. They provided him with some headphones so that he could speak with them and also listen to their contacts with the air traffic control. That really didn't help, as everything was done in German language. Watson also noted that behind the pilots, there was a bank of weapons—including rifles, handguns, shotguns—and other incendiary devices in some well-constructed and secure racks. Watson's initial reaction to this was that there were enough armaments there to support a small uprising on a Caribbean island!

They took off and rose quickly to an altitude of about 3,000 to 3,500 feet, and this gave Watson an overview of the city of Hamburg, which looked spectacular from that height. The flight took them over the large Elbe River, which was situated in the city, and then they flew toward the Alster Lakes and its two tributaries, the River Alster and the River Bille. Next they saw the vast Port of Hamburg, which was the biggest seaport in Germany and probably rated very highly in the world. It was mesmerizing to Watson to see the sights below him. They then flew following the flow of the Elbe River toward the North Sea. A large tanker of some sort was slowly wending its way up the Elbe River toward the Port of Hamburg, which got the attention of the helicopter crew. The pilot took the helicopter down and noticed that some of the hatches on the ship were open, and under local ordinance, they should have been tightly closed. The pilot got on the radio and connected with the tanker and its captain. In a stern and straightforward manner, he told them to close the hatches or they would face serious prosecution. Watson could not understand what message came back from the ship, but suffice to say, quite a few men were seen to emerge onto the decks and started scurrying around on the tanker. The hatches were being closed in very short order. *There is no doubt*, Watson thought, *that they got the message— loud and clear.* Watson was then treated to more views of the Elbe before they landed on a small island in the North Sea, near where the Elbe flowed into the North Sea. A small package was delivered by the second officer to an individual there, and then the helicopter was quickly back in the air. During the flight back toward the airport, the pilot asked Watson if he felt okay. Watson replied in the affirmative and said that he was enjoying the ride very much. The pilot said, "That is good. I will now show you what the helicopter can do!" Watson noticed they were traveling above a heavily wooded area, and the altitude was showing about 3,500 feet.

What happened next got Watson's attention in a heartbeat or perhaps two. The plane dropped like a stone from 3,500 feet to perhaps about thirty or forty feet above the ground—Watson had no idea, as his stomach was still following him from the 3,500 feet. There was a grass road-type clearing between the densely planted trees that was in a direct straight line. As the helicopter reached thirty to forty feet altitude, it was then flown by the pilot at about 120 knots in a direct line between the trees. Watson's stomach had still not caught up with him! After flying like that for a short while, the pilot put the nose of the helicopter up and quickly gained altitude. Watson was now feeling somewhat queasy, which was only increased as the pilot almost totally rolled the helicopter into an inverted position. He quickly put the craft back into normal straight-line flight and asked Watson how he felt. Watson, who did not know or understand helicopters could fly in such a manner, responded asking if the pilot had a bag on board, and the pilot directed him to bags in the back of the copilot's seat. Watson quickly regurgitated his lunch but felt much better afterward and then enjoyed the rest of the flight back to the airport. He was sure that the pilot and the copilot had broad smiles on their faces. Upon landing at the Flughafen, the pilot got out of the aircraft and helped Watson deplane. He then gave a thumbs-up to his police colleagues who were waiting for Watson, which indicated to them that Watson had thrown up during the flight. Apparently, a bet had been laid beforehand, and the pilot had collected on the bet! Notwithstanding the slight problem, Watson had thoroughly enjoyed the flight, seen lots of Hamburg, and thanked everyone for giving him the wonderful opportunity.

The very next day, Watson duly returned home to Cayman in a much more sedate flying style to update the team on a need-to-know basis and see where else the inquiry might have been taking them during his absence.

One of the members of the house-to-house teams, a young woman constable, after a few days beating the streets and houses in West Bay, quickly reported back to Watson, as she had been briefed to do. She had visited an older property in West Bay and met a woman there who, unusually for followers of the practice, followed and declared her affinity to Santeria, a religion that offered living animals, such as goats or chickens, as a sacrifice in one ceremony. Watson was perplexed. Yet again, Northern England was missing out on another practice; and Watson thought if they sacrificed living animals in Northern England, they would usually eat them. Watson discovered that Santeria (the Way of the Saints) was an Afro-Caribbean religion based on Yoruba beliefs and traditions, with some Roman Catholic elements added. Santeria had originated in Cuba and, over the years, had become a religion in its own rights and a powerful symbol of the religious creativity of Afro-Cuban culture. Although the center of the religion is Cuba, it had apparently spread to the USA and other nearby countries, particularly after the Cuban Revolution in 1959. For many years, it was a secretive underground religion, but it was becoming increasingly visible in the Americas and the Caribbean, attracting a following among middle-class professionals, including white, black, and Asian Americans. Watson learned that it was difficult to know how many people follow Santeria, as there was no central organization, and the religion was often practiced in private. However, some well-placed resources estimated that there were as high as a hundred million Santeria believers and followers worldwide. Watson had listened intently to all he had been told and asked, "How can this be connected to our case?" The woman constable said that a day or two earlier, the potential witness had been in a local restaurant near the entrance to West Bay when she had seen a local woman, whom she knew was also a follower of Santeria, dining with two younger men, both Caymanians she thought, and one had some scratches visible on his face and neck. They were also speaking to the woman about some new jewelry that they had just acquired. Watson pricked his ears up at this, as the police had not issued any press release or information regarding the tennis bracelet that Heinrich had acquired. Watson asked the constable if she thought she could persuade the lady to come with her and speak to Watson to see what evidence could be properly gained and documented from her. The policewoman stated that she thought the woman would happily come with her, but if not, she would tell her that DCI Watson would come to see her, no ifs or buts, and she could assure her she didn't want the DCI coming to see her. Watson liked the policewoman's style. The woman had asked for total anonymity, which the police lady had promised.

The witness was brought in by the woman constable, and Watson could see that the constable had already established a good relationship with the woman. Accordingly, he told the constable, "If and when needed, please feel free to interrupt or interject if you feel the woman needs comfort, reassurance, or support from you." The witness happily recounted to Watson what she had already told the constable, and Watson extracted more details on the two men she had seen with her Santeria friend. Since the original meeting, she had been doing her own digging around and believed that the two men worked together at a diving school and dinghy rental place on the north end of Seven Mile Beach. The woman constable suggested the name of the diving school and rental place and said she had a relative who worked there; she was willing to approach him in the strictest secrecy and see what she could find out, if Watson wanted her to. Watson was delighted for that to happen but first instructed her to take a full and complete witness statement off the witness and then drive her home and tell her to do nothing further. Watson would try to keep her name out of it.

Watson had received the records of Heinrich's bank account in the Cayman Islands, and sure enough, they showed large sums of money deposited from a number of banks in Germany and even more in France, plus one or two deposits from the USA, Antigua, St. Bart's, and Anguilla. This had been going on over some four to five years. Withdrawals were often made, and looking at the records of Heinrich's visits to Cayman courtesy of the *Caribbean Wanderer*, they often coincided with his visits. Heinrich also had a credit card issued by the bank that he had used throughout the world, and the outstanding balances held each month on the card was paid off by money being automatically transferred from his bank account in Cayman to satisfy the same. Watson decided to get a forensic accounting analysis completed of the account(s) over the life span of them, and he would then send those details to the detectives in Germany to research further. The German police confirmed that Heinrich had vanished from Germany about four to five years ago, having lived at various addresses in Hamburg. He did not currently have or apparently own any property in Germany that the police could determine. In Watson's absence, the teams working on the house to house had also researched other possible assets or wealth of Heinrich on the island. They had discovered that Heinrich apparently owned a two-bedroom condominium at Villas Pappagallo, which had been built in 1986 or '87. Heinrich had bought the property in 1987 and appeared to have paid cash for it, around $350,000. He also, on a fairly regular basis, had used the Ristorante Pappagallo, which was nearby, both for meals in-house and also takeouts. Inquiries made at the Villas showed Heinrich had not been seen for many months, but his yearly fees and the like were consistently paid from an associated bank account established and held in Germany. Under the authority of a search warrant, his apartment was searched; but other than usual day-to-day items, nothing of any probative value was found.

Another interesting result that came from the house-to-house inquiries in West Bay also indicated that an elderly female resident in the area since birth, who lived near some dense vegetation on the coast and near the Boatswain Bay area, on the late afternoon that Heinrich had gone missing, had heard some loud men's voices and then a few screams before the order of the area was quickly restored. She thought nothing of it at the time, as the area was used by young men and women who, in her words, "got up to all sorts of nonsense there, and none of it good." She had heard of Heinrich going missing but never thought for a minute that anything like that would happen or be connected to West Bay since he went missing near the port terminal in George Town. When Watson saw this information, he immediately, along with the other senior officers, put together a team to search the area near the resident's home. The area was marked off in quadrants to be searched, and step by step, in pretty harsh conditions, the search took place. It was about seven hours or so into the search when one of the search parties found a small aluminum watercraft, with an outboard motor attached, some one hundred yards from the beach and pulled over the beach into the densely wooded area. It looked in fairly good shape and quite clean, but on closer examination using a chemical luminol, traces of a number of small areas of blood spatter were discovered. Luminol was frequently used as a searching or enhancement method at a crime scene. The primary test was based on the ability of the luminol molecule to be oxidized by the reaction of sodium perborate with an oxidizing agent such as hemoglobin. Watson thought this was progress, but of course, at this time, no one knew whose or what blood was being indicated—perhaps it was a yellowfin tuna, a swordfish, or perhaps Heinrich? Watson made the decision to secure the boat for forensic examination at the Central Police Station. This caused many problems for the police charged with preserving and recovering the boat from where it was found, but to their credit, it was eventually protected, secured, and removed from the dense undergrowth. The boat turned out to have been owned by another resident of West Bay who lived about four hundred yards from where it was found. The resident believed that it had been stolen or borrowed on the day before or the same day that Heinrich was reported missing, but the resident, for some reason, had not yet reported it! Apparently, friends in the area would often borrow his craft without any authority from him to do so. *How strange,* Watson thought. He was sure friends would replace it back attached to the buoy in Boatswain Bay, not drag it into dense undergrowth and trees.

Watson and the team, who had been updated on the progress, decided to wait before doing anything further until the identity of the two men whom the woman constable was investigating had been determined. Watson called her, and she confirmed that the inquiry had been placed and that she was just waiting for a response from her relative. She stated she would get back to Watson within forty-eight hours. She did. She identified the two men, but Watson thought he had to wait until further information was received regarding the evidence that the boat was providing. Watson did take the precaution of putting the two suspects on the stop list at the immigration department to ensure that they did not leave the island prior to the determination of the ongoing various tests and inquiries. It had been established that the traces of blood identified had been confirmed to be a human's, but the investigators were still awaiting corroboration of any sort linking it to Heinrich. They had also found some fingerprints on the boat that appeared recent and were running them through various databases to try to get a match. Watson asked the woman constable to run the two men's names in the local crime index, which she did, and one came back with a hit for a petty theft a year or so earlier. Watson then asked the Fingerprint Department to run the prints off the boat with those on record in Cayman for petty theft. Based on the mounting pressure to resolve the matter and find out what happened to Heinrich, an operation was put together to arrest the two men simultaneously and see how they would explain some of the links discovered and where the interviews might take them. Watson also spoke to his friends in the Drug Squad and asked them, on a confidential basis, to dig around among the drug fraternity in West Bay and see what they could dig up on the two individuals. The inquiries that were completed bore fruit and suggested that they were both well-known by some people of a similar ilk in West Bay as primary distributors of certain drugs in Cayman.

They were both duly arrested, and their homes and workplace in West Bay were thoroughly searched. Much evidence was recovered from the homes, including some clothing at one that showed what appeared to be slight blood traces. Photographs were taken of the head and neck plus arms of both the prisoners. One had scratches that were almost fully recovered and healed, just scars remained. Also, there was a lot of financial evidence showing income far more than their day jobs at the beach would be reasonably expected to provide. Evidence also confirmed that the day after Heinrich had withdrawn money in Cayman, they had deposited substantial amounts in their separate accounts immediately afterward. The link between Heinrich and the men was appearing to draw ever closer. When asked about meeting him on the day in question, they said the name meant nothing to them. When asked about the boat that had been recovered, it seemed to shake them, and it sure as hell, from their body language, gave them things to think about. The evidence of the blood found in the boat possibly being connected to Heinrich caused them further apparent distress, and when Watson introduced the information received from drug informants in West Bay about the two of them running the operation in the Caymans, they were seen to be weakening and wondering to themselves how they were going to talk their way out of this. The final straw that broke the camel's back with them was when Watson introduced evidence of one of their fingerprints being found on the boat, and he also asked what would the result of the blood analysis on the clothing found during the searches be. It was not long thereafter that one gave a voluntary statement first, closely followed by the other person, admitting their involvement in the whole affair. They made the suggestion that Heinrich was a controller of theirs and that he helped them regarding ensuring product availability of the drugs and also financing and payments regarding the same. If they got lax in their duties of providing the drugs or failing to ensure their market was properly supported, Heinrich would contact them and, in their words, "blast them out." He was a person they described as a hard-task master who demanded subservience but one who would reward them appropriately.

On the day of his disappearance, they had met with him in West Bay and went, in their vehicle, to a secluded beach near Boatswain Bay. They were expecting an update from Heinrich on the drug business being conducted in Grand Cayman and Cayman Brac, but the first thing he told them was he had no money available for them that day as the drug lord was concerned over the diminishing market in Cayman. They got into an argument with Heinrich over the position in Cayman, and Heinrich told them he wasn't there to argue and that if they wanted to withdraw from the operation, he would look elsewhere for the proper and consistent support he required and cut the two of them out of the market, plus the local police might be provided with some evidence showing their local involvement over the past few years in the trafficking. Heinrich made a mistake in talking to them when he mentioned the amounts of money they had been provided with over the years. The only problem was that the amounts he quoted them were what they should have had. Unbeknown to them and his cartel seniors, Heinrich had been creaming off at least 50 percent of their payments for a considerable time and keeping it for himself. When the Caymanians realized this and bearing in mind his threat to tell the police and set them up, they both became enraged to the point of losing control. The younger man had taken hold of Heinrich and was hitting out at him with both force and anger. Heinrich tried to fight back and clawed wildly at him, which caused the scars that the witness had mentioned, which were now almost healed. Both persons then continued to assault Heinrich in a vicious attack, and they stated that during the fight, he fell and struck his head on some large boulders nearby on the seashore. They then hit Heinrich further on the head with some nearby stones, and they suspected that that had broken his skull, and he started bleeding profusely. They had seen a small watercraft nearby, and they quickly brought the craft ashore and loaded a by-now unconscious Heinrich into the boat. They started the boat's outboard motor and took Heinrich about one hundred yards beyond the eight-thousand-foot drop-off on the northside of Cayman. He appeared by then, they stated, to have succumbed to his terrible injuries. They lifted the body over the edge of the boat and slowly but deliberately slit open his stomach with a sharp hunting knife they possessed before dropping the body into the water, loaded down with a couple of the heavy rocks from the shore to ensure he did not reappear. As local residents and fishermen, they knew full well that the blood and guts from his injuries would quickly attract predators in the water for a quick fresh meal. After dropping him in the water, they made their way ashore further up the coastline, brought the boat ashore, and dragged it across the sand and into the woods and nearby dense undergrowth. They obtained some basic cleaning materials from home, which was not far away, and cleaned the boat to the best of their abilities. Watson asked what they had done with Heinrich's blue rucksack. After taking the money out of it and a couple books, plus the tennis bracelet, they had put a rock in it and thrown it into the sea at the place where they disposed Heinrich's body. Both of the men stated that they also threw into the deep water the knife that had been used to slit open Heinrich's stomach. They had kept some of the cash, and some had been banked. They had used the cash over the next few days, and then they spent the time doing their usual jobs but otherwise laying low, wondering what might happen regarding the drug business and how they were going to keep their customers satisfied. Also, what would Heinrich's drug employers do when Heinrich had suddenly vanished? Would they come to Cayman looking for him and them? They knew he would be certainly missed on the cruise ship. The tennis bracelet had earlier been given to a young American lady who worked at the diving and surfing center where the two men worked.

Watson, upon the police finding the boat, spoke with local fishermen and determined where they thought the body might have been dropped in the water so as not to yield any evidence. Most of them identified a place nearby where the depth of the drop-off and the currents would almost ensure the body would never be found. Watson also arranged for a search to be made of the area near Boatswain Bay to see if any trace of blood could be find on the rocks there, but there was no such luck; the search came back negative.

Watson contacted the woman constable again, and at his request, she and another police constable went to the diving school and dinghy rental place and saw the young American lady who had been given the tennis bracelet. She was visibly stunned by what the woman constable told her but confirmed that she had been given the bracelet by the younger of the two men whom she stated had aspirations on dating her and having a sexual relationship with her. Eventually she voluntarily agreed to take the woman constable to her apartment where she handed over the tennis bracelet, still in the very distinctive Kirk Freeport box and bag. A statement was then taken from her by the woman constable setting out in total the circumstances by which she had become the temporary holder of the bracelet. The girl further voluntarily agreed to remain on the island until the case was fully finalized, and to this end, she surrendered her passport temporarily to the police constable.

Watson and his team were feeling fairly good about the case now being built regarding Heinrich's disappearance but, in an effort to further collect persuasive evidence, discussed other potential ways by which any remaining evidence might be found to definitively answer many questions they still had.

There was a business in Grand Cayman at the time called Research Submersibles that had deployed many three-person submersibles in the Caribbean for deep-diving purposes for people who didn't scuba dive. The submersibles had originally been designed for use in the North Sea during the early days of offshore oil exploration there. Some of the senior officers approached the business and asked if they would kindly assist the police with an inquiry by allowing them to be a passenger on the submersible near the wall off Northwest Point and to see if anything could be found related to the suggestion that Heinrich's body had been disposed in that area. The business quickly came back and willingly agreed to help with the search. Watson, who was not in the least disappointed, and one of the other senior detectives were selected for the inquiry.

The front of the submersible was a clear dome, like a large bubble. Watson and his colleague sat immediately inside the bubble in a rather cramped space, and the pilot, one of Research Submersibles's older pilots sat behind them. It was like being on an airplane, as the pilot pointed out the sources of emergency air should it become necessary and also the means by which Watson or his colleague could operate the submersible to cause it to rise to the surface should it be necessary in an emergency. Watson thought this differed from an airplane in that he was sure the passengers wouldn't be invited to fly the plane in an emergency! They began the descent down the wall, and there were hundreds of plants and flora attached to the wall. And at one stage, a large moray eel watched as they slowly descended past him. A couple of turtles also swam alongside, wondering, *What the hell is that!* Behind the bubble, the curvature made everything look quite small; but if you maneuvered yourself to look through the area where the pilot was in the cone of the submersible, everything looked so much bigger. At about four hundred feet, the light was fading, but it was not dark. And when they reached about eight hundred feet, it was still not dark, but visibility was lessened greatly. The pilot turned on the lights on the outside of the submersible, and everything looked so different. Pure-white coral abounded, and there were many organisms growing in and on the coral and rocks. A number of fish passed their path, and some were almost transparent. The pilot was steering the submersible along the face of the wall while still descending, but there was absolutely nothing that stood out, although the whole experience was so interesting and exciting. They turned to go back along the wall and came up a few feet. Suddenly Watson and his colleague shouted "Stop!" in unison. Something of a mid-dark-blue color was snagged on some of the coral. The pilot stopped the submersible and slowly maneuvered it to face the wall while remaining about five feet away. Watson said, "They look like some mangled jeans." He turned to the pilot and asked if he could recover the item for them.

The pilot responded, "Watch and yee shall learn." Slowly but surely the craft edged toward the wall, and then a small arm emerged from the side of the submarine and grabbed the jeans. As they came away from the wall, there was a small cloud of debris and sand that fell away, but the jeans, or what remained of them, had been secured. The search continued along the wall for a little longer, but nothing else was found. The submersible then began its slow ascent to the surface, and both Watson and his colleague were feeling pretty happy and thought that the whole episode had been well worth the trouble. Watson noticed that at different depths on the wall, the underwater life varied as the amount of penetrating sunlight increased or decreased. It really was an education seeing this, and Watson was getting paid for it! Once back at the surface, the jeans that had been recovered were bagged and ready to be properly dried and prepared for forensic examination. Due thanks were proffered by Watson and his colleague to all the staff at Research Submersibles, and Watson made a note to ensure that the commissioner of police sent a nice letter of thanks and appreciation to the company for their valued assistance. It really had been a first-class experience and potentially yielded some good corroborating evidence.

Once on shore and back at the police station, after the jeans had been properly documented and dried by the scenes of crime officers, numerous photographs were taken of the jeans and sent by secure fax to the cruise line captain, who was at that time moored during a day stop in Aruba. The captain called Watson on the ship-to-shore phone connection, and Watson asked him that if the pictures were clear enough, could he kindly show them to Anneka ten Velden as soon as possible and see if she could recognize the jeans as the ones she had purchased in the recent past for Heinrich during a cruise stop in possibly Miami or Fort Lauderdale. Within two hours, a further call came from the captain to Watson, and the captain said that Anneka, upon viewing the photos, primarily from the embroidery displayed on the jeans, had recognized them as being identical to the jeans she had purchased for Heinrich in Miami. The captain also queried whether or not he could tell Anneka anything at this stage, but Watson asked him to tell her that the police would contact her in due course, probably the next time they visited Grand Cayman. This part of the inquiry was duly completed the next time the *Caribbean Wanderer* berthed in Grand Cayman, which was about three weeks later. Further evidence was then taken from Anneka, and following her viewing of the recovered jeans, an additional witness statement was completed regarding her purchase of and identification of the jeans. Following this interview, officers who were going to Miami on another inquiry visited the store where the jeans had been purchased and obtained evidence from the store identified by a receipt that Anneka still had of Anneka purchasing the jeans on the date she said she had, and also they provided a photograph of the same design of jeans that she had bought. All the embroidery was identical to those on the jeans that had been recovered from the drop-off.

Also, Watson and his team noticed that the jeans bore what appeared to be some bite marks, plus there was some distinctive tearing not readily associated with pulling them off the wall by the submersible. Accordingly, at Watson's request, the team then contacted the Oceanography and Marine Research Institute connected with the University of Miami and situated in the Florida Keys. They happily volunteered to examine the jeans and see if they could learn anything from the apparent bite marks thereon. The jeans were subsequently taken to the laboratory, and after review and examination by a number of marine and biological experts, their considered view was that the bite patterns on them were probably made by a tiger shark, possibly about nine feet or so in length. Tiger sharks were well-known to live along with a number of other species of shark in Caymanian waters and had been found at depths up to and including nine hundred feet in Cayman. The scientists stated that a human body dropping down the face of the drop-off toward eight thousand feet with the stomach slit open would quickly attract the attention of numerous predators, such as a tiger shark, and consequently, the body could be quickly ripped apart and devoured. This was all both persuasive and corroborative circumstantial evidence to confirm the sad and final disposal of Heinrich's body.

The interactions between the German police and Cayman continued, and following on from what had been learned in Cayman and also the history that was found from the forensic examination of Heinrich's financial affairs, the German and French Police executed numerous search warrants and made many arrests. Also, almost overnight, a large proportion of the cartel was closed down and put out of business. The drug lord was arrested and sentenced to many years in prison. Many of his close associates also suffered the same fate. The two drug distributors in Cayman were subsequently arrested and charged with an offense of murder, unlawful disposition of a body, and some drug distribution offenses. The murder charges were later reduced in court to charges of manslaughter. Watson had no doubt that the entire operation had seriously impacted the supply and distribution of illegal drugs into the islands for quite some time. The sad part was that as one operation left the island, invariably another one or more would fill the vacuum that had been created.

CHAPTER 26

A Trust Company—
Not to Be Trusted

In the late 1980s, a senior bank official, Barry Berridge, at a Swiss bank in the Cayman Islands came under suspicion and subsequent investigation by Detective Superintendent Goodley of the CCB following a complaint being received by the police from the family of an elderly construction builder who lived in Central Florida on the East Coast. The man had established previously an account at the Swiss bank in Cayman and had used it to save surplus funds he relocated over the years from the USA. The primary complaint was received following an attempt by the man's son, who was then managing the affairs for his father, to withdraw some funds and discovering that a substantial amount of money that the family believed was being held in the account was no longer there. The police commenced their investigations and took the required witness statements and documentary evidence, along with other persuasive evidence from the parties who were identified during the progress of the investigation. A substantial amount of the documentary evidence came under review by various handwriting experts to try to determine the authenticity or otherwise of various signatures and instructions allegedly provided to the bank. The total value of the thefts in question was about $200,000. Following the banker, Berridge, being interviewed by Superintendent Goodley and a criminal report being submitted to the Legal Department of the Caymanian government for consideration of prosecution, Berridge was charged, and a lengthy trial at the Grand Court in Cayman took place at the end of 1991. During the trial, the evidence and its presentation contained a lot of assumptions, and the defense lawyer used numerous tricks to try to help the banker. It led to both the prosecution and the judge being misled, and both came out with statements and assessments that were discriminatory against both Berridge and the defense lawyer. Following the evidence being presented and final speeches being made, the jury subsequently found Berridge guilty of ten of the criminal charges alleged. He was sentenced the following day on the tenth of December 1991 to a total of three years imprisonment. The sentences were of varying lengths, but all were ordered to run concurrently by the court.

The banker's defense lawyer, who was well-known to Watson, lodged a notice of appeal, and after what seemed an eternity, the matter came up before the Cayman Islands Court of Appeal. The grounds for the appeal were basically that because of this alleged and perceived discrimination the banker, Berridge had not received a fair trial, which was the cornerstone of the British judicial system. In the hearing of the matter, among other matters, a number of handwriting analysts had given evidence for each side, the prosecution and the defense. Some had said various signatures were not made by the owner of the assets, and others said the signatures were not made by the banker. It was suggested by the defense that the elderly owner of the assets had forgotten that he had made withdrawals. Because handwriting analysis was by no means an exact science, the Court of Appeal, in their wisdom, decided that the findings of guilt should be set aside, and this was consequently what happened. Watson did not know too much about the case, as it had been investigated by the superintendent, but he believed that there was more than prima facie evidence to show that the banker had indeed committed such egregious acts of dishonesty. Nonetheless, the Court of Appeal determined the matter differently, and the convictions were set aside.

Watson, by contrast, noted that after the banker's alleged actions came to light, he left the employ of the Swiss bank and established a duly registered and licensed trust company in the Cayman Islands styled CTC. He was the managing director and minority shareholder in CTC, which was incidentally duly liquidated after news of the banker's new acts of misfeasance broke. Watson started to receive complaints from various individuals who had placed investments and other assets under the control of CTC regarding their investments not being made available or, in some cases, missing. The company had first come to Watson's notice in late 1989 when Watson began receiving complaints from individuals and corporations concerning the MD's misuse of the trust company and the fiduciary duties, or lack thereof, that he owed to the trust clients.

After speaking with the Crown Counsel at the Legal Department, Watson, aided by some of his officers in the CCB, commenced inquiries worldwide to trace and identify a number of potential complainants and obtain the necessary evidence to put together a case against the managing director, Berridge, of CTC, the disgraced former banker at the Swiss bank. The complainants were spread far and wide in Asia, the USA, Canada, the Channel Islands, and Europe. Watson spent some days in Hong Kong with DS Raymond Collinson accumulating evidence regarding the largest individual crime alleged against Berridge. When Watson arrived there, the eight hundred workers plus at the Hong Kong firm originally thought he was Berridge, the man who had defrauded them, and DS Collinson was his lawyer! Watson could feel the perceived hostility in the workplace initially. However, after quickly realizing it was Watson who was trying to help them, the workers went out of their way to ensure Watson and Collinson enjoyed their stay in the Hong Kong area. One place they recommended that Watson and Collinson visit was Ned Kelly's saloon in Wan Chai. Watson took them up on their suggestion and had a nice evening in the saloon, drinking some strong Australian beer. The next morning, Collinson came down to breakfast but took one look at breakfast and went back to his room! Later in the morning, he rose again very slowly but surely, and together with Watson, they went back to the firm to continue assembling the primary witness statements and pertinent documents relating to the same.

Watson and his team slowly but surely gathered the necessary evidence and documents from various parts of the world to pursue potential criminal charges regarding the actions taken by the managing director. Watson had a great deal of difficulty in understanding how Berridge had been allowed by the Swiss bank to take clients from the Swiss bank to his new venture, CTC. Watson was firmly of the belief that when a trust officer would move and take any clients with them, the trust company that they were being taken to should be on a par with the trust company from which they were being transferred. It was an essential part of a trust company's fiduciary duties. A trust company must ensure that they were of the same standing. How this could be stated by the Swiss bank and their worldwide resources to a new startup one-man business was not quite immediately clear to Watson. Allied also to the fact that Berridge had already had serious criminal problems at the Swiss bank made it even more incomprehensible. It was inconceivable to Watson how they could allow such a thing to occur without any form of notice to their clients regarding his immediate past actions, or how they could allow their international presence to be compared to a one-man startup trust company was also a mystery. Watson thought that Berridge was fortunate that Watson had not chosen a banking profession and been in charge of Berridge. The fur would have been flying if that were the case.

The criminal inquiries were made as quickly as possible and as extensively as possible. Following on from these inquiries being completed in July 1989, Watson and a team of officers under his control executed a search warrant at the home of Berridge, the former banker. A large number of documents were seized pertaining to the complaints that the police were investigating, along with a personal computer that was also seized for analysis by computer technicians employed by the Cayman government. Much useful evidence was found in hard copy form and also in the records held on the computer, which were ultimately used to support criminal charges being made against Berridge and another co-accused.

Following the search made and the examination of the electronic and documentary evidence, Berridge and his attorney visited with Watson at the CCB offices, and the banker was duly interviewed at length under caution. The interview went on for two hours plus, and DS Johns made notes of responses given by Berridge in response to the questions asked by Watson and the documents produced to him. Basically, Berridge declined to answer the vast majority of the questions asked, as was his right under the law. At the end of the interview, Berridge and his attorney were provided with a copy of the contemporaneous notes made. The following day, the banker again returned to the CCB and handed Watson another page of evidence relating to one particular aspect of the matters that had been covered the day previously.

Once all the evidence and documentary evidence had been collected, Watson compiled and submitted a report and statements, together with a copy of the documents, to the Legal Department for their consideration as to what criminal charges should be considered in this matter. Following a couple of case conferences Watson had with the lawyers, they gave their instructions to charge Berridge with a number of separate criminal offenses. A barrister who was well-versed in serious fraud prosecutions was brought in from Jamaica to prosecute the case, and Watson spent quite some time with him and a barrister from the Legal Department to help him prepare for the upcoming trial, as Berridge was entering a plea of not guilty to the allegations they laid out. Having been instructed by the Legal Department to charge Berridge, Watson therefore made all the arrangements necessary to comply with their instructions. However, they did instruct Watson to temporarily hold on formally presenting the charges against the banker until such time as the ongoing trial at the Grand Court regarding his alleged thefts from the Swiss bank and the Florida construction builder or owner had been completed.

Accordingly, following Berridge being found guilty at the Grand Court of the Swiss bank allegations, it was not until mid-December 1991 that the new charges, involving in excess of $1.8 million, were laid against the banker. During the inquiries made, another Caymanian businessman, Ernest Proctor, had been found to have committed some criminal offenses regarding the matters complained of by the Hong Kong retirement fund, and he also was to be charged with three separate offenses involving the theft of some $750,000.

They both appeared simultaneously at court later that same month to commence the criminal proceedings against each of them. Berridge was remanded to jail, as he was already serving his first sentence for the Swiss bank matters, and his accomplice, Proctor, was bailed in his own recognizance along with a substantial surety. Based on arguments his lawyer made to allow him to continue his extensive business interests in Cayman and also the USA, Proctor was ordered to notify the police (DCI Watson) at least twenty-four hours in advance of him leaving the island and also his return date plus set out his reasons for needing to leave Cayman. This request by Proctor's lawyer was most useful to the Caymanian police and, by progression, the US federal agents who were obviously well-aware of the money laundering inquiries being made in the USA regarding Proctor, and by virtue of the lawyer's request, this thereby allowed surveillance to be kept on the individual on the dates and times provided by him. Watson thought that perhaps Proctor's lawyer never thought this part of his request through, but then again, he probably didn't know or reasonably suspect that Proctor was laundering money. Watson assumed that Proctor never told his Caymanian lawyers that he was also laundering money from the USA.

In due course, Proctor, who was charged shortly thereafter, was well-known to Watson as an individual who had a substantial number of contacts in the business, banking, and financial communities in Cayman. At one time, Watson recalled he had been the head of the Cayman Olympics Committee. He had been of interest to the US authorities for many years and had access to a number of cash businesses on the island, an ideal background and structure for potential money laundering operations. Accordingly and assisted by information and evidence received from the Caymanian authorities, plus a well-placed informant who brought the parties together, USA law enforcement agents named Clay and Tim had diligently and professionally set up two or three meetings in the USA with Proctor on the pretext that they were wealthy individuals who had inherited a large ranching operation and wanted to launder some of the excess money they were receiving through the business. Also, they professed at one of the meetings that took place between the three of them that they

held ownership over a large marijuana operation and that with the
volume of cash it was generating, they could not get it inserted easily
into the US banking system. Proctor declared that he could route
it through Cayman and continually professed that he could get it
into the Caymanian banking system and subsequently back into the
US system. Basically, whatever Clay and Tim needed doing with the
money, he was the man to help. He smiled and agreed that whatever
they needed could be done basically. This was all done, of course,
for an agreed percentage fee of the deposit due to Proctor, which
was based on the total amount of money laundered. Accordingly,
during a meeting in a US undercover motor vehicle, the two agents
gave Proctor US $50,000 in cash, and then both agents held their
breath that they would, in the fullness of time, see it again! As government agents, they knew that there would be lots of questions to
answer from their senior officers and the bean counters at headquarters should the money go missing!

Proctor duly returned to Cayman with the money he had been
provided with and subsequently inserted the same into the Caymanian
banking system before, a few days later, wiring it back to the USA
account specified, which was, in fact, an undercover account used
by the US federal authorities for just such circumstances. The agents
breathed more easily now that the money had been repatriated, less
Proctor's commission, and quickly set up a further meeting with
Proctor to speak about much larger volumes of the monies that he
would be required to launder going forward. Unfortunately for him,
this was where Proctor's enterprises came to a sudden and screeching
halt. He was duly arrested prior to the next meeting and interviewed
and then formally charged in the Southern District of Florida with
a number of money laundering charges and other related matters,
all arising from the actions he had taken part in with the US federal
agents. Interestingly, Watson learned that Proctor did not say a word
during his interviews with the law enforcement officers who processed him. This was similar to his responses when interviewed by
Watson in December 1991 over the allegations relating to CTC and,
in particular, the retirement fund account. He did not utter one word
then; he neither denied nor admitted the allegations being made

against him! In the USA, the matter was quickly processed following his arrest; and following a guilty plea in court, he was sentenced to a total of fourteen years imprisonment in the USA for those offenses.

By the time the trust company charges against Berridge arrived at Grand Court for trial, it was a few years after the initial charges had been laid against the banker; the wheels of justice sometimes turned very slowly but, assuredly, very deliberately! The trial lasted a total of forty-one court days, and the sums involved in the five counts of the indictment sent for trial totaled over $1 million. The offenses took place between May 1988 and March 1989 while Berridge was the managing director of CTC. He was found guilty of stealing assets valued at $750,000 (the property of a retirement plan in Hong Kong), a further $106,000 belonging to the beneficial owner of a Caymanian exempt corporation, and finally obtaining some $500,000 by criminal deception from an American businessman. Following his conviction by the jury, the judge stated that the defense lawyer had tried to defend the indefensible. He continued that the accused was both intelligent and clever, but he had not used those gifts for any constructive purpose but had used them in a totally shameless manner. The banker had drained the lifeblood out of the retirement company, and even when the Inspector of Banks and Trust Companies had sent experts to CTC to determine what was happening, Berridge had outwitted them and withheld existing documentation to frustrate and obstruct the experts. The judge stated he had lied from beginning to end and had not shown any contrition to assist in depriving people of their assets. The judge sentenced Berridge—the banker and, latterly, trust officer—to sentences ranging from three years to four and a half years of imprisonment, making the sentences to all run concurrently.

The sentence was subsequently appealed by the defense to the local Court of Appeal but was rejected by that court, and therefore the defendant then went to Privy Council in London to lodge an appeal where the council accepted all the evidence that had been provided as very persuasive. However, the Privy Council reversed the decision because they opined that the prosecutor who had been brought in from Jamaica to prosecute the case had been too aggressive during various exchanges in the course of the trial and also the judge had not stamped down on the supposed aggression, and therefore they felt the conviction was unfair. This all happened after the defendant had finished serving his sentence of imprisonment in the jail at Northward in Cayman.

Watson noted that the Privy Council, the highest court in the UK, in reaching their decision on the appeal and having reviewed in its entirety all the facts pertaining to the trial and the conduct of the same made, inter alia, the following points that they considered in their judgment:

> A contested criminal trial on indictment is adversarial in character. The prosecution seeks to satisfy the jury of the guilt of the accused beyond reasonable doubt. The defense seeks to resist and rebut such proof. The objects of the parties are fundamentally opposed. There may well be disputes concerning the relevance and admissibility of evidence. There will almost always be a conflict of evidence. Some witnesses may be impugned as unreliable, others perhaps as dishonest. Witnesses on both sides may be accused of exaggerating or even fabricating their evidence. Defendants may choose to act in an obstructive and evasive manner. Opposing counsel may find each other easy to work with, or they may not. It is not unusual for tempers to become frayed and relations strained. In a fraud trial, the pressure on all involved may be even more acute than in other trials. Fraud trials tend to involve a great deal of documentation, which is particularly cumbersome to handle in a jury trial. They involve much unfamiliar detail, often of a technical nature, which is difficult for many people to understand, assimilate, retain, and recall. And fraud trials can be very long, which in itself tends to increase the strain on all involved, whether the defendant,

witnesses, jurors, counsel, or the judge. This trial in question is said to be the longest criminal trial ever held in the Cayman Islands.

There is, however, throughout any trial and not least a long fraud trial, one overriding requirement: to ensure that the defendant accused of crime is fairly tried. The adversarial format of the criminal trial is indeed directed to ensuring a fair opportunity for the prosecution to establish guilt and a fair opportunity for the defendant to advance his defense. To safeguard the fairness of the trial, a number of rules have been developed to ensure that the proceedings, however closely contested and however highly charged, are conducted in a manner that is orderly and fair. These rules are well-understood and are not in any way controversial. But it is pertinent to state some of them.

The Board sees great force in many of the points made for the prosecution. The case against the accused does indeed appear to have been a very strong one, and the explanations proffered by him might well have been properly rejected by a jury. On the material before the Board, there would appear to be grounds for criticizing the conduct of the defense and the evidence of the accused. It would be quite wrong to infer that all the faults in the conduct of this trial lay with the prosecution, which had to overcome a series of unnecessary obstacles. The duty of prosecuting counsel is not to obtain a conviction at all costs but to act as a minister of justice.

However, this was still not the end of the matter for Watson. After Watson left Cayman and the police service following his retirement in 1993, he became a duly licensed and accredited investigator first in the state of Florida and, latterly, in the state of Texas. While he was in Florida, he was approached and contacted by a Hong Kong firm with a view to assisting them to compile a case on behalf of the retirement fund based in Hong Kong. Watson, using information he already possessed and further assistance and documents that were rendered to him by the attorney general of the Cayman Islands, produced a report and attachments for the client that allowed the retirement fund in September 1999 to file a civil action against the Swiss bank for misappropriation of $775,000 in client trust funds. Much of the information provided and unearthed details originally provided to Watson during the criminal inquiry established clearly that the bank had failed to live up to their fiduciary responsibilities and allowed the banker to take the trust account with him when he left the bank. Consequently, the retirement fund, in mounting their lawsuit, stated that the banker had handled the account while he worked at the Swiss bank and that when he left their employ, the bank had allowed him to transfer the account to CTC without the bank informing the retirement fund of the alleged criminal actions the officer had been involved in at the bank. It was alleged, but in Watson's view, the evidence clearly established that the bank had not fulfilled their fiduciary duties to the trust fund. Although in this matter, Watson was not called upon to testify, as he was during the criminal proceedings. The matter was eventually settled by agreement out of court in favor of the retirement fund.

It caused Watson a wry smile when in late 1997, the two primary parties, Berridge and Proctor, were reunited at Northward Prison in Grand Cayman. On humanitarian grounds, the associate of Berridge had been returned to Cayman from the USA to serve out his remaining prison sentence imposed for money laundering. Watson was using his vivid, if somewhat exhausted, imagination to wonder what type of business the two of them would now become involved in and run the same from the confines of Her Majesty's Northward Prison. He was sure that in the fullness of time, they would become involved in some type of scheme; it was obviously a part of their inherent nature!

ISLAND JUSTICE

Even this was not the end of Watson's interactions with the banker or managing director. Watson, who had lived with these various actions on and off from 1989, still received further potential action and inquiries in 2019 when a complaint was filed in St. Lucie County, Florida, by a Caribbean real estate entity against Berridge who was now publishing a Caribbean news entity from his home in the USA and allegedly falsely accused the real estate corporation of falsely misappropriating funds, defrauding investors, and misleading the government of two Caribbean islands regarding a proposed luxury resort to be built on one of the islands. However, only two months after the lawsuit was filed, the banker passed away unexpectedly at his home in Florida; and consequently, the lawsuit was amended by the plaintiffs with the banker named being replaced by his estate as a party in the same.

CHAPTER 27

A Sad Farewell to the Cayman Islands

During this final year of his wonderful and memorable secondment to the Cayman Islands, Watson had been thinking long and hard about what actions to take as he neared thirty years of service in the police, the optimum time to retire from the UK police. Watson was enjoying what he was doing, but as he was fast approaching the thirty-year mark, a decision had to be made. He had been married to Sarah for some four years plus, and together they debated the pros and cons of retiring. They were living in a nice apartment in beautiful Cayman, and Sarah was still flying for United out of their base at Miami International Airport, which meant commuting to and from Miami when she had a trip to work and then flying back once the trip was finished. Sarah's mother and stepfather lived in a condominium in some apartments at Leisure Gardens, Pompano Beach, Florida, just north of Fort Lauderdale, and as both were aging, they needed some regular help and support. Watson mused over the fact he could retire from the Bilberry Police as he had completed thirty years of service and draw his police pension from them. Additionally, he could then sign perhaps a two- or three-year contract to continue serving with the Caymanian police. A number of senior Caymanian officers had made that suggestion to him, and Watson was very tempted by the same, as he thoroughly enjoyed the work and also the camaraderie of the Cayman police and the friendship of its people.

Both Watson and Sarah ultimately decided that the time had perhaps come for Watson to retire from the police work that had consumed him and a lot of his time for thirty years and for the two of them to move to a house in Florida to be near her mother as she grew older.

During a trip to Florida, Watson and Sarah found a new building site located in Lauderhill, Florida, just off Commercial Boulevard and east of University Drive. It was a heavily wooded area with sabal palms and bald cypress trees, and some nice single-story homes were being built by a national building company, Centex. Watson and Sarah decided to purchase there, the primary reason being Sarah's mother lived in Pompano Beach, which was but a small fifteen-minute drive away. This place was also handy for Sarah who was flying her trips out of Miami Airport at that time, about a thirty-five-minute drive from Lauderhill. In early August 1992, they purchased a specific lot and then set in motion the style and design of the house to be built there. It was to be a three-bedroom, two-and-a-half-bath, one-office, double-garage home of about 2,200 feet. By overlaying an outline of the house on a plan of the lot, they were able to position the house exactly where they wanted it, and the builders knew which trees had to be removed to allow for the property and entranceway to be built. Planning and efforts were set underway to have the house ready for occupation in August 1993, about one month before Watson was due to retire. Sarah and Watson returned to Cayman, and Watson duly informed the commissioner that at the end of his contract in September 1993, he would be leaving Cayman and also retiring simultaneously from the British police. The news was received with disappointment by many, but all understood Watson's reasoning for retiring at that time, and Watson was certainly leaving the CCB in a healthier position than when he joined. The building site supervisor in Florida was a former University of Florida Gator, David Wagie, and he was most amenable to Watson and Sarah as the building process commenced, although the ground would probably not be cleared or broken until the beginning of 1993.

Hurricane Andrew plowed through the Bahamas and came ashore in the USA on the twenty-fourth of August 1992 just south of Miami and continued on to Homestead and that specific area.

It was a devastating hurricane, and at least forty-four people were killed in Florida along with millions of dollars of damage caused by the extremely high winds. Wind speeds reached over 140 mph. Watching from Cayman, Watson and Sarah were concerned that although Andrew had come ashore further south than Lauderhill, the outer wind bands might have damaged their building site and it might no longer be heavily wooded. Accordingly, a few days later, they contacted David Wagie by telephone; and after inquiring about his health and any damage he had possibly sustained during the storm, Watson asked him, "How is our lot, David? Is it still heavily wooded?"

David laughed and said, "Yes, it is. A few branches are off some of the taller trees, but it is still very heavily wooded."

Watson said, "That's good, but are the trees still vertical, or are they now horizontal?"

Wagie laughed and responded that they were still vertical and added that their breaking ground might start in December, as the schedule currently showed. Watson reminded him that he wanted to take possession in August 1993, and Wagie said he totally understood and that he would ensure Watson and Sarah would take possession by then, barring any further natural disasters! Sarah and Watson were excited at this new step in their lives, and many evenings were spent planning the same, mainly by Sarah with the occasional input from Watson.

Because of Watson's impending retirement, the RCIP conducted a new recruitment search in the UK for his replacement. A Detective Inspector Robert Week was finally selected from the South Yorkshire Police Department as Watson's replacement. DI Week was very experienced in fraud and major crime matters, and it was arranged that he would arrive in Cayman with his lovely wife, Norma, about two weeks before Watson was scheduled to leave. The idea was that there would be an indoctrination period for him and Watson could also brief and update him on all the inquiries that were proceeding at that time, together with introducing him to people whom Watson had found to be of great benefit in traversing the idiosyncrasies of the islands.

Also, a number of people in the police force wanted to have a going-away party for Watson and his wife, Sarah. Watson spoke with his work and resident neighbor, Mr. Smithley, and he volunteered to organize the evening after Watson had arranged—through some friends at the rugby club, Janet and Dave Robinson—to utilize the rugby clubhouse premises for the evening.

Watson also arranged with a representative of the local liquor providers to purchase beer and some wines that would be provided to guests at the function from the bar, staffed by rugby club members. Mrs. Smithley, Sarah, and other wives of police officers kindly agreed and made the food that was available for the evening. The evening of Thursday, August 26, 1993, was set for the day of the event, and invitations were sent to many agencies and corporations not only in Cayman but also in the USA, other Caribbean islands, the UK, Sweden, and Canada. Over 120 people turned out at the function, including numerous guests from the USA, Canada, the Caribbean, and the UK. Mr. Smithley opened the evening by welcoming one and all and then spoke briefly about Watson's journey in the police service. Smithley then touched on a number of occasions in the police in Bilberry that showed Watson's ability to get things completed and also Watson's tendency to always see the funny side of things. Based on the facts he was revealing, Watson immediately knew he had spoken to two former colleagues of Watson, Detective Sergeant Dave Chambers and probably also Detective Sergeant Dave Coote. Watson was pleased that neither of his former colleagues appeared to have disclosed any really embarrassing details of Watson's past as a detective in Bilberry.

Following on from this, some thirteen people—headed by the commissioner of police, plus other public and private dignitaries—made speeches of thanks to Watson that evening, while another thirty-nine faxed or mailed letters of thanks for inclusion by Smithley who put the whole program together in a binder that he used to MC the evening, much in the manner of the binder used in the ages old British TV program *This Is Your Life*, hosted by Eamonn Andrews. One presentation was made by a leading defense attorney who spoke on behalf of all defense attorneys whose paths had crossed with Watson by wishing him and Sarah much good fortune in the years ahead and saying how excited the defense attorneys were that Watson was now leaving the island. That effectively was a badge of courage now worn by Watson, and in Watson's speech of response, he assured the defense attorneys that he had enjoyed every minute of causing them grief! It was a nostalgic evening for Watson and much enjoyed by one and all. Lots of gifts of cut glass, other mementos from Cayman, commemorative plaques, and a large limited-edition painting (measuring twenty-eight by thirty-nine inches) by Debbie Van Der Bol entitled *Bodden Town Home* was presented by the CID Department to Watson. One speaker suggested that the exclusive Kirk Freeport store in George Town had done a roaring business in cut glass and bone china prior to the function, which were now presented to Watson and Sarah. Wonderful memories and lots of sentiments were expressed that evening by many individuals whom Watson and Sarah would treasure for years way beyond his police service in Cayman and the United Kingdom. Watson provided floral bouquets to the ladies who had helped Sarah prepare for the evening, and he also presented British police memorabilia to Cayman officers he had interacted closely with. An added bonus for Watson was having his lovely stepdaughter from Dallas, Texas, Stacey there, and she was blown away by the evening and the people who both attended and spoke during the evening. Stacey had come to Cayman to help her mother pack belongings and other associated matters and be ready for the move to the new property in Lauderhill, Florida, which had been completed as promised by David Wagie.

About a week before Watson's final day in Cayman, a cargo carrier from Cayman arrived at the apartment to collect about 1,200 lbs. of household goods and items that were subsequently loaded, packed, and secured on two wooden pallets for shipping to Florida. Watson could not comprehend how he arrived in Cayman with two suitcases full of clothing and here he was about six and a half years later leaving Cayman with two large loaded pallets of stuff plus other items to be carried personally when he'd leave Cayman. *What happened?* he thought, although he would never suggest the same publicly that Sarah bore some responsibility for this.

While Watson was working up until the day he left Cayman, Sarah and Stacey were packing suitcases and other items for the journey to Florida. Following on from the retirement party, they now had thirteen bags to check, including one large framed painting and twelve bags to carry on, on the aircraft. There were a lot of pieces of cut glass and bone china to be carried on plus one pet carrier holding Patch, the Caymanian calico cat, who was going to a new country! Watson had made a lot of inquiries regarding taking Patch to the USA, and as a result, he had spent a substantial amount of time with island vets ensuring Patch was current on various vaccinations and also getting the required paperwork in hand to present upon arrival in the USA for her. The paperwork alone cost Watson fifty dollars! He thought for fifty dollars and the time he had spent, it had better have been necessary for Patch to enter the USA.

Leaving on the end of a contract, the Cayman government would always reasonably expect a retiree to use Cayman Airways for the first part of their trip; but as Sarah was a United employee and United had been flying from Miami into Cayman since January 1992, Watson and her, plus Stacey, were allowed to use United Airlines to fly to Miami. The Cayman Islands station manager of United knew both Watson and, of course, Sarah, as she had often used their computer system at the airport to submit her bids for lines of flying that she wanted to fly each month. He was delighted to welcome them aboard a flight to Miami on a Boeing 737 and allocated them three seats in first class, along with Patch who was in her pet carrier beneath one of the seats. The manager was quite shocked, however, to be asked to check thirteen bags, but due to the extenuating circumstances, he did graciously accommodate them. He was then further surprised at the twelve carry-ons, including Patch, but again in the circumstances, he was sympathetic to the cause and again thankfully accommodated them, hoping to protect the cut glass and bone china from damage during the flight. Watson and Sarah had just left some of their closest friends and colleagues in the terminal concourse, and it was a time and mixture of sadness and nonetheless anticipation, as they were looking immensely forward to what the future would hold for them.

The manager was most helpful and assisted Watson and his menagerie to stow their items ready for takeoff and did suggest that upon arrival in Miami, they might want to kindly let the other passengers exit the plane before they left with their twelve bags! Shortly thereafter, the aircraft was pushed back and set off down the runway toward the cricket pitch that Watson had been on so many times. At the end of the runway, the aircraft did a 180-degree turn and waited for permission to take off. Once given, the two engines roared into life and the aircraft went down the runway past the terminal buildings and started to climb. As it gained height, it turned slightly to the left and set course for a flight over Cuba and over the Florida Keys before lining up to land at Miami Airport from the west. This was yet another step in Watson's life, and now he was already beginning to wonder what the future would hold for Sarah and himself. He knew it would be good and that it would be a happy time for the two of them.

After landing and arriving at a gate and after most of the passengers had deplaned past them, Watson, Sarah, and Stacey collected their twelve carry-on bags and slowly but surely made their way off the airplane, with both the pilots looking and broadly smiling while wishing Watson and Sarah a long and happy retirement. Obviously, the Cayman station manager had forewarned the pilots and flight attendants about this crazy police detective and his United flight attendant wife plus their obvious inability to count carry-on bags!

The three of them went through the immigration process quite quickly and then went to the area where hopefully all thirteen checked bags would appear. They did! As the carousel slowly went around, one by one the bags and the painting were recovered, and Watson had obtained five baggage carts to carry the items through the customs check areas and present them to the customs officer. The baggage carts were slowly and carefully loaded with the bags, including the carry-ons, and on top of one of the carts and its baggage was Patch in her carrier, taking in everything and anything that was happening. Heaven knows what she must had been thinking at this time. Watson had already completed the customs declaration form as best he could with the amount of items being presented in preparation for the officer and also had Patch's paperwork readily available for production.

Slowly but surely they made their way, pushing the five carts, toward the lines to clear the customs officer and then to exit the Customs Hall. Watson could only imagine what the other passengers must have thought; the baggage carts were all fully loaded! He did notice that no other passengers in line were behind him. They had all gone to other lines! Watson was cursing himself for not remembering to tell his US Customs friends that he and Sarah were returning to the USA that day; they might well had been able to expedite their passage through the process. Watson did, however, anticipate some questions being asked, and accordingly, he wore an FBI polo shirt that had been given to him when he spoke during a meeting on offshore matters a month or so previously at the FBI Academy in Quantico, Virginia. He thought that this might help to smooth his path and transition during their landing processes in Miami.

They got to the head of the line, and a customs officer, who looked quite experienced, quizzically looked at the five carts and the copious amounts of luggage on them. And after a few moments to consider the scene, he asked Watson in a somewhat circumspect way, "Are you three together with all that stuff?"

Watson responded that they were and was then asked where they were arriving from. Watson replied, "Grand Cayman. We have been down there for a couple of days."

The officer smiled, laughed, and continued, "Okay, thank goodness you weren't there for a week or so" before continuing to ask, "What is the true story then?"

Watson, smiling, said, "I was a detective chief inspector in the Royal Cayman Islands Police for almost seven years on loan from the United Kingdom Police. Now I have retired after thirty years of total service, and my wife and I—plus our cat, Patch, for whom I have documents, you know—are moving to Florida, Fort Lauderdale actually, where we have bought a plot of land and just built a house."

The officer said, looking at the five loaded carts, "I am purely guessing, but I suspect that you had a leaving or retirement party of some sort before you left?"

Watson responded in the affirmative and explained that accordingly, most of the packages contained cut glass and bone china figures that were given as both leaving and retirement presents, plus the painting that was in its own package was from the entire Detective Department. The customs officer said without hesitation that that was fine, and he initialed the card to be handed in at the exit to the Customs Hall. Watson was genuinely concerned that the officer had not mentioned Patch though, nor did he look at the cat's documents and letters. Accordingly, he asked in his usual direct manner, "What about the papers for the cat? I have them here."

The customs officer responded, "I don't want to see them. They are not necessary."

Watson said, "They told me in Cayman I needed all these certifications and other related documents, and I had to get the cat examined and vaccinated plus also pay fifty dollars for some of these documents. I spent an inordinate amount of time and effort plus money getting these things together just for you. Please, please, please, if for no other reason than to just make me happy, at least pretend to have a look and examine the documents and certifications."

The officer said, "No, I don't want the documents, nor do I even want to see them. I can see the feline in the crate! Just wait here a moment." He immediately turned and walked purposefully and quickly away from the desk. Sarah looked in her special way at Watson as if to say, *What the hell have you done or said now?* Even if she had asked the question of Watson who was pretty quick on his feet in normal circumstances, he could not have answered it because he had absolutely no idea what was now happening. It was not as though the three humans in the party, plus the cat and the five carts, could sprint away with their belongings out of the Customs Hall. The officer quickly returned with two other uniform customs officers and said, "My colleagues and I will help you get your carts out curbside so you can then go on to wherever you want." Watson was dumbfounded by this. They were most gracious and accordingly helped Watson and Sarah push the carts out of customs and then totally outside of the terminal to the curbside. Watson thanked them profusely and thought that was so kind of them to go way beyond their normal scope of duty. He made a mental note to let his US Customs friends know of that good deed by their uniform colleagues the next time he spoke with them.

Watson, Sarah, and Stacey now stood curbside with a total of twenty-five bags, including one cat, stacked on five carts, and they attracted quite a few strange looks from people, most of them looking in sheer disbelief. You could see their minds racing and wondering, *Where the hell has all that come from?* Watson mentioned that it must look like a small cargo plane had just landed and disgorged its cargo. Sarah, who had been professionally flying out of Miami for some time, had her car, a Nissan Maxima, parked in the staff car park. She stated that she would go and fetch her car. Watson added quickly, "I think we need something else as well to get these bags to Lauderhill. These bags won't fit in your car along with the three of us and Patch!" Sarah asked if he was sure, and Watson said he was 110 percent sure. Watson suggested that while Sarah fetched her car from the staff car park, he would go to a car and truck rental company and rent a small truck or van if possible. Stacey and Patch could stay at the curbside and zealously protect the bags, and then Sarah could return with her car and Watson with a rented van.

As it turned out, Sarah was back before Watson by about ten minutes, and Stacey and Sarah had already put some of the more delicate smaller boxes and items in the car along with Patch. Watson arrived with a small van a short time later, and they finished loading the van with the remaining cases and packages. They then set out to drive the thirty-five minutes or so out of the airport and then north on I-95 toward Commercial Boulevard and then on to Lauderhill and their new home. Upon arrival at their new home, they emptied the car and the van; settled Patch in one small room with her kitty litter, bedding, food, and water; and then went off for a nice dinner and a drink in a nearby restaurant to celebrate this new chapter in their lives and their relationship. It was both a sad yet incredibly happy time, and everyone was full of anticipation. No one needed any rocking that night to sleep, including Patch.

The next day, Watson returned the van to the rental company, and the packages were slowly but surely unwrapped and placed in their assigned storage areas in the new home, as indicated by Sarah. The pallets from Cayman were not expected to be delivered for another week or so, and also en route from Dallas were the remaining items that Sarah had had in storage from the sale of her home in Roanoke some four years previously. Watson and Sarah would shortly be flying to England to formally tender Watson's retirement from the UK police and sign the especially important and very necessary documents to obtain his well-earned police pension from the United Kingdom, which would be then be implemented and operative from that date onward.

As Watson, together with Sarah and Stacey, thoroughly relaxed that next day, he knew he was going to be busy in the days, weeks, and months ahead now that he was living in a new country in a brand-new house along with Sarah. Patch spent the whole day busily exploring all around the house and making sure it was to her standards—plenty of places to continue her routine of hourly naps—and also identifying weak spots in the construction where geckos might invade the house and thereby need her predatory skills to repel them.

Many times throughout this day and in the days and weeks ahead, Watson reflected on his police career in its totality and how, during the thirty years of service, he had been so fortunate in the postings he had received and the numerous colleagues who had worked with him and for him during those years in the United Kingdom and especially Bilberry. There was a great camaraderie and esprit de corps in the police force, and the friendships formed subsisted way beyond the years of work, toil, frustrations, and often happiness. They lasted a lifetime, even if former colleagues didn't see one another every day. Watson had been so fortunate to see and apply for the post in the Cayman Islands and the fact that he had been appointed to the position. Although it was initially a short-term attachment for him, it had turned into almost seven years and dramatically changed his whole life in ways he could not have comprehended initially. He had been given opportunities he could only dream about because of policing, and over those years in Cayman, he had many new and other exciting opportunities placed before him. Watson reminisced over the many new friends he had made in Cayman and in other countries, worldwide. In Cayman, he was most fortunate to be surrounded by a group of officers who were always willing to learn, commit to each and every task given to them, and enhance their own skill sets. They had received Watson with an openness and friendship that was so praiseworthy and heartwarming that it would be difficult to forget; no, on second thoughts, he would never forget this part of his life. The people of Cayman, at all levels, had invariably opened their arms and hearts to him and shown great friendship. They made him feel most welcome to their most beautiful home, the three Cayman islands. In Watson's vernacular, he had also rattled a few cages; and as he expressed to the defense lawyers at his going-away party, he had reminded them that he loved every minute of it. He secretly hoped that DI Week would keep up the tradition! Now those days were over, but Watson had left a piece of his heart and soul in beautiful Cayman with his many acquaintances and experiences there. Words could not express either his debt or his eternal gratitude to them. Watson was truly humbled by them and the six years plus he had been there. He would never forget those experiences and all that had taken place during that time—good, bad, hilarious, and indifferent. He believed he had generally contributed on many levels in many areas during his time in Cayman and that perhaps because of those various interactions, some of the locals would remember him—even the defense lawyers!

Over the following weeks, Watson mused many times of what possible new career he would now become involved in and hoped that it would be as happy and as fulfilling as the one he had just left. He enjoyed traveling the world and had enjoyed many new places during his time in Cayman. He secretly hoped that the new job, whatever it might be, would allow that passion and enjoyment of his to continue. He wondered how the next twenty or thirty years of his working life could even come close to rivaling what he had now enjoyed, savored, and left. Watson genuinely and earnestly believed that with his background, many experiences of all sorts, and well-placed contacts all over the world, he could perhaps easily fall into a new vocation as...?

ABOUT THE AUTHOR

John Boaden has been a British police detective for twenty-three years plus then a detective on loan to the Cayman Islands for almost seven years prior to retirement. Additionally, for a further twenty-two years, he has been a licensed investigator in Florida and latterly Texas, including four years working for a renowned worldwide asset recovery lawyer in Tortola, British Virgin Islands. He has been fortunate to have traveled the world extensively in both the public and private sectors, along with various sporting events that he has been heavily involved in. Over the years he has experienced in the private sector, he has spoken at many conferences and events worldwide on the subject of asset recovery and techniques used to fulfill the same and has coauthored an article on *The Language of Hiding*. He also wrote a manual setting out the requirements to establish and process serious crimes. The procedure was subsequently taught and adopted in the British Dependent Territories throughout the West Indies. He and his wife now live in beautiful South Carolina near Hilton Head Island and have a blended family of five children and nine grandchildren, plus a mini goldendoodle named Riley. Because of their primary work backgrounds, they both have an extraordinary background of interactions with numerous people on the various continents in all manner of places. They are currently both kept busy with a number of positions for which they volunteer, plus they maintain an active social life in the vibrant community where they live.

This is John's first book, and he has used as his primary character Detective Chief Inspector Christopher Watson, who, after years in the British police, needed to get out of a task he had been involved in, one which did not allow him to operate on the front line. Accordingly, Watson applied for and was given a posting in the Cayman Islands. John's first book solely covers the application to the Cayman Islands and the almost seven years he spent working there before finally retiring from the police and moving on to new pastures in the USA. The seven years in Cayman were ultimately dramatically life-changing.

CPSIA information can be obtained
at www.ICGtesting.com
Printed in the USA
FSHW011925160321
79546FS